# THE
# ATLANTIS
## WORLD

A.G. RIDDLE spent ten years starting and running internet companies before retiring to focus on his true passion: writing fiction. He grew up in a small town in North Carolina and attended UNC-Chapel Hill, where he founded his first company with one of his childhood friends. He currently lives in Parkland, Florida and would love to hear from you: agriddle.com

T0033362

# THE ATLANTIS TRILOGY

The Atlantis Gene
The Atlantis Plague
The Atlantis World

# THE ATLANTIS WORLD

HEAD
ZEUS

First published in the USA in 2014.

First published as an ebook in the UK in 2014 by Head of Zeus Ltd.
This paperback edition first published in the UK in 2015
by Head of Zeus Ltd.

Copyright © 2014 by A.G. Riddle

The moral right of A.G. Riddle to be identified as
the author of this work has been asserted in accordance with
the Copyright, Designs and Patents Act of 1988.

All rights reserved. No part of this publication may be reproduced,
stored in a retrieval system, or transmitted in any form or by
any means, electronic, mechanical, photocopying, recording,
or otherwise, without the prior permission of both the copyright
owner and the above publisher of this book.

This is a work of fiction. All characters, organizations,
and events portrayed in this novel are either products of the author's
imagination or are used fictitiously.

9 7 5 3 4 6 8

A catalogue record for this book is available from the British Library.

ISBN (PB) 9781784970130
ISBN (E) 9781784970123

Printed and bound by CPI Group (UK) Ltd,
Croydon, CR0 4YY

Head of Zeus Ltd
First Floor East
5-8 Hardwick Street
London EC1R 4RG

WWW.HEADOFZEUS.COM

*For my parents, who encouraged me to never give up.*

# THE
# ATLANTIS
# WORLD

# PROLOGUE

For the last forty-eight hours, Dr. Mary Caldwell had spent every waking second studying the signal the radio telescope had received. She was exhausted, exhilarated, and sure of one thing: it was organized, a sign of intelligent life.

Behind her, John Bishop, the other researcher assigned to the observatory, poured himself another drink. He had gone through the scotch, the bourbon, then the rum, and all the other booze the dead researchers had stockpiled until he was down to the peach schnapps. He drank it straight since they had nothing to mix it with. He winced as he took the first sip.

It was nine a.m., and his revulsion at the liquid would only last another twenty minutes, until his third drink.

"You're imagining it, Mare," he said as he set the empty glass down and focused on refilling it.

Mary hated when he called her "Mare." No one had ever called her that. It reminded her of a horse. But he was the only company she had, and the two of them had reached an understanding of sorts.

After the outbreak, when people across Puerto Rico were dying by the tens of thousands, they had holed up in the observatory, and John had promptly made his first pass at her. She had brushed it off. The second followed two days later. After that, he made a move every day, each more aggressive than the

I

last, until she had kneed him in the balls. He had been more docile after that, focusing on alcohol and snide remarks.

Mary stood and walked to the window, which looked out on the lush, green Puerto Rican hills and forests. The only hint of civilization was the satellite dish that lay recessed into a plateau in the hills, pointed straight up at the sky. The radio telescope at Arecibo Observatory was the largest radio telescope in the world, a triumph of human engineering. It was a marriage of sciences that represented the pinnacle of human achievement embedded in a primitive landscape that symbolized humanity's past. And now it had fulfilled its ultimate mission. Contact.

"It's real," Mary said.

"How do you know?"

"It has our address on it."

John stopped sipping the drink and looked up. "We should get out of here, Mare. Get back to civilization, to people. It will do you good—"

"I can prove it." Mary moved from the window back to the computer, punched a few keys and brought up the signal. "There are two sequences. I don't know what the second one is. I admit that. It's too complex. But the first sequence is composed of a simple repetition. On-Off. 0–1. Binary digits."

"Bits."

"Exactly. And there's a third code—a terminator. It appears after every eighth bit."

"Eight bits. A byte." John set the bottle aside.

"It's a code."

"For what?"

"I don't know yet." Mary walked back to the computer and checked the progress. "Less than an hour before the analysis is complete."

"It could be random chance."

"It's not. The first part, what's decoded, begins with our address."

John laughed out loud and grasped his drink again. "You

had me for a minute there, Mare."

"If you were going to send a signal to another planet, what's the first thing you would put in? The address."

John nodded as he dumped more schnapps into the glass. "Uh huh, put the zip code in too."

"The first bytes represent two numbers: 27,624 and 0.00001496."

John paused.

"Think about it," Mary said. "What's the only constant across the entire universe?"

"Gravity?"

"Gravity is constant, but its measure depends on the curvature of spacetime, how close one object of mass is to another. You need a common denominator, something that any civilization, on any planet, no matter its mass or location, anywhere in the universe would know."

John looked around.

"The speed of light. It's the universal constant. It never changes, no matter where you are."

"Right…"

"The first number, 27,624, is Earth's distance from the center of our galaxy in light years."

"That distance could apply to a dozen planets—"

"The second number, 0.00001496, is the exact distance of Earth to the sun in light years."

John stared straight ahead for a long moment, then pushed the bottle and half-empty glass out of his vision. He focused on Mary. "This is our ticket."

Mary bunched her eyebrows.

John leaned back in his chair. "We sell it."

"For what? I think the malls have all closed."

"Well, I think the barter system is still in place. We demand protection, decent food, and whatever else we ever want."

"This is the greatest discovery in human history. We're not selling it."

"This is the greatest discovery in human history—at the moment of our greatest despair. This signal is hope. Distraction. Don't be a fool, Mare."

"Stop calling me Mare."

"When the plague broke out, you retreated here because you wanted to do something you loved until your time came. Me, I came here because I knew it was the biggest stockpile of booze anywhere in walking distance, and I knew you would come here. Yes, I've had a crush on you since I landed in San Juan." He held his hands up before Mary could say anything. "That's not my point. My point is that the world as you know it is over. People are desperate. They act out of self-interest. Sex and alcohol for me. For the folks you're going to call, it's about preserving their power. You're giving them the means to do that: hope. When you've delivered that, they won't need you anymore. This world isn't the one you remember. It will chew you up and spit you out, Mare."

"We're not selling it."

"You're a fool. This world slaughters idealists."

Behind her, the computer beeped. The analysis was complete.

Before she could read the results, a noise from the other side of the building echoed through the hall outside the office. Someone banging on the door? Mary and John's eyes met. They waited.

The banging grew louder, ending in the sound of glass breaking, scattering across the floor.

Footsteps, pacing slowly.

Mary stepped toward the door of the office, but John caught her arm. "Stay here," he whispered.

He picked up a baseball bat he had brought with him during the outbreak. "Lock this door. If they're here, the island's out of food."

Mary reached for the phone. She knew who she had to call now. Her hands shaking, she dialed the only person who could save them: her ex-husband.

4

# PART I
# RISE & FALL

# 1

*Alpha Lander*
1,200 Feet Below Sea Level
Off the Northern Coast of Morocco

David Vale was sick of pacing in the small bedroom, wondering if, or when, Kate would return. He glanced at the bloody pillow. The pool that had started as a few drops ten days ago was now a river that stretched from her pillow halfway down the bed.

"I'm fine," Kate had said each morning.

"Where do you go every day?"

"I just need some time. And space."

"Time and space for what?" David had asked.

"To get better."

But she hadn't gotten better. Every day when Kate returned, she was worse. Each night brought more violent nightmares, sweats, and nosebleeds that David thought might not stop. He had held her, and he had been patient, waiting, hoping the woman who had saved his life, whose life he had saved two weeks ago, would somehow turn the corner and pull through. But she slipped away a little more each day. And now she was late. She had never been late before.

He checked his watch. Three hours late.

She could be anywhere in the massive Atlantean ship, which covered sixty square miles and was buried just off the mountainous coast of Northern Morocco, directly across from Gibraltar.

David had spent the last fourteen days, while Kate was away, learning how to operate the ship's systems. He was still learning

7

them. Kate had enabled the voice command routines to help with any commands David couldn't figure out.

"Alpha, what is Dr. Warner's location?" David asked.

The disembodied computer voice of the *Alpha Lander* boomed into the small room. "That information is classified."

"Why?"

"You are not a senior member of the research staff."

It seemed Atlantean computer systems were not immune to stating the obvious. David sat on the bed, just beside the blood stain. *What's the priority? I need to know if she's okay.* A thought occurred to him.

"Alpha, can you show me Dr. Warner's vital signs?"

A wall panel opposite the small bed lit up, and David read the numbers and chart quickly—what he could understand.

```
Blood Pressure: 92/47
Pulse: 31
```

*She's hurt. Or worse—dying. What happened to her?*

"Alpha, why are Dr. Warner's vitals abnormal?"

"That information is class—"

"Classified." David kicked the chair into the desk.

"Does that conclude your query?" Alpha asked.

"Not by a long shot."

David stepped to the double doors, which hissed open. He paused, then grabbed his sidearm. Just in case.

David had been marching down the dimly lit corridors for almost ten minutes when he heard a figure moving in the shadows. He halted and waited, wishing his eyes would adjust to the faint lights at the floor and ceiling. Maybe the Atlanteans could see in less light or perhaps the ship—the piece of the ship they occupied—was operating in power-saving mode. Either way, it made the alien vessel seem even more mysterious.

A figure stepped out of the shadow.

Milo.

David was surprised to see the Tibetan teenager this deep in the ship. Milo was the only other person who shared the ship with Kate and David, but he spent most of his time outside of it. He slept outside, just beyond the inclining shaft that led from the buried ship to the mountaintop, where the Berbers left food for them. Milo loved sleeping under the stars and rising with the sun. David often found him sitting cross-legged, meditating when he and Kate went to join him for dinner each night. Milo had been their morale officer for the last two weeks, but through the dim light, David now saw only concern on the young man's face.

"I haven't seen her," Milo said.

"Call me on ship's comm if you do." David resumed his rapid pace.

Milo fell in behind him, pumping his legs to keep up. David's muscular frame and six-foot three-inch height dwarfed Milo, who was a full foot shorter. Together, they looked like a giant and his young sidekick barreling through a darkened labyrinth.

"I won't need to," Milo said, panting.

David glanced back at him.

"I'll be with you."

"You should go back up top."

"You know I can't," Milo said.

"She'll be angry."

"If she's safe, I will not care."

*Same here*, David thought. They walked in silence, the only sound the rhythmic beating of David's boots pounding the metallic floor followed by Milo's fainter footfalls.

David stopped before a large set of double doors and activated the wall panel. The display read:

Auxiliary Medical Bay 12

It was the only medical bay in their part of the ship, and it was David's best guess about where Kate went each day.

He moved his hand deeper into the green cloud of light that emerged from the wall panel, worked his fingers a few seconds, and the doors hissed open.

David crossed the room quickly.

There were four medical tables in the center. Holographic wall displays ran the length of the room—the empty room. Could she have already left?

"Alpha, can you tell me the last time this bay was used?"

"This bay was last used on mission date, 9.12.38.28, standard date 12.39.12.47.29—"

David shook his head. "How many local days ago?"

"Nine million, one hundred twenty eight thousand—"

"Okay, fine. Is there another medical bay within our section of the ship?"

"Negative."

*Where else would she go?* Maybe there was another way to track her.

"Alpha, can you show me which sections of the ship are currently consuming the most power?"

A wall screen lit up, and a holographic model of the ship materialized. Three sections glowed: Arc 1701-D, Auxiliary Medical Bay 12, and Adaptive Research Lab 47.

"Alpha, what is Adaptive Research Lab 47?"

"An Adaptive Research Lab can be configured for a variety of biological and other experiments."

"How is Adaptive Research Lab 47 currently configured?" David braced for the response.

"That information is classified—"

"Classified," David muttered. "Right…"

Milo held out a protein bar. "For the walk."

David led Milo back into the corridor, where he ripped the wrapper open, bit off a large chunk of the brown bar, and chewed in silence. It seemed to help with the frustration.

David stopped in the corridor, and Milo almost slammed into the back of him.

David squatted and examined something on the floor.

"What is it?" Milo asked.

"Blood."

David walked faster after that, and the blood on the floor increased from a few drops to long stretches.

At the double doors to Adaptive Research Lab 47, David worked his fingers in the green light of the wall panel. He entered the open command six times, and each time, the display flashed the same message:

```
Insufficient Access
```

"Alpha! Why can't I open this door?"

"You have insufficient access—"

"How can I get inside this door?"

"You cannot," Alpha's voice echoed through the corridor with finality.

David and Milo stood for a moment.

David spoke quietly. "Alpha, show me Dr. Warner's vital signs."

The wall display transformed, and the numbers and charts appeared.

```
Blood Pressure: 87/43
Pulse: 30
```

Milo turned to David.

"Dropping," David said.

"What now?"

"Now we wait."

Milo sat cross-legged and closed his eyes. David knew he was seeking the stillness, and in that moment, David wished he could do the same, could put everything out of his mind. Fear clouded his thoughts. He desperately wanted that door to hiss open, but he dreaded it as well, dreaded finding out what had happened to Kate, what experiment she was running, what she was doing to herself.

David had almost fallen asleep when the alarm went off. Alpha's voice thundered through the cramped corridor.

"Subject medical emergency. Condition critical. Access overrides executed."

The wide double doors to the research lab slid open.

David rushed in and rubbed his eyes, trying to understand what he saw.

Behind him, Milo spoke in awe, "Whoa."

# 2

*Alpha Lander*
1,200 Feet Below Sea Level
Off the Northern Coast of Morocco

"What is this?" Milo asked.

David scanned the research lab. "No idea."

The room was vast, at least one hundred feet long and fifty feet deep, but unlike the medical bay, there were no tables in the room. In fact, the only things on the floor were two glass vats, at least ten feet in diameter. Yellow light glowed inside, and sparkling white elements drifted from the bottom to the top. The vat on the right was empty. The other held Kate.

She floated a few feet off the ground, her arms held straight out. She wore the same plain clothes she had left their bedroom in this morning, but there was something new: a silver helmet. It covered her entire face, even the bottom of her chin. Her recently dyed brunette hair fell out of it and onto her shoulders. The small visor that covered her eyes was black, revealing no clues about what was happening to her. The only hint was a stream of blood that flowed out of the helmet, down her neck, and stained her gray t-shirt. The stain seemed to grow with each passing second.

"Alpha, what's... going on here?" David asked.

"Specify."

"What is this experiment? Procedure?"

"Resurrection memory simulation."

*What does that mean? Is the simulation what's hurting her?*

"How can I stop it?"

"You cannot."

"Why not?" David asked, growing impatient.

"Interrupting a resurrection memory sequence would terminate the subject."

Milo turned to David, fear in his eyes.

David searched the room. What to do? He needed some clue, somewhere to begin. He threw his head back, trying to think. On the ceiling, a single small dome of black glass stared down at him.

"Alpha, do you have video telemetry of this lab?"

"Affirmative."

"Begin playback."

"Specify date range."

"Begin the second Dr. Warner entered today."

A wave of light emanated from the left wall, slowly forming a hologram of the lab. The vats were empty. The double doors slid open, and Kate strode in. She marched to the right wall, which lit up and began flashing a series of screens full of text and symbols David couldn't make out. Kate stood still, her eyes darting slightly left and right, reading, taking in the screens, each of which remained for less than a second.

"Cool," Milo whispered.

David felt himself take a step back. In that moment, he realized some of what Kate had become, the growing gulf that existed between the power of her mind and his.

Two weeks ago, Kate had found a cure for the Atlantis Plague, a global pandemic that had claimed a billion lives in its initial outbreak and countless more during its final mutation. The plague had divided the world. The survival rate was low, but those who survived were changed at the genetic level. Some survivors benefited from the plague—they grew stronger and smarter. The remainder devolved, receding back to a primitive existence. The world's population had rallied around two opposing factions: the Orchid Alliance, which sought to slow and cure the plague, and Immari International, which had unleashed the plague and advocated letting the genetic transformation run its course.

Kate, David, and a team of soldiers and scientists had stopped the plague and the Immari plan by isolating the pieces of a cure: endogenous retroviruses left by past Atlantean interventions in human evolution. The retroviruses were essentially viral fossils, the genetic breadcrumbs from instances where Atlanteans had modified the human genome.

In the final hours of the plague, with millions dying each minute, Kate had found a way to reconcile all the viral fossils and cure the plague. Her therapy had created a stable, unified Atlantean-Human genome, but she had paid a high price for the breakthrough.

That knowledge came from repressed memories within Kate's subconscious—memories from one of the Atlantean scientists who had conducted the genetic experiments on humanity over the course of thousands of years. The Atlantean memories enabled her to cure the plague, but they had also taken much of her own humanity—the part of Kate that was distinctly Kate and not the Atlantean scientist. As the clock had ticked down and the plague had spread around the globe, Kate had chosen to keep the Atlantean knowledge and cure the plague instead of ridding herself of the memories and protecting her own identity.

She had told David that she believed she could repair the damage the Atlantean memories had done, but as the days had passed, it became clear to David that Kate's experiments weren't working. She got sicker each day, and she refused to discuss her situation with David. He had felt her slipping away, and now, as he watched the playback, Kate reading the screens instantaneously, he knew that he had underestimated how drastic her transformation was.

"Is she reading that fast?" Milo asked.

"It's more than that. I think she's learning that fast," David whispered.

David felt a different kind of fear rising inside him. Was it because Kate had changed so much or because he was realizing how far over his head he was?

*Start with the simple stuff*, he thought.

"Alpha, how can Dr. Warner operate you without voice or tactile input?"

"Dr. Warner received a neural implant nine local days ago."

"Received? How?"

"Dr. Warner programmed me to perform the implant surgery."

Just one more thing that hadn't come up during their nightly *Honey, what did you do at work today?* discussion.

Milo cut his eyes at David, a slight grin forming on his lips. "I want one."

"That makes one of us." David focused on the holomovie. "Alpha, increase playback rate."

"Interval?"

"Five minutes per second."

The flashing screens of text morphed into solid waves, like white water sloshing back and forth in a black fish tank. Kate didn't move a muscle.

Seconds ticked by. Then the screen was off, and Kate was floating in the glowing yellow vat.

"Stop," David said. "Replay telemetry just before Dr. Warner enters the round... whatever it is."

David held his breath as he watched. The screen with text went out, and Kate walked to the rear of the room, just beside the vats. A wall slid open, she grabbed a silver helmet, and then walked to the vat, which slid open. She stepped inside, donned the helmet, and after the glass vat sealed, lifted off the ground.

"Alpha, resume accelerated playback."

The room remained the same with a single exception: slowly, blood began trickling out of Kate's helmet.

In the last second, David and Milo entered, and then three words flashed on the screen.

```
End of Telemetry
```

Milo turned to David. "Now what?"

David glanced between the screen and the vat that held Kate. Then he eyed the empty one.

"Alpha, can I join Dr. Warner's experiment?"

The panel at the back of the room slid open, revealing a single silver helmet.

Milo's eyes grew wide. "This is a bad idea, Mr. David."

"Got any good ideas?"

"You don't have to do this."

"You know I do."

The glass vat rotated, its glass opening. David stepped inside, pulled the helmet on, and the research lab disappeared.

# 3

It took a few seconds for David's eyes to adjust to the bright light beaming into the space. Directly ahead, a rectangular display flashed text he couldn't make out yet. The place reminded him of a train station with its arrivals/departures board, except that there seemed to be no entrance or exit to the cavernous space, just a solid white floor and arched columns that let light shine through.

Alpha's booming voice echoed. "Welcome to the Resurrection Archives. State your command."

David stepped closer to the board and began reading.

```
Memory Date     (Health)      Replay
============    ========      ======
12.37.40.13     (Corrupted)   Complete
13.48.19.23     (Intact)      Complete
13.56.64.15     (Corrupted)   Complete
```

A dozen rows continued—all complete. The last entry was:

```
14.72.47.33     (Corrupted)   In progress
```

"Alpha, what are my options?"

"You may open an archived memory or join a simulation in progress."

*In progress*. Kate would be there. If she was hurt... or under attack. David glanced around. He had no weapons, nothing to defend her with. It didn't matter.

"Join simulation in progress."

"Notify existing members?"

"No," he said on instinct. The element of surprise might preserve some advantage.

The lighted train station and board faded and a much smaller, darker place took form. The bridge of a spaceship. David stood at the rear. Text, charts, and images scrolled across the walls of the oval room, covering them. At the front, two figures stood before a wide viewscreen, staring at a world that floated against the black of space. David instantly recognized both of them.

On the left stood Dr. Arthur Janus, the other member of the Atlantean research team. He had helped David save Kate from Dorian Sloane and Ares in the final hours of the Atlantis Plague, but David still had mixed feelings about Janus. The brilliant scientist had created a false cure for the Atlantis Plague that erased seventy thousand years of human evolution—reverting the human race to a point before the Atlantis Gene was administered. Janus had sworn that rolling back human evolution was the only way to save humanity from an unimaginable enemy.

David felt no such conflicting feelings for the scientist standing beside Janus. He felt only love. In the reflection of the black areas of space on the screen, David could just make out the small features of Kate's beautiful face. She concentrated hard on the image of the world. David had seen that look many times. He was almost lost in it, but a sharp voice, calling out from overhead, snapped him back.

"This area is under a military quarantine. Evacuate immediately. Repeat: this area is under a military quarantine."

Another voice interrupted. It was similar to Alpha's tone. "Evacuation course configured. Execute?"

"Negative," Kate said. "Sigma, silence notifications from military buoys and maintain geosynchronous orbit."

"This is reckless," Janus said.

"I have to know."

David stepped closer to the screen. The world was similar to Earth, but the colors were different. The oceans were too green, the clouds too yellow, the land only red, brown and light tan.

19

There were no trees. Only round, black craters interrupted the barren landscape.

"It could have been a natural occurrence," Janus said. "A series of comets or an asteroid field."

"It wasn't."

"You don't—"

"It wasn't." The viewscreen zoomed to one of the impact craters. "A series of roads lead to each crater. There were cities there. This was an attack. Maybe they carved up an asteroid field and used the pieces for the kinetic bombardment." The viewscreen changed again. A ruined city in a desert landscape took shape, its skyscrapers crumbling. "They let the environmental fallout take care of anyone outside the major cities. There could be answers there." Kate's voice was final. David knew that voice. He had *experienced it* several times himself.

Apparently Janus had as well. He lowered his head. "Take the *Beta Lander*. It will give you better maneuverability without the arcs."

He turned and walked toward the door at the rear of the bridge.

David braced. But Janus couldn't see him. *Can Kate?*

Kate fell in behind Janus but stopped and stared at David. "You shouldn't be here."

"What is this, Kate? Something is happening to you outside. You're dying."

Kate took two more long steps toward the exit. "I can't protect you here."

"Protect me from what?"

She took another step. "Don't follow me." She lunged through the exit.

David charged after her.

He stood outside. On the planet. He spun, trying—

Kate. She was ahead of him, in an EVA suit, bounding for the crumbling city. Behind them, a small black ship sat on the red rocky terrain.

"Kate!" David called, running toward her.

She stopped.

The ground shook once, then again, throwing David off his feet. The sky opened, and a red object poured through, blinding David and smothering him with its heat. He felt as though an asteroid-sized fire poker were barreling toward him.

He tried to stand, but the shaking ground pulled him down again.

He crawled, feeling the heat from above and the sizzling rocks below melting him.

Kate seemed to float over the shaking ground. She loped forward, timing her landings to the quakes that shot her up and forward, toward David.

She covered him, and David wished he could see her face through the mirrored suit visor.

He felt himself falling. His feet touched a cold floor, and his head slammed into the glass. The vat. The research lab.

The glass swiveled open, and Milo rushed forward, his eyebrows high, his mouth open. "Mr. David..."

David looked down. His body wasn't burned, but sweat covered him. Blood flowed from his nose.

*Kate.*

David's muscles shook as he pushed himself up and staggered to her vat. The glass opened, and she fell straight down, like a contestant in a dunking booth.

David caught her, but he wasn't strong enough to stand. They spilled onto the cold floor, her landing on his chest.

David grabbed her neck. The pulse was faint—but there.

"Alpha! Can you help her?"

"Unknown."

"Unknown why?" David shouted.

"I have no current diagnosis."

"What the hell's it going to take to get one?"

A round panel opened, and a flat table extended into the room.

"A full diagnostic scan."

Milo rushed to pick up Kate's feet, and David gripped under her armpits, straining with every last ounce of strength to lift her onto the table.

David thought the table took its sweet time gliding back into the wall. A dark piece of glass covered the round hole, and he peered inside at a line of blue light that moved from Kate's feet to her head.

The screen on the wall flickered to life, its only message:

```
DIAGNOSTIC SCAN IN PROGRESS…
```

"What happened?" Milo asked.
"I… We…" David shook his head. "I have no idea."
The screen changed.

**Primary Diagnosis:**
Neurodegeneration due to Resurrection Syndrome

**Prognosis:**
Terminal

**Predicted Survival:**
4-7 local days

**Immediate Concerns:**
Subarachnoid hemorrhage
Cerebral thrombosis

**Recommended action:**
Surgical intervention

**Estimated Surgical Success Rate:**
39%

With each word David read, more of the room disappeared. Feeling faded. He felt his hand reach out and brace the glass vat. He stared at the screen.

Alpha's words beat down upon him, smothering him like the heat from the fire poker on the ruined planet. "Perform recommended surgery?"

David heard himself say yes, and vaguely, he was aware of Milo putting his arm around him, though it barely reached the top of his shoulder.

# 4

The screams served as Dorian's only guide through the ship's dark corridors. For days, he had searched for their source. They always stopped as he drew near, and Ares would appear, forcing Dorian to leave the Atlantean structure that covered two hundred fifty square miles under the ice cap of Antarctica, making him return to the surface, back to the preparations for the final assault—grunt work that was beneath him.

If Ares was here, spending every waking hour in the room with the screams, that's where the action was. Dorian was sure of it.

The screams stopped. Dorian halted.

Another wail erupted, and he turned a corner, then another. They were coming from behind the double doors directly ahead.

Dorian leaned against the wall and waited. Answers. Ares had promised him answers, the truth about his past. Like Kate Warner, Dorian had been conceived in another time—before the First World War, saved from the Spanish flu by an Atlantean tube, and awoken in 1978 with the memories of an Atlantean.

Dorian had Ares' memories, and those repressed recollections had driven his entire life. Dorian had seen only glimpses: battles on land, sea, air, and the largest battles of all, in space. Dorian longed to know what had happened to Ares, his history, Dorian's past, his origins. Most of all, he longed to understand himself, the *why* behind his entire life.

Dorian wiped away another bit of blood from his nose. The nose bleeds were more frequent now, as were the headaches and

24

nightmares. Something was happening to him. He pushed that out of his mind.

The doors opened, and Ares strode out, unsurprised to see Dorian.

Dorian strained to see inside the chamber. A man hung from the wall, blood running from the straps cutting into his out-stretched arms and the wounds on his chest and legs. The doors closed, and Ares stopped in the corridor. "You disappoint me, Dorian."

"Likewise. You promised me answers."

"You'll have them."

"When?"

"Soon."

Dorian closed the distance to Ares. "Now."

Ares brought his straightened hand across, striking Dorian in the throat, sending him to the ground, gasping for air.

"You will give me exactly one more order in your life, Dorian. Do you understand? If you were anyone else, I wouldn't even tolerate what you just did. But you are me. More so than you know. And I know you better than you know yourself. I haven't told you about our past because it would cloud your judgment. We have work to do. Knowing the full truth would put you at risk. I'm depending on you, Dorian. In a few short days, we will control this planet. The survivors, the remainder of the human race—a race, I remind you, that I helped create, helped save from extinction—will be the founding members of our army."

"Who are we fighting?"

"An enemy of unimaginable strength."

Dorian got to his feet but kept his distance. "I have quite an imagination."

Ares resumed his brisk pace, Dorian following at a distance. "They defeated us in a night and a day, Dorian. Imagine that. We were the most advanced race in the known universe—even more advanced than the lost civilizations we had found."

They reached the crossroads where an enormous set of doors opened onto the miles of glass tubes that held the Atlantean survivors. "They're all that's left."

"I thought you said they can never awaken, that their trauma from the attacks was too great for them to overcome."

"It is."

"You got someone out. Who is he?"

"He's not one of them. Of us. He's not your concern. Your concern is the war ahead."

"The war ahead," Dorian muttered. "We don't have the numbers."

"Stay the course, Dorian. Believe. In a few short days, we will have this world. Then we will embark on the great campaign, a war to save all the human worlds. This enemy is your enemy too. Humans share our DNA. This enemy will come for you too, sooner or later. You cannot hide. But together, we can fight. If we don't raise our army now, while the window exists, we lose everything. The fate of a thousand worlds rests in your hands."

"Right. A thousand worlds. I'd like to point out what I see as a few key challenges. *Personnel.* There are maybe a few billion humans left on Earth. They're weak, sick, and starving. That's our army pool—assuming we can even take the planet, and I'm not even sure of that. So a few billion, not necessarily strong, in our 'army.' And I use that term loosely. Up against a power that rules the galaxy... Sorry, but I don't like our chances."

"You're smarter than that, Dorian. You think this war will resemble your primitive ideas about space warfare? Metal and plastic ships floating through space shooting lasers and explosives at each other? Please. You think I haven't considered our situation? Numbers aren't our key to victory. I made this plan forty thousand years ago. You've been on the case three months. Have faith, Dorian."

"Give me a reason."

Ares smiled. "You actually think you can goad me into giving you all the answers your little heart desires, Dorian? Want me to make you feel good, whole, safe? That's why you came to Antarctica originally, isn't it? To find your father? Uncover the truth about your past?"

"You treat me like this—after all I've done for you?"

"You've done for yourself, Dorian. Ask me the question you really want to ask."

Dorian shook his head.

"Go ahead."

"What's happening to me?" Dorian stared at Ares. "What did you do to me?"

"Now we're getting somewhere."

"There's something wrong with me, isn't there?"

"Of course there is. You're human."

"That's not what I mean. I'm dying. I can feel it."

"In time, Dorian. I saved your people. I have a plan. We will establish a lasting peace in this universe. You don't know how elusive that has been." Ares stepped closer to Dorian. "There are truths I can't reveal to you. You're not ready. Have patience. Answers will come. It's important I help you understand the past. Your misinterpretation could sink us, Dorian. You're important. I can do this without you, but I don't want to. I've waited a long time to have someone like you by my side. If your faith is strong enough, there's no limit to what we can do."

Ares turned and led them out of the crossroads, away from the long hall that held the tubes, toward the portal entrance. Dorian followed in silence, a war beginning in his mind: blindly obey or rebel? They suited up without another word and crossed the ice chamber beyond, where the Bell hung.

Dorian lingered, and his eyes drifted to the ravine where he had found his father, frozen, encased in ice within the EVA suit, a victim of the Bell and his Immari lieutenant, who had betrayed him.

Ares stepped up onto the metal basket. "The future is all that matters, Dorian."

The dark vertical shaft passed in silence, and the basket stopped at the surface. The rows of pop-up habitats spread out across the flat sheet of ice like an endless flow of white caterpillars dug into the snow.

Dorian had grown up in Germany and then London. He only thought he knew cold. Antarctica was a wilderness with no equal.

As he and Ares strode toward the central ops building, Immari staffers clad in thick white parkas scurried between the habitats, some saluting, others keeping their heads down as the winds hit them.

Beyond the caterpillar habitats, along the perimeter, heavy machinery and crews were building the rest of "Fortress Antarctica" as it had become known. Two dozen rail guns sat silently, pointed north, ready for the attack the Immari knew would come.

No army on Earth was prepared to wage war here—even before the plague. Certainly not after. Air power would mean nothing in the face of the rail guns. Even a massive ground assault, with cover from artillery from the sea, would never succeed. Dorian's mind drifted to the Nazis, his father's successors, and their foolish winter campaign in Russia. The Orchid Alliance would face the same fate if, or more likely, when, they landed here.

Soldiers greeted Dorian and Ares inside central ops and lined the hallways, standing at attention as the two leaders passed. In the situation room, Ares addressed the director of operations. "Are we ready?"

"Yes, sir. We've secured the assets around the world. Minimal casualties."

"And the search teams?"

"In place. They've all reached the specified drill depths along the perimeter. A few had trouble with pockets in the ice, but we sent follow-up teams." The director paused. "However, they haven't found anything." He punched a keyboard, and a map of Antarctica appeared. Red dots littered the map.

*What's he looking for?* Dorian wondered. *Another ship? No. Martin would have known, surely. Something else?*

Ares stared back at Dorian, and at that moment, Dorian felt something he hadn't in a long time, even in the corridor below, when Ares had struck him. Fear.

"Have they lowered the devices I supplied?" Ares asked.

"Yes," the director said.

Ares walked to the front of the room. "Put me on base-wide comm." The director punched a few keys and nodded to Ares.

"To the brave men and women working for our cause, who have sacrificed and labored toward our goal, know this: the day we have prepared for has arrived. In a few minutes, we will offer peace to the Orchid Alliance. I hope they accept. We seek peace here on Earth so that we can prepare for a final war with an enemy who knows no peace. That challenge is ahead. Today, I thank you for your service, and I ask you to have faith in the hours to come." Ares focused on Dorian. "And as your faith is tested, know this: if you want to build a better world, you must first have the courage to destroy the world that exists."

# 5

Dr. Paul Brenner rolled over and stared at the clock.

5:25

It would ring in five minutes. Then he would turn it off, get up, and get ready—for nothing. There was no job to get to, no work to do, no list of urgent matters to get through. There was only a broken world grasping for direction, and for the last fourteen days, that direction had nothing to do with him. He should have been getting the best sleep of his life, yet something was missing. For some reason, he always awoke just before five-thirty, just before the alarm rang, ready, expectant, as if today everything would change.

He threw the covers off the bed, shuffled to the master bathroom, and began washing his face. He never took a full shower in the morning. He liked to get to the office quickly, to be the first there, getting a head start on the staff who reported to him. He always hit the gym after work. Ending the day that way helped him relax at home, helped him separate. Or try to. That was tough in his line of work. There was always a new outbreak, a suspected outbreak, or a bureaucratic mess to handle. Directing the CDC's Division of Global Disease Detection and Emergency Response was a tough job. Contagions were only half the problem.

And then there were the secrets Paul kept. For the last twenty years, he had worked with a global consortium, planning for the ultimate outbreak, a pandemic that could wipe out the human race—a pandemic that came in the form of the Atlantis Plague. All his years of hard work had paid off. The global task force,

Continuity, had contained the plague and finally found a cure—thanks to a scientist he had never met, Dr. Kate Warner. So much about the Atlantis Plague still remained a mystery to Paul, but he knew one thing: it was over. He should have been overjoyed. But mostly, he felt empty, without purpose, adrift.

He finished washing his face and ran a hand through his short, black, wiry hair, patting down any signs of bed head. In the mirror, he saw the empty king bed and briefly considered going back to sleep.

*What are you getting ready for? The plague is over. There's nothing left to do.*

No. It wasn't entirely true. She was waiting for him.

His bed was empty, but the house wasn't. He could already smell breakfast cooking.

He crept down the stairs, careful not to wake his twelve-year-old nephew Matthew.

A pot clanged in the kitchen.

"Good morning," Paul whispered the second he crossed the threshold of the kitchen.

"Morning," Natalie said, tipping a pan and letting scrambled eggs flow onto a plate. "Coffee?"

Paul nodded and sat at the small round table next to the bay window that overlooked the sloping yard.

Natalie set the plate of eggs down alongside a large bowl of grits. The bacon completed the buffet. It was covered with foil, keeping the heat in. Paul served their plates in silence. Before the plague, he usually watched TV while he wolfed down his breakfast, but he much preferred this—having company. He hadn't had company in a long time.

Natalie added a dash of pepper to her grits. "Matthew had another nightmare."

"Really? I didn't hear anything."

"I got him calmed down around three." She ate a bite of eggs mixed with grits and added some more salt. "You should talk to him about his mother."

Paul had been dreading that. "I will."

"What are you going to do today?"

"I don't know. I thought about going to the depot." He motioned to the walk-in pantry. "We could run out of food in a few weeks. Better to stock up now before the Orchid Districts empty and there's a run."

"Good idea." She paused, seeming to want to change the subject. "I have a friend named Thomas. He's about my age."

Paul looked up. *Your age?*

"Thirty-five, for the record," she said with a small smile, answering his unspoken question. She focused on her food, the smile fading. "His wife died of cancer two years ago. He was devastated. He kept the pictures up around the house. He never really got better until he talked about her. For him, that was the key to moving on."

*Did her husband die? In the Atlantis Plague? Before? Is that what she's telling me?* Paul was an expert at unraveling retro-viruses, or anything in a lab for that matter. People, especially women, were a real mystery to him. "Yes, I agree. For anyone who has... lost someone, I think talking about it is very healthy."

Natalie leaned in, but across the room, an alarm rang out, piercing the moment. Not an alarm, a phone. Paul's landline.

Paul rose and picked up the phone.

"Paul Brenner."

He listened, nodded several times, and tried to ask a question, but the line was dead before he had a chance.

"Who was it?"

"The Administration," Paul said. "They're sending a car for me. There's some kind of problem in the Orchid Districts. "

"You think the plague has mutated? Another wave of infection?"

"Maybe."

"You want me to come with you?"

Natalie was the only remaining member of the Continuity research staff—the team that had coordinated the global efforts to cure the Atlantis Plague. Before that, she had been a researcher working in a lab at the CDC. She likely couldn't add anything research-wise, but for some reason, Paul did want her along. But there was a more important issue. "I need someone to stay here with Matthew. I can't ask you—"

"You don't have to. We'll be here when you get back."

Upstairs Paul dressed quickly. He wanted to get back to his conversation with Natalie, but he had to admit: it felt good to be getting dressed for work, to be needed, to have somewhere to go. He heard a horn honk outside. He glanced out the window and saw a black sedan with tinted windows, idling, sending clouds of exhaust into the cold, barely lit morning.

At the front door, he jerked his trench coat out of the closet. On the opposite side of the foyer, a small table held a picture frame with a wedding photo of Paul and his wife. Ex-wife. She had left four years ago.

*Is that what she thinks? That my wife is dead?*

Of course. All the pictures were still up, scattered around the house.

Paul had the irresistible urge to set the record straight before he left. "Natalie."

"Just a minute," she called from the kitchen.

Paul glanced at the wedding picture again. The last conversation with his wife ran through his head.

"You work too much, Paul. You're always going to work too much. It just can't work."

Paul had sat on the couch—ten feet from where he now stood—staring at the floor.

"Movers are coming tomorrow for my things. I don't want to fight."

And they hadn't. In fact, he still held no hard feelings. She had moved to New Mexico, and they had stayed in touch over the years, but he hadn't taken the pictures down. It had never even occurred to him. For the first time, he regretted that.

Natalie's voice interrupted his memory. "In case they don't feed you."

33

Paul took the brown paper bag. He motioned to the picture on the table. "About my wife—"

The horn rang out, a long blow this time.

"We can talk when you get back. Be careful."

Paul began to reach for her but hesitated. He reached for the door instead and trudged toward the car. Two Marines exited, and the closest opened the door for him. They were off several seconds later.

Paul turned and looked back through the rearview window at his two-story brick home, wishing he'd had more time there.

# 6

Paul Brenner stared out the window of the fourth-floor conference room, trying to understand. Rows of people lined the streets. Medical staff processed the lines, taking readings and directing people to different buildings, where they wandered out exhausted. It was almost as if everyone were undergoing a physical.

"What do you think, Paul?"

Paul turned to find Terrance North, the new Secretary of Defense, standing in the doorway. North was a former Marine, and although he wore a close-fitting navy suit, he still looked like a soldier, his face lean, his posture rigid. Paul had met North several times via video conference during the Atlantis Plague but never in person, where he was certainly more imposing.

Paul pointed to the street below. "I'm not sure what I'm looking at."

"Preparations for war."

"War with whom?"

"The Immari."

"Impossible. The Europeans crushed them in Southern Spain. They're in shambles, and the plague is cured. They're no threat."

North closed the door behind him and activated the large screen in the conference room. "You're talking about organized warfare. A war that resembles any past war."

"What are you talking about?"

"A new kind of conflict." North worked his laptop, and a series of videos appeared on the screen. Armed forces in black with no insignia assaulted a series of industrial buildings and warehouses. Paul didn't recognize the locations. They weren't army bases.

"These are food depots," North said. "They have been under light guard since Orchid governments nationalized the food supply in the opening days of the outbreak. This last video is of the Archer Daniel Midland facility in Decatur, Illinois. Immari militia units seized it and a dozen other major food processing plants a week ago."

"They intend to starve us?"

"That's only a piece of their plan."

"You can't retake them?"

"Of course we can. But they'll destroy them if we attack. That puts us in a tough spot. We can't rebuild the food processing plants fast enough."

"Can you get people to process the food?"

"We've looked at that. That's not why you're here."

"Why am I here?"

"I'm going to lay out all the pieces, Paul. Let you make an informed decision."

*Decision about what?* Paul wondered.

North worked the keyboard again. A scan of a crumpled document appeared. "This is an Immari manifesto that's been circulating. It predicts a coming collapse of humanity. A day of reckoning when a cataclysm will occur. It calls for all those who wish to see the human race survive to rally behind the Immari cause. It lays out a strategy. The first step is the seizure of the food supply—everything from large food processing plants to farms. Second: the power grid."

Paul began to ask, but North interrupted. "They've taken control of eighty percent of our coal reserves."

"Coal?"

"It still produces over forty percent of American power. Without the coal, the power plants will go dark soon. Nuclear and hydro-electric plants will be online, but taking the coal facilities out will do us in."

Paul nodded. There had to be some viral or biological component. Power and food... he wasn't here for that. "Is there a third step in the manifesto?"

"Wait. The Immari promise that those loyal to their call will receive help—an attack on a scale the world has never seen. They promise the Orchid Alliance will be crushed in a single day and night of destruction."

"A nuclear attack?"

"We don't think so. Those locations are well-guarded. And it's too obvious. It's something outside the box. We have one clue. The satellites. Last night, we lost contact with every satellite controlled by the Orchid Alliance as well as the International Space Station. Private satellites are unresponsive as well. The first satellites entered the atmosphere this morning. The last of them will burn up and crash to the Earth by nightfall."

"Someone shot them down?"

"No. They were hacked. A very sophisticated virus got into the control software. We're blind. The only reason to do that is if they're ready to attack. The cataclysm, the Immari attack, whatever it is, begins soon."

"You think it might be biological? Another outbreak?"

"It's possible," North said. "In truth, we have no idea. The president wants to be ready for anything."

One of North's staff members entered the conference room. "Sir, we need you."

North left Paul alone to contemplate what he had seen. If the attack were biological, Paul would be the logical choice to lead the global response. He began mentally preparing himself. Scenarios flashed through his mind. His thoughts went to Natalie and Matthew. He would transfer them to Continuity—

The door opened, and North walked in slowly. "It's started."

# 7

Walking the halls of Continuity was bizarre for Paul. In this section of the CDC, he and the Continuity staff had managed a global pandemic that lasted eighty-one days and claimed the lives of almost two billion people. Eighty-one days of sleeping on the couch in his office, drinking coffee endlessly, shouting matches, breakdowns, and one final breakthrough.

The faces walking the halls were different now: soldiers, DOD staff, and others Paul couldn't identify.

Secretary of Defense North was waiting for him in the main Continuity situation room. The glass doors parted and closed behind Paul, and the two men were alone. The screens that covered the far wall showed the same display they had when Paul had walked out fourteen days ago: casualty statistics from Orchid Districts around the world. They ranged from twenty to forty percent. All except one: Malta. Dr. Warner and her team had found the last piece of the cure there. It glowed green, the text "0% Casualty Rate" floating beside it.

North took a seat at one of the rolling tables. "One of my teams just picked up Natalie and your nephew, Paul. They'll be here soon."

"Thank you. I've contacted the members of my staff—what's left. Once they're here, I'll start making calls to my foreign counterparts."

"Excellent. I know they're having similar conversations right now. So, first thing's first. We need to get your root-level access code to the Continuity control program."

Paul squinted. "My access code?"

North took out a pen and nodded casually. "Uh huh."

"Why?"

"I was told only your codes could push a new therapy out to the Orchid implants."

"That's true," Paul said, alarm bells ringing in his mind.

"It's for security, Paul. You're a point of failure. If you die, those codes are lost with you—and for all intents and purposes, Continuity with it. The whole system is worthless if we can't administer a new therapy. We need redundancy."

"We have redundancy. Two people have the access codes: someone on the team—someone I select—and me. No one knows that person's identity. *For security purposes.* Imagine if the Immari were to learn the Continuity access codes. They could wipe us out in hours."

"And who is that other person?"

Paul rose and paced away from North, whose expression had now changed. The other code keeper was dead. He had died with many of the other staff in the final hours of the plague. Paul had intended to select a new code keeper when the remaining staff arrived, but now he wasn't so sure. "That's all I can say regarding the code. But you have my word that we won't lose access to Continuity."

North stood as well. "We never finished our conversation at the Orchid District. We're officially at war. We're working on ways to communicate with our naval fleets, but they have standing orders to launch an attack if they lose contact with the Pentagon for an extended period of time. The bombs should begin falling on the Immari central headquarters in Antarctica soon. They've evacuated their facilities in Cape Town, Buenos Aires, and others, but they will be hunted. Fighting the Immari head-on isn't what we're worried about. It's the coming war here at home. We estimate Immari strength here in the US at forty thousand, maybe a little more, possibly less. It was enough to take our food chain and cripple the power grid, but they can't do much else."

"Exactly."

"I read your file, Paul. You're a smart guy. A good scientist. I was a good Marine. It took me years to get up to speed on politics. It's a different game. But you know that. You were upper management here at CDC. You've played the game. You can see where this is going."

"Obviously I'm not as smart as you think."

"They cut the power and food to the Orchid Districts to make us empty them. When we do, the Immari will start converting the tired, hungry masses that flow out. Their message will appeal to the millions of people we release. We'll be fighting a propaganda war. Their ideology against ours. We aren't fighting the Immari Army. We're fighting their message. It boils down to the elimination of the welfare state. The Immari want a global state built with people who can fend for themselves, people who don't rely on the government to live. A lot of people like that idea. They don't want to go back to the way things were. And there's the simple reality from our end: we can't fend off the militia and care for those too weak to fight anyway. The US has about a ten-day supply of insulin left. Antibiotics are practically gone; we only use them in extreme cases now. We've been burning the dead outside the Orchid Districts, but we can't keep up. With the close quarters, a new antibiotic-resistant superbug is likely already loose in an Orchid District somewhere."

"We can handle superbugs. That's why Continuity exists."

"It's only a fraction of what we face. Even without the Immari threat, we're looking at a humanitarian crisis on a global scale. We have to rebuild the world, and we've got too many mouths to feed. We have an opportunity. We can eliminate some of our own who we can't care for *and at the same time*, convince the Immari sympathizers not to go over. It's our only play. Continuity and the Orchid implants are the key. We've got to build an army of our own—from the strong within our ranks."

Paul swallowed. "I... need some time to think—"

"Time is one thing we don't have, Paul. I need those codes. I'll remind you that I have Natalie and your nephew."

Paul felt himself involuntarily step back. "I... I want to know the plan."

"The codes." North glanced at the soldiers outside the glass doors.

Paul took it as a threat. He took a seat at the table and spoke softly. "I assume you've been trying to crack the codes?"

"For over a week now. NSA says they could be in within a few days, but when the satellites went down, we decided to call you. We'd really like to get those codes the easy way."

Paul nodded. He knew what *the hard way* would be. He tried to push the idea of being tortured out of his mind and focus on what would happen if he turned over the codes. He saw two possibilities. One: North was an Immari agent and he would use the codes to kill countless people. Two: America and the Orchid allies were about to make the greatest mistake in human history. And they were possibly going to frame Paul for it. He needed to know more. He needed time to form a plan. "Okay. Look, I've been at home for two weeks. I didn't know any of this was going on. I agree that our back is against the wall. I will turn over the codes, but you should know that the Continuity program has multiple levels of security, including trap doors and protocols that ensure Continuity staff are the only ones who can send new therapies to the implants each Orchid District resident has. You need me. I now understand the threat we're facing. All I ask is that you make me part of the solution."

North took a seat and pulled a keyboard close to him. "Now we're getting somewhere." The screen changed to show a series of statistics. Paul recognized some of them.

"You've done a physical—"

"A short one, yes. We've done a large-scale inventory of the entire human race—everyone under the Orchid flag."

"To what end?"

41

"There are two lists here. Those we can save—the ones fit to fight or contribute. And those who aren't."

"I see."

"We need to use the Euthanasia Protocol on the unfit list, and we need to do it now."

"People won't stand for this. You'll have riots—"

"We intend to blame the Immari. They've taken the food and power. This isn't a stretch. If they could take Continuity, this is exactly what they would do: euthanize the weak. The death of millions will energize the survivors to stand against the Immari threat. And it would take away the Immari selling point: eliminating the welfare state. With the weak gone, we can offer everything they can. The world the Immari sympathizers want would already be here." North moved closer to Paul. "With a few keystrokes, we can win this war before it begins, before the cataclysm. Now I need your answer."

Paul glanced out the glass doors. His staff was arriving, but the guards were directing them away. There was no way out of this room.

"I understand," Paul said.

"Good." North motioned to the guard, and a skinny young man carrying a laptop entered. "This young man has been working on the Continuity database. He's going to follow along with you, Paul. He'll be watching and taking notes, including your access code. For redundancy, of course."

"Of course."

Paul began typing on the keyboard while his new "assistant" got set up.

A few minutes later, Paul opened the main Continuity control program and began walking him through it. "The Euthanasia Protocol is actually a pre-programmed therapy..."

Fifteen minutes later, Paul entered his final authorization code and the main screen began blinking:

```
Euthanasia Protocol Transmitted to Population
Subset
```

Paul stood and said, "I'd like to be alone in my office now."

"Sure, Paul." North addressed one of the soldiers. "Escort Dr. Brenner to his office. Remove his computer and phone and see that he has any food and drink he requests."

In his office, Paul sat on the couch and stared at the floor. He had never felt worse in his life.

# 8

Paul Brenner checked his watch for the hundredth time, then got up from the couch and paced to the window. The three rings of military vehicles barricading the CDC tower sat silently, some of the soldiers standing and smoking, most sitting in their Humvees or slumped against the sandbags.

Shouts erupted in the reception area outside his office. The door handle rattled then shook as someone began pounding on the solid wood door.

"Unlock this door, Brenner!" North's voice was hoarse but strong enough to strike fear into Paul.

*He's alive.* Paul checked his watch again.

"Three seconds, Brenner! Or we open this door without you."

Paul froze.

Behind the door, he heard something that amounted to "aim down, we need him alive." Shots sprayed splinters into the room, and the door swung open.

Terrance North staggered in, clutching his chest. "You tried to kill me."

"You should get to the infirmary—"

"Don't play games, Paul." North jerked his head to the guards. "Take him."

Guards seized Paul's arms and dragged him down the hall.

In the Continuity situation room, the young computer programmer silently watched North throw Paul against the wall and spit words slowly in his face. "You stop this now, or I swear I'll have these soldiers shoot you."

Paul couldn't believe the man could still stand. North's cardiovascular health had kept him alive far longer than Paul had anticipated. His mind grasped for any diversion that might buy time.

In his peripheral vision, he saw Natalie enter the hall with Matthew. He tried to look away, but it was too late—North had seen them.

"I'll execute the boy first. You can watch." He gasped for breath. He released Paul and collapsed onto the table, panting now. "Major—"

Paul swallowed and spoke to the three soldiers. "Stop. Major, I believe you swore to defend this country against enemies foreign and domestic. That's all I've done. Thirty minutes ago, the Secretary forced me to use Continuity to execute millions of our own citizens."

"He's lying!"

"He's not," the skinny programmer said. "North gave me the same orders. I wouldn't do it either. I cracked the access codes days ago. I've been lying about it."

North shook his head and stared at Paul with disgust. "You're a fool. You've killed us all. When the Immari come, they'll wipe us out."

The soldiers slowly lowered their rifles. Paul exhaled as he watched Terrance North convulse and fall to the floor, taking his last breaths. It was the first life Paul Brenner had ever taken, and he hoped it would be his last.

---

Paul was rubbing his temples, staring out the window, when the shattered door to his office creaked open.

Natalie came in and stood beside him for a moment, gazing at the rings of military outside the building. Finally, she said, "How can I help?"

"We're in a tough spot. It depends on what the White House does next. The Marines inside Continuity will follow Major Thomas, who's supporting me for now, but if the Administration orders a full assault on the building, we won't last long."

"So…"

"We need to get Matthew out of here. I don't want you here either."

"How? Where can we go?"

"The Orchid Districts won't be safe. Or the cities. Probably not the roads for that matter. My grandmother has a cabin in the mountains of North Carolina." He handed her a map with highlighted directions. "Take Matthew and a few Marines and get there as quickly as you can. The stock room is still pretty full here. Take food and water—as much as you can pack into a Humvee and get out before the next shoe drops."

"What about—"

"There's a call for you, sir." Susan, Paul's secretary, was leaning in the door frame.

Paul hesitated. Was it "the call"—the surrender or face the firing squad call? "Is it…"

"It's your ex-wife."

His nervousness turned to surprise.

Natalie's face was even more surprised.

Paul raised a finger. "Yes, my ex-wife is alive and well, *and* I haven't talked to her in years." He turned to Susan. "Tell her I can't talk—"

"She says it's important. She sounds scared, Paul."

Paul walked into the outer office and picked up the phone. He hesitated, not sure how to start. He settled on, "Brenner." It came out harsher than he intended.

"Hi, it's, um, Mary, I'm… I'm sorry to call—"

"Yeah, Mary, it's… a really bad time."

"I found something, Paul. A signal on the radio telescope. It's organized. A code of some type."

"What kind of code?"

When the conversation was over, Paul hung up the phone and glanced out the window at the soldiers waiting outside the building. He needed to get out of Atlanta, possibly the country, and if the code was real, it could change the entire equation. It had to be connected to the Atlantis conspiracy, though Paul wasn't sure how. The timing, it arriving just as the plague had been cured couldn't be a coincidence. He addressed the Marine standing in his office. "Major, assuming we can get out of here, can you get me a plane?"

———————— ❀ ————————

Three hours later, Paul was standing in Mary's office, trying to understand what she was saying.

"Stop." He held up his hand. "Is it one code or two?"

"Two," Mary said. "But it could be the same message encoded in two formats—"

"Don't say another word, Mare!" John Bishop, Mary's colleague, placed his hand on Mary's forearm and focused on Paul. "We need to talk turkey first."

"What?"

"We want ten million dollars." John hesitated. "No—a hundred million!" He pointed his index finger down at the table. "Seriously. A hundred million—right now or we delete this thing."

Paul looked at Mary, confused. "Is he drunk?"

"Very."

Paul gave the Marine a quick nod, and he and another soldier dragged John, kicking and screaming, out of the room.

Now that they were alone, Mary's expression changed. "Paul, I appreciate you coming, really. I'm surprised. I actually was just hoping to get out of here."

"We will." He pointed at the screen. "Now what is the code?"

"The first part is binary. Just numbers—Earth's location relative to the center of the galaxy and our solar system."

"The second part?"

47

"I don't know yet. It's a sequence with four values. The first just had two values—zero and one, on and off. I think the second sequence could be an image or a video."

"Why?"

"CMYK. Cyan, magenta, yellow, key—or black. It would be an accurate way to transmit a high-res image or video. The image could be a message or even a universal hello. A greeting. Or instructions on how to transmit a message back."

"Uh huh. Or a virus."

"It's possible. I hadn't thought of that." Mary chewed her lip. "In the first part of the message, the binary code was readable to us. It indicates that we have binary computing ability, that we could store the CMYK image as a computer file, but I don't see how it could—"

"No, I mean an actual virus, a DNA virus. A.T.G.C. Adenine, thymine, guanine, and cytosine are the four nucleobases that form DNA. Or it could be RNA, with uracil standing in for thymine. The code could be a genome. It could be an entire life form or a gene therapy."

Mary raised her eyebrows. "Oh. Yeah. Maybe. That's… an interesting theory."

"Or their DNA could be composed of other nucleobases." Paul paced away, deep in thought.

Mary glanced around. "Did you… think of that before you decided to come here?"

"No."

"Then…"

"I think this signal could be connected to the Atlantis Plague and possibly a war that's starting as we speak."

"Oh." Mary paused. "Wow."

"There's someone we need to talk with. She's probably the only person on Earth who could tell us what it is."

"Great. Let's call—"

"All the satellite phones are down."

"They are?"

"We'll have to go to her. She was in Northern Morocco last I heard."

Twelve hundred feet below sea level, just off the coast of Northern Morocco, David Vale sat at a small metal table, staring at the flashing words on the wall panel.

```
Surgery in progress...
```

A countdown ticked the seconds away.

```
3:41:08
3:41:07
3:41:06
3:41:05
```

But David could only think of one number: 39%. A 39% chance Kate would survive the surgery.

# 9

Ares was sitting at the back of the situation room with Dorian and the operations director when the analyst approached them.

"Sir, we have the Chinese response."

"And?"

"They say, 'There can be no peace with any enemy who threatens to destroy the Three Gorges Dam. China's walls have held barbarian invaders at bay for centuries. This will be no different—'"

Ares held his hand up. "Okay. For future reference, a simple 'no' will suffice."

"Actually, sir, we see this as an opening, a possible clue to a bargaining point—something they want in order to talk. We release the Three Gorges Dam and maybe—"

"Stop talking. You're making everyone who can hear you dumber. It was an *unconditional* demand to surrender."

The analyst nodded. "Of course, sir."

Several minutes later, the same analyst returned. This time, he avoided making eye contact with Ares as he placed a sheet of paper on the desk in front of Dorian. "The American response, sir."

The man was gone before Dorian looked up. He snatched the page and read the single word. The sides of his mouth curled. *Fools.* No, *brave fools.*

He handed the page to Ares, who read the single word.

"Nuts. What does that mean?"

"It's a historical reference."

Ares stared at Dorian.

Dorian smiled, satisfied to be the one withholding the answers for a change. He decided to give Ares some of his own treatment. "I'm afraid you don't know enough history to understand."

"Perhaps you could grace me with a history lesson, Dorian. If that's not too much to ask."

"Not at all. We're on the same side. As you know, it's imperative for us to share information with each other. Don't you agree?"

Ares stared at him.

"Let's see… In 1944, during World War II, in the Battle of the Bulge, the American 101st Airborne Division was trapped in the Belgian city of Bastogne by heavy German artillery. They received a surrender demand from the German commander. They were starving, tired, and outgunned. It was hopeless, but their response was simply: Nuts!"

Ares continued staring, waiting with an impatient look on his face.

"The Germans shelled the town, nearly leveled it, but the Americans held on. Patton's Third Army linked up with them less than a week later. The Allies won the war."

Ares clinched his jaws. "What does it mean, Dorian?"

"It *means* that they intend to fight to the very last man."

"So be it." Ares stalked toward the door. "Yours is a very foolish race, Dorian."

*Yes*, Dorian thought. But they were brave fools. That distinction was important to him. And at that moment, for some odd reason, he felt a bit of pride at their response, as *nuts* as it was.

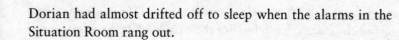

Dorian had almost drifted off to sleep when the alarms in the Situation Room rang out.

"We've got incoming," one of the techs called out. "Over a hundred planes."

The massive screens in the center of the room switched to a map of Antarctica and the Atlantic Ocean beyond. Light green dots pulsed in the blue sea, just outside a round white line that radiated out from the Immari base. The Orchid Alliance fleet, composed mostly of American, British, Australian, Japanese, and Chinese aircraft carriers and destroyers, inched closer to the line, but none crossed it. Smaller yellow dots, which represented the planes, ticked toward the white continent.

"All the ships are still outside the rail guns' firing radius, sir. The planes just entered. Should we engage?"

"How soon until they can fire on us?" Ares asked.

"Five minutes."

"Launch the drones," Ares said.

Dorian turned to him. "Drones?"

"Patience, Dorian."

The screen changed. Three of the smaller green dots broke from the fleet, moving south, across the white line.

"Three destroyers inbound." The tech paused, studying the screen. "We can hit them with the forward rail gun battery, sir."

"How long before the destroyers can fire on our guns?"

The tech worked the keyboard. "Twenty minutes. Thirty tops."

"Ignore them," Ares said.

Two minutes passed with hardly anyone saying a word. Dorian felt the tension in the room.

Another group of yellow dots sprang from the fleet. Hundreds of points, like sand from an hourglass, falling across the firing line, toward the white landmass and the Immari base.

"Second wave of planes. Three, no, four hundred this time." Alarm spread across the tech's face. "They've launched cruise missiles. We need to—"

"Hold your fire."

Dorian eyed Ares. What was his plan? The rail guns could shoot the planes down but not their payload. If the first wave of planes fired, the Immari base would be essentially defenseless. And even if they survived the first wave of bombs and shot those planes down, the rail guns had a limited amount of power—and it took hours to recharge. They needed to be firing now.

"Show me the drone telemetry," Ares said.

The right-hand section of the massive screen switched to a series of tiles that showed video feeds of the American, Indian, and British planes in the distance. Three of the video blocks were black squares.

"They've shot down three drones."

Two of the lead planes launched missiles.

The tech turned to Ares and Dorian. "We've got incoming. They're targeting the rail gun batteries. We can—"

Ares held up his hand. "That's enough. Turn the drones around. Keep recording." He walked to the front of the room and stood before the group. "They started this war. Now we will finish it—in the most humane way possible: with one strong blow. A strike that takes their very will to fight."

Dorian took a step closer to him. *What's he talking about?*

Ares tapped at a console on his wrist. The drone telemetry revealed the result. Massive fissures of light rose from the ice and then every square on the far right of the screen went black.

On the map, the hundreds of yellow dots that represented the planes went out.

The map flickered, then froze.

Dorian stared, finally realizing the truth. The drill teams. The devices Ares had buried had melted the ice along the perimeter of Antarctica, away from the Immari base, close to the fleet. The drones. The photos and video. He would try to use it as proof that the Orchid Alliance had started the war and caused the flood. Would the world believe it? How much ice had Ares melted? A flood of historic proportions would engulf the world.

*Humane.* That was Ares' description. Dorian wasn't so sure.

# 10

"Hungry?" Milo asked.

"No." David had no idea if it were true or not.

Milo nodded.

"You should go," David said, his voice hollow, his eyes on the floor. "Bring some back. She might be hungry when it's over."

"Of course."

David didn't remember Milo leaving. He blinked, and the teenager was gone. He was only vaguely aware of himself sitting at the metal table that had risen out of the floor in the adaptive research lab where he and Milo had found Kate. Two glass vats towered in the middle of the room, and just beside them, lights flickered in the cylindrical bay where Kate lay, undergoing surgery at the hands of the mysterious ship.

David's eyes drifted down, the room faded, and the countdown seemed to jump forward in leaps.

3:14:04
2:52:39

*What's happening to me?*

David put his head on the table and glanced up at the countdown only occasionally.

2:27:28

54

Milo was back, sitting at the table. A series of packages spread out. He asked a question. And another.

```
2:03:59
1:46:10
1:34:01
1:16:52
0:52:48
0:34:29
```

Milo sat silently.
David stood and paced, staring at the countdown.

```
0:21:38
0:15:19
0:08:55
Surgery complete
```

The words blinked for a moment; then, when the next words appeared on the screen, David exhaled deeply and smiled as Milo jumped into his arms.

```
Survival probability: 93%
Post-op Recovery Procedures Commencing
Maintaining medically induced coma
Time to completion: 2:14:00
```

David hadn't considered that there would be a post-op period. This was the first time a loved one had been operated on by an ancient Atlantean ship. He would have to do a blog post about it afterward—for everyone out there who might go through the same thing. His grin widened. His giddiness had turned to foolishness. He tried to focus. "Alpha, what happens after post-op?"

"The procedure will be complete."

David glanced at the Immari military MREs. He realized he was famished. He grabbed the closest pack and ripped it open. "Have you eaten?"

"I was waiting for you."

David shook his head. "Dig in. You must be starving."

Milo shoveled a mouthful of the closest ration pack into his mouth without even reading the label.

"Want it heated?" David asked.

Milo stopped in mid-chew and spoke with his mouthful. "Don't you eat yours cold?"

"I do. But it's just an old habit."

"Because your enemies could see a fire?"

"Yeah, and the dogs could smell the food. Better to eat it cold and quick, then bury it and move, if you can."

"I like to eat mine like you eat yours, Mr. David."

They both finished two ration packs.

David didn't notice the countdown anymore. He felt different now. He was confident Kate would live, though he didn't know how long. Alpha's prognosis, the result of the initial scan, had been four to seven local days. They would cross that bridge together. For now, he knew he would talk to her again, feel her in his arms.

A flood of memories came back to him—thoughts he wouldn't let himself think during the surgery. It was like his mind had been holding every memory of his time with her at bay. The day he met her, how they had argued in Indonesia, only hours before he had saved her. His extensive wounds in China. And then it was her saving him, practically bringing him back from death's doorstep.

They had truly sacrificed for each other, laid it all on the line when the stakes were highest. That was the definition of love.

At that moment, he knew that whatever she was doing, she was protecting him. But from what?

When the round portal slid open, David and Milo both rushed to it.

They stepped aside as the flat table extended.

Kate opened her eyes and stared at the ceiling… confused?

Her expression changed upon seeing David and Milo. She smiled.

Milo glanced back and forth between Kate and David. "I'm

very glad you're okay, Dr. Kate. I… need to do something on the surface now." He bowed and exited.

David was actually impressed at the young man's intuition. Milo never ceased to amaze him.

Kate sat up. Her face was fresh, the blood gone, her skin glowing. David spotted a small area, just beyond her ear, where Alpha had shaved the hair to access her brain.

Kate quickly pulled some of her brunette locks over it and turned her head away, hiding it. "How'd you find me?"

"The power."

"Clever."

"I was due." David sat on the rigid table and put his arm around her.

"You're not angry."

"No."

Kate narrowed her eyes. "Why?"

"I have some bad news." David took a breath. "Alpha did a scan before your surgery. You have a neurological condition. I can't remember the name. The life expectancy… Alpha could be wrong, but it said four to seven days."

Kate displayed no emotion.

"You knew?"

Kate stared at him.

David hopped off the table and faced her. "How long?"

"Does it matter?"

"How long?"

"The day after the plague."

"*Two weeks ago?*" David shouted.

"I couldn't tell you," Kate said, sliding off the table and closing the distance to him.

"Why not?"

"I have a few days left. If you knew, every day would be agony for you. This is better. Sudden. You can move on when I'm gone."

"I'm not interested in moving on."

"You have to. That's your problem, David. When something bad happens, you refuse to move on—"

"What's happening to you?" He pointed to the vats. "What is this? Why are you dying?"

Kate stared at the floor. "It's complicated."

"Try me. I want to hear it all. From the beginning."

"It won't change anything."

"You owe me this much. Tell me."

"Okay. I was conceived in 1918. My mother died in the Spanish flu pandemic, a pathogen my father unknowingly unleashed when they uncovered an Atlantean ship buried off the coast of Gibraltar. He placed me in a tube, where I remained until I was born in 1978. What I didn't know, until a few weeks ago, is that those tubes were used for resurrecting Atlantean scientists in the event that they died unexpectedly."

"You're one of those scientists."

"Close. Biologically, I'm the child of Patrick Pierce and Helena Barton, but I have *some* of the memories of one of the scientists on the Atlantis expedition. What I didn't know is that Janus—"

"The other member of the Atlantean research team."

"Yes. Janus erased some of his partner's memories. I only got some of the memories. Janus' partner had been killed by Ares."

"Another Atlantean."

Kate nodded. "A soldier. A refugee from their fallen home-world. Thirteen thousand years ago, off the coast of Gibraltar, he tried to destroy the scientists' vessel—this vessel. He only split it in half. Janus was trapped in the section on the Moroccan side of the Straits of Gibraltar. He longed to resurrect his partner, but he had a secret, something I didn't realize until two weeks ago."

"Which was?"

"He wanted to bring her back without some of her memories."

"The corrupted resurrection files."

"Yes. I think they're about something she did. I believe those memories take place on the Atlantean homeworld or possibly on their expedition."

"Why hide the memories from his partner?"

"It's something that damaged her beyond repair, changed her."

"Why didn't you know about the memories before? Why now?"

"I think her memories were always there, driving me, influencing my decisions. My choice to become an autism researcher, my quest to isolate the Atlantis Gene—it all makes sense in light of these repressed memories. But I think they were activated by the Atlantis Plague. I was only able to see the repressed memories after the final outbreak."

David nodded, prompting Kate to continue.

"The Atlanteans isolated the genes that control aging. They're disabled for deep-space explorers. The resurrection process takes a fetus, then implants the memories and matures it to around my current age."

"Then you emerge from the tube, ready to pick up where you left off," David said.

"Right. But for me, it didn't happen. I was a fetus, trapped inside my mother's body. I got the Atlantean memories—those Janus wanted me to have—but the tube couldn't develop me to standard age. I was born as a human and lived a human life. I formed my own memories." She smiled. "Some with you. And then the Atlantis Plague hit. I think the radiation retriggered the resurrection process, the evolutionary components. It's trying to overwrite the memories I formed, but it's failing. The resurrection process has a failsafe. If the brain is damaged or resurrection fails, the tube destroys the biological matter and recycles it. It starts over."

"You're not in a tube."

"Correct. But the hard-wired processes are the same. My brain, specifically my temporal lobe, will shut down in a few days, and then my heart will stop. I will die."

"Won't you resurrect?"

"No. The tubes in this part of the ship are destroyed."

David's mind flashed to a memory of four tubes cracking and crumbling to the floor in a pile of white dust.

"It's better this way. If I resurrected, I would be the same age, with the same memories and neurological condition. The outcome would be the same. I would die an endless number of times."

"Purgatory. Like the Atlanteans in Antarctica."

Kate nodded. "This will be better. I will die here and never resurrect. It will be very peaceful."

"The hell it will."

"There's nothing I can do about it."

"So why all this?" David pointed to the glass vats.

"I've been trying to access the lost memories, hoping they could correct my condition."

David stared at her. "And?"

"They're gone. Janus must have deleted them. I don't see how—there are strict regulations around resurrection memory storage. The computer core may have been damaged during the attack. Some memories are corrupted. I had hoped I could find some clue about the enemy that destroyed the Atlantis world, the enemy that could one day come for Earth. It's the best thing I can do with my time."

"Not true."

"What would you have me do?"

"Leave."

"I can't—"

"I won't watch you die here, in a lab, floating in a vat like some experimental rat. Leave with me—"

"I can't."

"You can. Look, I grew up on a small farm in North Carolina. I have about half a PhD in Medieval European History, and I'm a really good shot. That about sums me up. I'm in so far over my head here I can't see the surface, but I will go wherever this road takes us—if we're together. I'm in love with you. In fact, you're the only thing I love in this whole world. We can leave here. I can take care of you. You can die like a human. We can enjoy

60

the time you have left, live every day to the fullest."

"I don't know..."

"What's to think about?"

Kate walked away from him. "I'm not going to run away and wither and die. I want to fight. I'm going to press on. I'm going to do whatever I can to help people. That's why I became a scientist. It's what I dedicated my life to, and I won't change in my final hour for a few days of comfort. This is how I want to spend my last hours."

"What about dying with dignity? About spending the time we have left together?"

"I want that too."

"I can haul you out of here if it would make you feel better."

Kate smiled. "I'm not scared of you."

David couldn't help but shake his head and grin. "I'd like to remind you that I'm a trained killer."

"I'm only afraid of untrained killers."

He laughed, almost against his will. "Unbelievable. Look, all I ask is that you consider it—leaving here. The Immari are defeated. The plague is cured. You've given enough. Sleep on it. Let's talk in the morning, and I hope, leave together."

He walked to the doors.

"Where are you going?"

"I need some fresh air."

---

Paul had been watching the weather system out the plane's window, wondering if it was a hurricane or just a bad storm. The rain came, first in sheets, then in a constant gale of water, pushing the plane down, bogging the engines and tossing him, Mary, and the three soldiers around.

The plane banked and plunged again, throwing Paul hard against the seatbelt. He felt Mary's hand cover his and squeeze hard. He wondered if they would make it to Morocco.

# 11

Where Kate had needed time and space before, David needed it now.

He tried not to think as he trudged down the ship's narrow corridors and up the lift to the dank, dark shaft that led to the surface. Against his will, his thoughts drifted to the looming decision. Stay or go.

It was Kate's decision to make, and he knew that whatever she chose, he would stay with her to the end, no matter what.

He hoped that end wouldn't be here—in this cold, dark, alien place. He imagined them sitting by the fire at his parents' home, him reading, her falling asleep in his arms, them sleeping until late in the day, not waking for anyone or anything, living without a care in the world. They deserved it. They had paid their dues.

The faint light of stars broke the total darkness of the round shaft, and David walked out into the moonlit night. Several crates of supplies sat on pallets, some cartons opened and picked over where David and Milo had brought MREs back. The Berbers who controlled Northern Morocco had kept them well-supplied, an obligation they felt they owed David, who had helped them take control of the Immari base at Ceuta. In the distance, the massive base glittered. The lights on the guard towers twinkled and probed the perimeter. The lights from the administrative buildings and houses burned beyond.

The moonlight from above and the burning lights from the base almost made David miss Milo sitting just beyond the farthest crate.

The teenager sat cross-legged, his eyes closed. For a moment, David thought he was asleep, but he opened his eyes slowly and drew a deep breath.

"You should get some sleep, Milo."

"I would like to. My mind refuses to cooperate." He stood. "Dr. Kate. Will she live?"

"I'm not sure."

"Please tell me."

"She says she won't recover. She says Alpha's diagnosis is correct."

Milo looked away. "There's nothing you can do?"

"Sometimes there's nothing left to do but enjoy the time you have left. There's nothing wrong with that."

Neither said anything after that. They simply lay on their backs, staring at the stars.

An hour passed, maybe longer. David lost track of time. He was barely awake when Milo broke the silence. "Will you stay here?"

"I hope not."

"Where?"

"America."

"Where you're from?"

"Mmm hmm. North Carolina. Where I grew up. If she'll go."

"I want to see America." Milo glanced over. "It's why I learned English."

"You should go."

In the distance, David heard the crack of a branch snapping. He focused, listened. No further sound came.

"Milo, you still have that radio?" David whispered.

"Yes," he said, patting his side.

"Go below. Don't come back until I call you."

Milo narrowed his eyes, then nodded, and snuck out of the clearing at the top of the mountain, back into the darkened shaft.

David receded behind the closest crate and gripped his sidearm. The footsteps had stopped, but someone was still there. He could feel it.

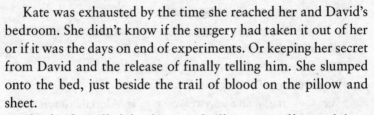

Kate was exhausted by the time she reached her and David's bedroom. She didn't know if the surgery had taken it out of her or if it was the days on end of experiments. Or keeping her secret from David and the release of finally telling him. She slumped onto the bed, just beside the trail of blood on the pillow and sheet.

Slowly, she pulled the sheets and pillow cases off, tossed them on the bed of the cabin across the hall and placed new sheets on the bed.

She was asleep the second her head hit the pillow.

Before she opened her eyes, Kate knew the bed was empty. The narrow crew quarter beds weren't designed for two, and they slept a lot warmer with both David and her present. Still, she reached her hand across and touched the cold space where he would have lain.

At that moment, she made her decision.

She would spend her last days with David, wherever he wanted. She was doing it for him, as much as for herself.

She closed her eyes again, and the sleep that came was the best she had had since... she could remember.

Waiting was a poor strategy. David assumed that the person beyond the tree line knew his general position and might not be alone.

He was about to dart to the next crate of supplies when a strong voice called into the night, a voice David knew. "It's nice to see that your instincts haven't faded."

David rose and found Sonja, the chief of the Berber tribe that now controlled Ceuta, emerging from the forest, an amused expression on her face.

"You could have announced yourself."

"Like you, I prefer the element of surprise."

David smiled, appreciating her reference to his surprise attack and takeover of the Immari base—with her and her tribe's help.

He motioned to the crates. "I think you've oversupplied us."

Sonja's playful smile faded. "Not for what's to come."

David glanced at the base. Yes, the lights were more than the usual night watch. They were preparing for an attack.

"How soon?"

"Days. Possibly even tomorrow. If the spies are right, the Immari counterattack will be global. A war on every continent."

"How? I thought they were finished."

"They've consolidated their forces. And they're attracting new devotees. They've begun taking power plants and food depots around the world."

"You can't be serious."

"Many don't want the world to return to the way it was. The Immari alternative, their worldview, appeals to many."

David scanned the base again. "You're not planning for the base's defense. You're planning for an attack."

Sonja nodded. "The Immari have been moving into the mountainous regions, trying to take the high ground where they can prolong the fight. The Spanish plan to drive them to the sea, to within range of our rail guns. We can finish them, force a surrender—assuming we can hold our ground here."

David nodded. "Good plan."

"It's part of a larger plan. The Orchid Alliance is contemplating a final offensive to finish the Immari once and for all." She pointed to a plane waiting on the runway. "I'm traveling

65

to America at first light. I'll be the representative for Northern Africa."

"Representative to what?"

"A global war council."

David had a feeling about what she was working up to. "Congratulations," he said, turning away.

"I was hoping..."

"That I would run Ceuta in your absence."

"You could save lives—again."

David's eyes lingered on the dark corridor that led to the ship and Kate. "I can't."

"The woman you came here to save."

"Yes. She's sick. She needs me."

"Watching a loved one suffer is the worst torture on Earth. If you stay here, you should take the supplies below. I don't know how long the offensive will last."

"We've considered spending her final days in America." David glanced back at the runway, at the plane he had flown to Ceuta from Malta. "But if you're taking the plane..."

Sonja smiled. "I'll drop you off. It's the least I can do for what you've done for my people."

"That's much appreciated."

It began raining, and they both gazed into the distance. The downpour seemed to gather strength by the second.

"Looks like a big one," David said.

Sonja turned her head sharply, as if she had heard something. David moved closer to her, his posture defensive.

She pressed a finger to her ear piece. "There's an incoming flight. American military transport requesting clearance to land. The person on board identifies himself as Dr. Paul Brenner. He wishes to speak with Dr. Warner. He says she can verify him."

David considered the request. He had never met Paul Brenner, and he wondered how he might verify his identity. With the looming war, David considered the possibility that the caller was an Immari impostor hoping his flight could slip past the rail guns to hit the base. "Ask him how Dr. Warner cured the plague."

A few seconds later, Sonja related Brenner's response: "He says it's a trick question. He doesn't know. Only that she found something in Malta and transmitted it to him at Continuity. He would like to ask her the same question."

"Ask him if that's why he's here."

"No," Sonja said. "He says it's about a code on a radio satellite, that it could be related to what was found in Gibraltar and Antarctica."

David frowned, the rain falling in sheets on him now.

"You want us to divert him?"

"No," David said. "Let him land. But guard him. Have several men bring him up here. Don't let him inside." For some reason, David thought it best to keep everyone out of the ship. "I'll bring Kate up."

# 12

David had tip-toed back into the bedroom, but it didn't matter.

He sat in the chair before the small table and faced the bed. "I can tell you're awake."

Kate sat up. "How do you always know?"

"You smile a little, like you're hiding something. You'd make a terrible spy."

Kate held that cute smile he liked so much for a few more seconds. Then it was gone, and it felt as though every last breath of air had been sucked out of the room.

"I've decided."

David eyed the floor.

"North Carolina sounds nice."

"It will be. And we'll be happy there."

"I know we will. Knowing I don't have much time left has given me some perspective, reminded me of what's important. That's you. I do have two requests."

David felt a little pit form in his stomach. "Go ahead."

"First, the two boys who were taken from my lab. I left them with a couple in Spain when the Immari invaded the Orchid District in Marbella. After... When I'm gone, I want you to find them and make sure they're safe and provided for."

"I will. The other request?"

When Kate finished telling him, David simply stared at her.

68

"That's a tall order."

"I'll understand if you say no."

"I'm saying yes. I'll do it, even if it kills me."

"I hope it won't."

———————————— ✿ ————————————

After the plane ride and landing, the Jeep ride through the Moroccan mountains felt like a picnic to Paul. He sat beside Mary in the backseat, two Moroccan guards in the front. They had made Paul's military escorts wait with the plane. The man staring back at them, holding a rifle that looked like it was from World War II, made Paul even more nervous than the torrential downpour and reckless driving.

In the distance, he heard a roll of thunder that nearly deafened him.

He looked back, but the rain almost blotted out the view. What little bit he saw horrified him. A wave of water twenty feet tall rose from the ocean and slammed into the sprawling army base. Another wave. It carried something. Paul tried to focus. It looked… like a cruise ship. It spun on top of the wave, like a plastic toy being washed ashore by the tide. It slammed into the base, flattening everything it rolled over.

Paul's mouth went dry.

Water rushed across the unpaved road, and he felt the Jeep skidding, losing traction as it climbed the mountain.

"Slower!" Paul shouted.

The soldier raised his rifle to Paul and yelled at him.

The driver accelerated even faster, and Paul motioned to Mary to buckle up. A wave caught the Jeep and tossed it off the muddy road a few seconds later.

———————————— ✿ ————————————

"What convinced you?" David asked.

"Let's see…" Kate pulled her shirt off. "I think it could have been the part about enjoying the time we have left."

David kissed her, and she reached for his shirt.

"You're very convincing, you know."

"Right…" David was about to slip his shirt off, but he stopped. "Wait. Almost forgot. Paul Brenner is here."

"What?"

"Yeah, I have no idea. We need to go up top to talk—"

The ship shuddered, throwing David across the room into the bulkhead, Kate landing on top of him.

Her hands were instantly around his head, feeling for blood.

He opened his eyes wide and shook his head once. Sounds and feeling converged, and he could focus again. "I'm okay."

"The ship's been hit with explosives," Kate said.

"What? How do you—"

"My neural implant."

Another shudder came, but David was ready. He held the desk attached to the wall with one hand, Kate with the other.

"Earthquake?" David yelled, over the din.

"No. I think it was the mines the British laid in the straits. Something pulled them down."

The ship shook again, this time more violently.

"They're destroying the ship," Kate said. "Alpha is unresponsive."

"Come on." David pulled her up, and they began staggering through the dark corridors, trying to make their way out.

Paul brushed Mary's hair out of her face, trying to get a look at the cut the blood was coming from. She opened her eyes, and he drew back instinctively.

"I'm okay," she said, peering into the empty front seat. "The guards."

"Gone. Thrown out."

Water washed into the floor board as Paul unbuckled first his, then Mary's seatbelt.

"What is it, Paul?"

"No idea."

"Hurricane?"

"Maybe," he said, hoping his lie would comfort her.

Mary's reaction told him she hadn't bought it. So she did remember something from being married to him.

"Let's go, we've gotta get to higher ground."

Mary grabbed her laptop bag.

"Leave it, Mary."

"I can't—"

"It'll be soaked and only slow us down. We have to go."

He pulled her out of the Jeep and into the muddy road, where a wall of wind and rain caught them, throwing them to the ground and rolling them twice before it abated.

Paul got to his feet and caught his first full view of the chaos below, what had been Ceuta only seconds ago.

He saw the expression on Mary's face, and that steeled him enough to grab her, turn her around, and yell, "Run."

# 13

The explosions were less frequent now, but David and Kate still ran cautiously.

"What could do this?" David asked.

"A tsunami could have washed the mines into the ship."

David's mind flashed to his conversation with Sonja. A tsunami—at the exact time of the Immari global attack? He didn't believe in coincidences. "Ares and Dorian did this."

"How?"

"The ice in Antarctica. They melted it. Does the ship there have any weapons?"

"No. Wait. It has emergency mines for asteroids and comets."

"Could they melt ice?"

"Definitely. Comets are mostly ice."

"How do you know that?"

Kate slowed her pace. "I don't." She thought for a second. "I know it because she did. That's weird." The tidbit about comets had come naturally to her—like her own memories. Previously, when she had cured the plague, she had focused on the science; remembering her Atlantean counterpart's knowledge had been an effort.

"Let's keep moving," David said.

They raced through the corridors, occasionally stopping to grab a bulkhead when an explosion rocked the ship.

At the surface, David instantly sensed how bad things were. It should have been morning, and the sun should have greeted them, but it was dark, almost pitch black, and he couldn't see a single star. The sound of destruction was complete: waves crashed into the rocks below, buildings crumbled in the distance, and thunder echoed across the sky and in their chests.

They stood for a moment, the hard-falling rain numbing them.

David leaned over and shouted, his voice barely audible against the clamor. "Get below. I'm right behind you."

He ran into the clearing, past the pallets of supplies. At the base of the mountain, at sea level, the crumbling ruin that had been the fortress of Ceuta was sustaining an onslaught beyond imagination.

The base was almost completely submerged; only a few buildings jutted out, but they were falling fast.

The jet that would have carried them away lay overturned, several hundred feet from the runway, which was also flooded.

The rain came in sheets, and David fought to keep it out of his face and his eyes open.

From his peripheral vision, he saw movement. Milo and Sonja. They ran to him, and the three of them took cover under the trees, just past the clearing. The wind gained steam, forcing each of them to reach for a tree, holding tight, bracing as it picked up speed.

"I came up to look for you," Milo shouted.

"That was smart," David said. "You did good."

Sonja leaned close to his ear. "It would seem we've underestimated our enemy."

"Badly."

Behind them, David heard a sucking noise that seemed to drain all the air and sound away. The rain nearly ceased. Through the darkness, he saw a wall of water rising, bearing down on the mountain. It would wash over it, taking everything—and everyone with it.

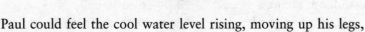

Paul could feel the cool water level rising, moving up his legs, like a countdown to his and Mary's death.

He tried to pump his legs faster, but it was like doing water aerobics in the shallow end of a mountain lake.

Mary was falling behind.

"I need to stop," she said, bending over to heave breath after breath.

Paul tried to estimate the distance to the top of the peak. Two, maybe three hundred yards?

The rain had almost stopped. Maybe the massive storm was ending. But the water still crept up his legs—it was almost to his knees now. If it leveled out eventually, maybe they could swim to land, pausing to rest by hanging on to the tree tops or floating debris from Ceuta.

But if the water topped the mountain, their only option would be to find something to make a raft out of and try to make landfall further inland. But where would the new coastline form? Miles, hundreds of miles away?

A sound, over the ridge—like the Earth was taking a deep breath. Paul could feel the wind rushing past him, flowing out to sea.

"Come on," he grabbed Mary's hand and pulled her toward a ridge, pushing his legs through now knee-deep water. It was all Paul could do not to reel back when he saw the wall of water rushing over the sea.

He thought Mary was going to release his hand for a moment, but she squeezed harder.

Paul looked from the mountain to the valley—which was fully submerged. They could run back, try to get under water, hold on to something. Would that be safe? He had absolutely no idea.

Or they could run to the mountain top. If the wave topped it…

He made his decision.

He tugged at Mary's hand, and she followed as fast as she could, not saying a word.

He pushed harder, feeling her strength draining as well as his own.

Finally, she fell in the water, and Paul jerked her up. "Keep going," he said, wrapping his arm around her, half-carrying her as her legs walked and kicked the water.

Ahead, the forest stopped and a clearing spread out. It wasn't the top of the mountain, but...

Figures, moving, heading toward a rock outcropping.

"Help!" Paul yelled. He released Mary, and she collapsed into the water on her hands and knees. Paul rushed forward, waving his arms back and forth in the air. "Hey!"

The figures stopped, then two of them were racing towards him, cutting through the water with breathtaking speed. The man was tall, over six feet and well-built. A soldier. And so was the woman, though she was trim, her skin dark caramel.

The man put his shoulder into Paul's stomach and hoisted him up, holding him by his legs while speeding back to the clearing, only slightly slower with Paul's added weight. Paul saw the woman lift Mary the same way, and then they were close behind them.

A skinny Asian teenager with short black hair was grabbing small packages out of massive crates stacked on pallets in the clearing.

"Time to go, Milo," the man called.

He set Paul down, and the woman released Mary. Their rescuers ran full on toward a rock wall and... disappeared.

The Asian teenager stopped just before it and waved his hand. "Come on." He turned and walked through the rock.

Paul and Mary charged after them and right through the wall, which was clearly a hologram of some kind.

The area beyond was almost pitch black, save for a tiny glowing yellow light at the end of the tunnel, like a train in the far distance.

"Come on!" A voice ahead of them called.

Paul again grabbed Mary's hand, and they lumbered through the dark on their exhausted legs.

The impact of the wave was deafening. Paul felt as though he were in the barrel of a gun that had been fired. The blow threw him and Mary against the left wall. They rolled to the ground, and water rushed over them. The shaft was on a downward incline. It would fill...

Paul again felt hands on him, and he was up, floating through the shaft, the soldier carrying him.

The yellow light grew brighter and the splash of water louder until he saw a set of doors part, and the five of them were out of the shaft, into an elevator of some sort. The man worked a panel that closed the doors quickly, but there was still three feet of water in the elevator. He seemed not to care. The lights in the elevator flickered, and it shuddered a few times. Paul wasn't sure if it was losing power.

He leaned against the wall, trying to take stock of his injuries. He hurt all over, and his muscles throbbed. It was hard to isolate any particular malady.

"I'm Paul Brenner," he said, to no one in particular.

"I thought you might be," the soldier said. "I'm David Vale."

"Thank you for saving us... twice."

"No problem." He stared at the water. "Just doing my job."

The teenager smiled at Paul. "I'm Milo."

The elevator doors opened, emptying the water into a dry hallway where a woman stood. Paul recognized her. He had seen her in months of videos during the Atlantis Plague clinical trials, talked to her several times on the phone, but he had never seen Kate Warner in person until this moment.

# 14

Paul unfolded the crisp, dry clothes Kate had provided and began stripping off his soaked shirt and pants. He threw them on the narrow bed and used the pillow to sponge some of the water off his body. He was so soaked he wondered if he'd ever be dry again.

"You knew about this?"

Mary was staring at him, still wearing her own soggy clothes, ignoring her clean set on the desk. They were alone in the small bedroom, and her voice boomed in the space.

"I did."

"When we were married?"

Paul could see where this was going. "I've known for twenty years—"

"You... knew about an alien spacecraft, buried outside Gibraltar, for twenty years, including the entire time we were married, and you said not one word about it to your astronomer wife who spent day and night searching for any shred, any minute sign of alien life?"

"Mary—"

"The sort of betrayal and lack of trust—"

"I took an oath, Mary. I knew the vessel existed, but I've never been inside until now. I knew nothing about it. I still don't. My part of the Continuity consortium was fighting the plague."

"They're connected?"

"Yes. The plague originated from this vessel, from the sentry device. It was extracted in 1918." Paul paused, watching Mary take off her clothes. "I'll wait outside."

"Stay. I want to hear this—while we're alone."

"I can..."

"It's nothing you haven't seen before, Paul."

Paul turned around just the same, and he could almost feel Mary smiling at his modesty.

"So whoever built this vessel caused the plague?" she asked.

"Yes. The Atlanteans have been conducting genetic experiments, guiding human evolution for seventy thousand years—since the Toba Catastrophe that almost caused humanity's extinction. We think the Spanish flu in 1918 was a mistake on their part, caused by the radiation from one of their devices, the Bell. Kate Warner, the woman you met, cured the plague. She's the daughter of a World War I soldier who found the Bell. During the Spanish flu, he placed her mother, who had died during the outbreak, in a resurrection tube in another section of this vessel. Kate was born in 1978. Her father went missing in the eighties. Dr. Martin Grey adopted her. He was the organizer and chairman of the Continuity group. He recruited me in the early nineties at a conference I attended. He died during the plague."

"You trust these people?"

Paul glanced back. "Yes. Well, Kate and after the rescue on the mountainside, I'd say I trust the others as well."

"You think we should share what we know with them?"

"I do. There's something else. Continuity, the plague, that's what I was always working on."

Mary was silent for a moment. "In that case, I would say it was worth it."

Paul watched her glide through the double doors and out into the corridor.

He had been certain that it was worth it too—until this moment.

Kate was reviewing the results of a full ship diagnostic when Paul and Mary entered the conference room wearing the dry clothes she had provided.

David, Sonja, and Milo were huddled at the end of the raised table, sorting their MREs, weapons, and supplies. Paul spoke to David first. "Thank you again for saving us out there."

"No problem."

"We'd like to share something, the reason we came here," Paul said, then nodded to Mary.

Mary introduced herself and her background: a radio astronomer focused on finding and analyzing signs of extra-terrestrial life.

"About two weeks ago, the radio telescope picked up an organized signal. A code."

"That's impossible," Kate said.

"I verified it myself."

"You have a copy of the signal?"

"Yes." Mary held up a USB key. "It has two parts. The first part, a binary sequence, is two numbers: Earth's exact location. The second part is a code made from four values."

Kate tried to access Alpha's link to the beacon, hoping to verify the signal.

David seemed to know what she was doing. He gave her a look that said, *Pay attention to our guests.*

Paul spoke before she had a chance. "Why did you say it was impossible?"

"Two Atlantean scientists came here one hundred fifty thousand years ago to study the early humans on this planet. As part of their routine procedures, they deployed a beacon. It filters the light we can see and blocks any signals either to or from Earth."

Kate thought Mary was on the verge of crying. "What's wrong?" Kate asked.

"Nothing... that's just my soul collapsing like a neutron star," Mary said.

Kate thought the comparison was a little dramatic.

"Why did they deploy a beacon? Why hide?" Paul asked.

"Protection. The scientists were aware of several threats in the galaxy—"

"What kind—" David began, but Kate cut him off. "I don't know. Not part of my memories."

Before anyone could ask, Kate explained that through a twist of fate, she had been born in 1978 with one of the Atlantean scientist's memories—the ones the other scientist, Dr. Arthur Janus, had wanted his partner to resurrect with.

"So..." Mary said. "The scientists or you—"

"The scientists," Kate corrected. "I've only seen memories of what they did."

"Right. Were they protecting us or themselves with the beacon?"

"Both."

"So how did this signal get through?"

Kate used her link to Alpha to connect to the beacon. The orbiting communications station had recorded an incoming signal and allowed it to pass. And there was something even more surprising. "It's true, there was a transmission two weeks ago. One outgoing. A message sent from the beacon."

"Who?" David asked.

"It had to be Janus," Kate said. "When you and he entered the Atlantean ship to rescue me. When Dorian rescued Ares."

"Can you see his transmission?" David asked.

"No. I should be able to, but access to the message is restricted from here. I don't know why. The damage to the ship may have disrupted the interface."

"What's the other signal?" Mary asked.

Kate tried to access the entry on the beacon, but it too had restricted access. But... "It's Atlantean."

"How is that possible?" David asked.

"It's not." Kate explained that the Atlantean homeworld had fallen fifty thousand years ago, and the sole survivors of the war had sought refuge here on Earth, under the protection of the beacon, where their enemy couldn't find them. General Ares, an Atlantean soldier, had brought the refugees here. Ares had joined the two scientists, colluding with Janus' partner in secret to control human evolution. Ares had ultimately betrayed the scientists, killing Janus' partner and injuring and trapping Janus.

"So Janus sent a transmission to someone—presumably an Atlantean," David said, "and it sounds like he got a response—that's how it got past the beacon."

"Yes," Kate said.

"Any ideas who it's from or what it is?" David asked.

"No." Kate said, lost in thought.

"It could be an ally," Sonja said. "Help."

"The world could use it." Paul proceeded to share his experience with the group, how the American government had tried to use Continuity to eliminate people it felt were too weak to fight or fend for themselves. "I assume other nations are looking at the same scenario. The global flood would presumably increase the urgency."

"Makes you wonder who to even pull for in this war," David said.

"Indeed."

"What's our status here?" David asked Kate.

"Dire. The ship is more or less offline. The main computer core is gone. We've got emergency power and communications; that's how I could access the beacon. We've got hull breaches all along the perimeter. The shaft leading out of the mountain is completely flooded.

"Assuming any of the mountain is still above sea level, we'd have to swim for it." Kate read David's expression. "No, there are no oxygen tanks down here. There are plenty of EVA suits, but they're in these sections." She brought up a map on the screen. "They were destroyed in the blasts."

"We're trapped," David said.

"Almost. There's a portal room at the other end of the ship."

"Similar to the one in the other section—that connected to the ship in Antarctica?"

"Yes. The portal can conceivably take us to two locations. Antarctica or the beacon. But access to Antarctica is closed from that end."

"Going there would be too dangerous anyway," David said.

"I agree. Ares would know the second we stepped through the portal. But we can go to the beacon. If we make it there, we can see the messages and send a response."

"I like it," David said. "A lot better than drowning."

"Me too. But, there may be a... slight problem with getting to the portal."

# 15

Through the habitat's large picture window, Dorian watched the Immari crews disassembling the white caterpillar shaped buildings, along with the rest of Fortress Antarctica. Ares' order to break down the camp was nearly as surprising as what he wanted them to do with it: drop it into the ocean.

For hours, the crews had been tearing apart the rail guns, buildings, and everything in between, loading the parts into the fleet of planes on the ice runway for disposal at sea.

*Why?* Dorian wondered. It made no sense—to build all this then toss it in the sea.

Ares had ordered Dorian to evacuate the remaining staff to the mountains of South Africa, where the new Immari headquarters would be established.

Behind him, a small group of middle managers, morons, and scientists argued over the details. Dorian had bowed out of the conversation early, unable to justify wasting his time. Their planning was pointless. They were simply doing Ares' bidding. He had planned this sequence of events thousands of years ago, and he didn't care to share any particulars of it, didn't think Dorian was worthy.

"If the Isthmus of Panama is underwater, the Atlantic and Pacific have been joined again. All our models are wrong. Global sea currents are…"

*Their models*, Dorian thought, smiling.

"The axis is a bigger issue. We know the weight of the ice at the South Pole tilts the Earth. If we've lost enough, the axis will shift. The equator moves—"

"Which would melt more ice."

"Yes. We could be looking at a complete melt off. That could be the reason for the full evacuation."

"Should we call up more personnel?"

"He didn't say to—"

"It's implied in our mandate. Full evacuation at best speed possible."

A technician approached Dorian. "General Ares has asked for you to join him in the ship."

Dorian desperately wanted to tell "Lord Ares" where to shove his summons, but he simply trudged out of the room.

———————— ❀ ————————

Fifteen minutes later, he was two miles below the surface, inside the expansive Atlantean ship, standing in a room he had never seen before. Ares stood at a terminal that scrolled text in a language Dorian couldn't read.

"I know you're not happy with me, Dorian."

"I salute your penchant for understatement."

"I saved lives today."

"Really? I'm sure my primitive Earthman math can't hold a candle to your advanced Atlantean calculus, but I count millions of bodies floating in a toxic soup all over the planet as *lives lost*. But hey, that's just me, your humble pet caveman here."

Dorian sensed that Ares wanted to reprimand him, strike back at him as he had in the corridor, but the Atlantean restrained himself. *He needs me for something*, Dorian thought.

"I didn't tell you the plan because you would have tried to stop me."

"No. I would have killed you."

"You would have tried. So in not telling you, I've saved your life—once again."

"Again?"

"I'm counting my genetic interventions that led to your species in the first place. Now for the matter at hand. We control the world, Dorian. We have won. Now we will build an army and win the future. There is an enemy out there. It's only a matter of time before they find this world. You will not survive—unless we work together. We can save the survivors of this flood. We can lead our people off this world to meet our enemy, surprising them, winning our right to exist in the universe." He turned, pacing away, letting the words sink in.

When Ares spoke again, his tone was gentler. "If I hadn't done what I did today, every person on this world would have perished. We've sacrificed lives today, but in war, you must sacrifice lives to win—and you must win to preserve your civilization and your way of life. Losers don't write history. They're burned, buried, and forgotten."

"You started the war out there."

"The war out there started thousands of years ago; you just can't see the battle lines. They reach the length of this galaxy, crossing every human world."

"What do you want from me?"

"You have a role to play, Dorian. You've always known that. When we've defeated our enemy, you can return here and do whatever you want with this world."

"Wow. Let me just thank you for slaughtering millions of my fellow humans and giving me our screwed up world. You've been so helpful."

Ares exhaled. "You still don't grasp the magnitude of what you're involved in, Dorian. But you will soon. Very soon."

"As much as I appreciate this post-apocalyptic pep-talk, I'm getting this sneaking suspicion that I'm here because you need me to do something. And that's the *only* reason I'm here."

"I've never lied to you, Dorian. I've kept things from you— for your own good. You're here because we have a problem."

"We or you?"

"My problems are your problems. Like it or not, we're in this together now."

Across the room, a panel flickered to life, and an image of what Dorian thought was a dark gray space station appeared.

"What is that?"

"The beacon."

"Beacon?"

"It's a specialized communications array. Research teams and our military deploy them. They shroud worlds, blocking all incoming or outgoing communications and light, essentially hiding what's occurring on that world. This beacon has been orbiting Earth for the last one hundred fifty thousand years. It's the only reason any of us are still alive."

"So what's the problem?"

"The problem is that our enemy is trying to disable it. And if they succeed, if that beacon is destroyed or turned off, they will be here in days, and they will slaughter every last one of us."

Dorian stared at the floating gray station. "I'm listening."

Ares walked closer to Dorian. "Let's try this your way. What would you like to know?"

"Why now?"

"A message was sent fourteen days ago."

"Janus."

"He used his access codes to send a message when he was on the scientists' deep space vessel just before he destroyed it."

"A message to our enemy?"

"I doubt it. I can't see his message, but I assume it was intercepted by our enemy. They likely know the general vicinity it came from but not the exact world. They sent their reply to every suspected world, customizing the address to make the recipient think it was tailored for them. They're just waiting for a response or for one of the beacons to go out. You have a term for this?"

"Yeah. Shaking the bushes."

"They're shaking the bushes," Ares said.

"What's the problem? As long as we don't respond or disable—"

"The problem is that someone just tried to access the beacon from the *Alpha Lander*—the scientist's ship off the coast of Morocco. What's left of it."

"Kate and David."

"I assume so. If I'm right, they're on their way to the beacon right now. There's a portal with access within the section of the ship they're confined to."

"Confined?"

"They should be completely submerged by now."

"If they reach the beacon..."

"They could either send a reply message—directed at the origin—or simply disable the beacon. If they do that, our enemy will be upon us in days. You must stop them from reaching the beacon."

"They have a head start."

"Yes. If you can't intercept them in the *Alpha Lander*, follow them to the beacon. The portal in the *Alpha Lander* is keyed for your Atlantis Gene print."

"Mission parameters?"

"Kill. We don't need them alive. Don't take chances, Dorian. The stakes are too high."

"Why can't we access the beacon from here? We have a portal too. I could wait for them."

"The portals here aren't keyed for the beacon—only the scientist's ships are. Access is strictly limited. But you have my memories and my access genes. You can follow them. The beacon is the absolute last place you can stop them. This mission will determine all of our fates, Dorian."

# 16

Kate was searching for just the right words when David rubbed his eyebrows and said, "I'm sorry, but when I hear 'we may have a problem,' it almost always, and I mean 99.9% of the time, means we're screwed."

"I... wouldn't go that far," Kate said. Kate brought up the schematic of the ship again. "Normally, we would take the outer corridors to the portal room. But they're flooded."

"What about the large chamber in the middle? 'Arc 1701-D.'"

"That's the *potential* problem—traveling through it."

"What is it?"

"Arc stands for Arcology. 1701 is the world it was collected from, and D is the size designation—the largest. This arc is five miles long and three miles wide."

"Arcology?"

"It's a self-contained ecosystem. The Atlanteans collected them from worlds they visited, almost like little snow globes. The landers, in this case, the *Alpha Lander*, carries the arc machines to the surface where it studies the world, collecting data. Then it gathers a subset of the planet's species and makes a balanced biosphere. The goal is to collect exotic species the Atlantean citizens might like to see when the arcs are exhibited back on the homeworld."

"So it's like a portable zoo exhibit," Sonja said.

"Yes. The scientists used it to generate support. Science was hard to fund, even on the Atlantis world."

David held his hand up. "I'm thinking the key words here are 'exotic species.'"

"Yes. That's one of the issues," Kate said.

"The other?"

"Usually when the arc is done with collection, the lander takes it back to the space vessel for storage. This arc hadn't been detached yet when the ship was attacked. Conceivably the arcologies should sustain themselves indefinitely—they're on a separate power source from the lander, and the arc computer is constantly taking readings, intervening to balance the biosphere."

"So if we enter, could it try to... balance us out?" David asked.

"If we traverse it fast enough, that won't be a problem."

"So speed is the issue?"

"Yes. Well, one of the issues but not the biggest. This arc has been tossed around—once thirteen thousand years ago when the lander was split in half by Ares' attack on the scientists, then again nine months ago when my father destroyed the other half of the ship off Gibraltar and pushed this half to Morocco, and today, when the mines rattled the ship. There's no telling what the environment is like inside. Some species could have died out, others mutated, to say nothing of the terrain, which could be impassable."

Paul stared from Kate to David. "Sorry but this sounds worse every second."

David rubbed his eyebrows again. "Let's back up. What was the arc like when it was collected? And please, please tell me exactly what the exotic creatures are."

"Okay." Kate took a deep breath. "World 1701 was basically a vast rainforest, like the Amazon."

"Snakes inside?" David asked quickly.

"Definitely."

"I hate snakes."

"They're low on the predator list," Kate said. "The research logs say that world 1701 was in a binary star system—that means it has two suns."

David and Mary both gave her a look that said, *We know what a binary star system is.* Paul stared at the floor, looking nervous. Sonja's expression was blank, utterly unreadable, and Milo struck a sharp contrast with them all: a wide grin on his face, like a kid waiting for an amusement park ride to start.

"The days are long in the arc," Kate said. "There's sunlight for about twenty hours. The overlap of the passing of the two suns in the middle of the day is extremely bright and hot. The night lasts about five hours. That's when things might get... dangerous."

"The exotic creatures." David said.

"Yes. The scientists had never seen anything like the predators on 1701. They're flying reptiles that hunt at night, but what they do during the long days is what makes them special. They spread out on mountain tops and collect sunlight. Their bodies are covered in scales that are essentially photocells. They charge during the day, collecting solar power that fuels the cells at night. They use the power to cloak themselves, essentially becoming invisible."

"Cool," Milo said.

"Can we cross in a single day?" David asked.

"I doubt it. If the terrain is like it was on 1701, it's dense. We'll have to cut our way through, camp for at least one night, maybe two."

"How smart are they?"

"Very smart. They have a social structure, hunt in packs, and adapt quickly."

"Can I talk to you?"

When Kate and David were alone in the bedroom, he said, "You've *got* to be kidding me."

"What?"

"We've been living next door to a Jurassic Park snow globe for two weeks, and you never bothered to mention it?"

"Well, I didn't... think it would come up."

"Unbelievable."

Kate sat on the bed and tucked her hair behind her ears. "I'm sorry, okay. I mean, didn't you ever wonder why the lander was so big? Sixty square miles?"

"No, Kate, I never really stopped to contemplate why the lander was so big." He paced the room. "I feel like Sam Neill in *Jurassic Park* when he realizes the raptor cage is open."

Kate wondered what part of the male brain prioritized movie scene storage above all other details in life. Maybe the answer was in the Atlantean research database somewhere. It was all she could do not to launch a query for the answer.

"Is there another arc?"

"Yes," Kate said. "The ship had two—one on the other side for balance—that's why 1701-D was attached. But the other one, which was destroyed thirteen thousand years ago, is empty. It would have contained an Earth arcology."

"The wooly mammoth/saber-toothed cat exhibit?"

"Something like that," Kate said dryly.

"Sorry, it's been a rough day." David massaged his eyelids. "Between your news and... I thought Dorian and Ares were contained..."

"If we can get to the beacon, and contact help, whoever sent the message, we can turn this around," Kate said. "There is one more issue." She read David's exasperated expression and spoke quickly. "But I think we can handle it. The arc access doors are jammed. Alpha can't open them."

"Why not?"

"I'm not sure. It could be the arc locking them down, preventing access, or something else."

David nodded.

"What do you want to do?" she asked.

"We don't have a choice. We grabbed as much food as we could from up top, but it won't last. We have to try to reach the beacon—for our sake and everyone else's. We'll blow the arc doors open and take our chances inside."

Thirty minutes later, David and Sonja were placing the last of the explosives on the door that led to Arc 1701-D.

"This is half of what we have," Sonja said. "If it's not enough, we won't be able to get out."

"We'll cross that bridge when we get there," David said.

They set the timer and retreated.

The echo of the blast was deafening, even far from the explosion. The group of six cautiously approached the dust cloud that spread out, filling the corridors on each side of the arc door. The beads of light at the floor and ceiling glowed through the gray-black cloud, guiding their way.

When David got his first glance at the arc door, he first felt relief: the explosions had punched through. But that was all the good news.

# 17

*My world is dying*, Dorian thought as he watched the storms over the sea form, rage, and fade just as quickly.

The flight had been like riding a roller coaster for hours: one second the plane was plummeting, diving into the dark unknown, the next it was coasting, sunlight shining through the windows. He and his six soldiers were strapped in tight, and no one had said a word since takeoff. Three of the men had thrown up about an hour in. Two still dry-heaved every fifteen minutes or so, when the turbulence was especially bad. The other three stared straight ahead, gritting their teeth.

At least he knew whom he could depend on now—when the fight began. And it would start soon. Somewhere under the vast sea that consumed more and more of his planet, David Vale was waiting on him.

Dorian had almost killed David twice—once in Pakistan, again in China, and Dorian *had* killed him twice: both times in the Atlantean vessel in Antarctica. The first time, David had resurrected in Antarctica, directly across from Dorian, thanks to David's Atlantis Gene, which Kate had given him. David was stronger, but Dorian was smarter. Or rather, willing to do things David wasn't. David wasn't a survivor. His moral compass had been his weakness. Dorian had killed him for a second time, but David had resurrected in the Atlantean structure off the coast of Morocco.

Today would be their final conflict.

But Kate Warner was smarter than both of them. She was sublimely clever, and she had knowledge Dorian didn't. That was their advantage: David's strength and Kate's brains. But Dorian had the element of surprise. And something else—the willingness to do what had to be done to save his people. He was the march of human history, embodied in one man. A survivor, standing against impossible odds, doing the things others, like Kate and David, turned their backs on. He was the essence of human survival.

A part of him was nervous about the final confrontation with David. That would be the true test—whether Dorian could win.

If he could, he would turn his sights on Ares. The Atlantean was a snake, a manipulator. Dorian didn't trust him. He would have to go next, after Dorian had learned the full truth, especially about this "enemy" Ares was so frightened of.

"Sir, we're at the drop zone," the pilot called into Dorian's headset.

Dorian peered out the narrow window. Water stretched out as far as he could see.

Dorian marveled. What he saw used to be the coast of Morocco.

"Drop the probe," he said.

He raised the tablet and watched the telemetry on the split screen, which showed a contour of the new sea floor on the right-hand side and a video feed on the left. Dorian recognized a mountain top, completely submerged. He tapped the tablet, directing the probe. A few seconds later, the Atlantean ship, the *Alpha Lander*, came into view. It was buried deep.

"Mark it," Dorian said.

They would find the airlock entrance after the dive.

"Form up for jump!" Dorian called to the six soldiers.

On the next pass, they spilled out of the aircraft, falling to the pitch-black sea at terminal velocity, their bodies formed into a dart, their hands held at their sides, oxygen tanks on their backs. Just as they reached the surface, the most recent storm receded and sunlight broke through, showering their entrance to the watery unknown with light.

Dorian plunged into the water and instantly spun himself about, searching for his men. One of them had veered too low and collided with the rocks just below the surface. His now broken body floated in the lighted murkiness.

The other five figures spread out, the sunlight carving their outlines in the water.

"Form up on me," Dorian called over his intercom.

As the soldiers swam toward him, Dorian surveyed the dark water between them. Something else floated in the space. Not debris.

The silence in the water shattered. An explosion, then an eruption of white bubbles and air engulfed him, throwing Dorian into the submerged mountainside. He rolled across the rock, trying to grasp a handhold. Finally, he came to rest. His hands instinctively reached for his oxygen tank. It was intact. He was safe. He turned, peering into the water. The chaos was clearing. Four of his men still floated in the abyss. They called over the radio, sounding off, then awaited his order.

"Don't move," he said. "I'll guide you around the mines."

One by one, Dorian directed his men down through the water, using his vantage point to spot suspected mines. He couldn't afford to lose any more men. When they were safely at the ship below, he followed them, pushing through the water, careful to avoid anything that could be a mine.

The darkness slowly consumed every bit of light from above, and the dark shapes that could be mines grew harder to spot. Dorian had only his memory and the narrow beams of light from his helmet to guide him.

Ahead, he saw the four soldiers floating. Forty feet. Thirty. Twenty.

He was there. The airlock control was similar to the portal in Antarctica. It opened for him as he drew close, and he and his men rushed in, out of the darkness.

The airlock flushed the water out, and Dorian shed his suit and approached the control panel. The green cloud of familiar light emerged. Dorian worked his fingers inside it, and the display flashed.

```
General Ares
Access Granted
```

Dorian pulled up a schematic of the ship.

It had been badly damaged, either from the nuclear blast Patrick Pierce, Kate Warner's father, had unleashed or by the mines. Entire sections were decompressed and flooded. The ship was on emergency power, and most importantly, there was only one route to the portal room.

Dorian pointed to the map. "Arc 1701-D. South entrance. That's our destination." Dorian chambered the first round in his automatic rifle. "Shoot to kill."

# 18

David was covered head to toe in dirt. His muscles had ached, and now they burned, but he kept digging, throwing shovel after shovel of dirt and rock down the tunnel where Milo, Mary, and Kate waited to haul it out, pail after pail.

He felt a hand on his shoulder, and he turned to find Sonja. "Take a break," she said.

"I can go another—"

"And then you'll be exhausted, and I'll be exhausted, and Paul will be exhausted, and we'll all have to wait." She took the shovel from him and began digging into the hard-packed ground, maintaining the upward slant they hoped would lead to the surface—an opening into the arc.

Kate had been right: the contents of the arcology had shifted over the last thirteen thousand years and not in their favor. The door was underground now, the Earth having slid to one side. How far under, they didn't know. It could be ten feet or a hundred. David wondered how long their meal rations would last, and what they would do if they didn't see the arc's artificial daylight soon.

At his and Kate's bedroom, he collapsed on the chair by the small metal table and dug into the MRE Kate had left out for him.

He was famished. He stopped eating only to breathe.

Kate entered and threw another MRE on the table.

"I'm not eating your ration," he said.

"Me either."

"You need your strength."

"You need it more," she said.

"I wouldn't if you could get that quantum cube Janus gave to Milo to work."

"We've been over this. Gaps in my knowledge. Big ones."

David held the fork up defensively. "Just saying." He finished the first MRE and eyed the second. "I feel like Patrick Pierce tunneling under the Sea of Gibraltar."

"That's a bit dramatic. I don't see why you don't use the explosives."

"Don't have enough. We used half to get in. Barely broke through. We'll need the other half—assuming we ever make it across."

Kate opened the second MRE. "Eat it, or it will go to waste."

She left before David could say a word. He exhaled and continued eating. He would pull a double shift next go round, whether Sonja stopped him or not.

The door slid open, and Milo rushed in. "Mr. David!" The teenager smiled. "We're through."

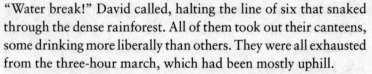

"Water break!" David called, halting the line of six that snaked through the dense rainforest. All of them took out their canteens, some drinking more liberally than others. They were all exhausted from the three-hour march, which had been mostly uphill.

David handed the machete to Paul, who took the lead position, ready to continue cutting their path through the thick green, red, and purple plants and vines that webbed between the trees which stretched to the dense canopy, blocking out much of the artificial sun. Or two suns in this case.

David studied the shadows on the forest floor, trying to get an idea of how much daylight they had left. *Night will be dangerous*, Kate had said.

"What do we call the flying invisible reptiles?" David asked her.

"Exadons."

"If we make camp here, will they attack us? In the thick forest?"

"I don't know. Possibly."

David sensed that Kate was holding back. "Tell me."

"They are predisposed to attack any new species in their habitat. It's an evolutionary response, a learning method for them. It's one of the reasons the scientists were interested in them."

"Wonderful."

David took his pack off and slung his sniper rifle around his shoulder.

"Where are you going?"

"To climb a tree."

***

The view from the top of the forest's canopy was breathtaking. The arc was an arena unlike any David had ever witnessed. He sat there for a few minutes, simply taking it all in. The ceiling of the dome simulated a sky with clouds and radiated heat. In the center of the floor, the rainforest stopped, and a green plain spread out, maybe a mile wide and slightly longer, followed by a smaller forest, this one more rocky and on declining terrain that ended in the exit. David was relieved to see that it wasn't blocked. The bottom layer of soil had completely shifted in their direction. In fact, they would need to build a ladder or stairway of some sort to even reach the door. And they'd have to blow it up, but there was another bright spot: they could use fewer explosives, which gave them a little extra to work with out here.

The green plain was surrounded on three sides by rainforest, but its right side ended in a wide stream with a slow-moving current. A herd of large, four-legged animals similar to hippopotamuses bathed and congregated where the water met the plain. Above the pool, a rock face covered the entire right side on the arc.

There, on one of the highest ledges of the rock face, David got his first look at the exadons. He counted eleven of them, spread out on the rock, unmoving, their eyes closed, their bodies glistening under the sun like silvery glass pterodactyls. Most exadons were entirely silver-glass except for two, who were covered in bright-colored tiles like a stained-glass window. He made a note to ask Kate about that. He estimated their wingspan at twelve feet, but from this distance, he couldn't make out any other details.

The first sun was setting now, and the edge of the forest cut two distinct shadows: one pointing to the open plain and the last stretch of forest before the exit, the other back into the forest, in the direction they came. And those were their options.

If nightfall arrived as they crossed the plain, the exadons could pick them off easily.

———————————❧———————————

"What did you see?" Sonja asked him.

She had continued hacking at the path during David's surveillance, and he was glad for that. She was every bit the leader he was, maybe more so: she had led her Berber tribe, composed of fighters and elders from the remnants of many disparate factions, to victory against the Immari in Ceuta. She was the definition of a self-starter.

David related their situation, and the six of them stood there in the dense, shaded forest, waiting for a decision. To David, the group looked like a motley crew of superheroes.

Milo, Mary, and Kate carried large packs that held the food and what Kate had only described as the scientist's expedition gear. It remained a mystery box to David, a surprise for the end of the day—if they lived that long.

The real question was Paul and Mary. They had been exhausted when they arrived, and David and Sonja had given Paul the shortest digging and machete shifts.

Paul seemed to sense the eyes on him and Mary. "We can keep up. I agree that we should make for the other forest at best speed."

"Sonja and I will take the packs when we cross the plain." Milo smiled, excited to keep his pack. The young man seemed to be a well of energy. David continued. "We'll hug the far tree line in hopes the exadons won't see us."

About an hour later, they cut the last of the plants and vines that held them in the rainforest and exited onto the plain. The packs came off Mary and Kate's backs, and the six of them began their march across the green plain to the trees in the distance. Everyone's focus was on the rock face to the right, and the predators that would soon take flight, hunting, invisible in the night. David had never dreaded nightfall so much.

Kate pulled up even with him. "I can take the pack."

"Not happening." At the back of his mind, he wondered how her condition was affecting her, if she was in any pain, if the exertion would limit her prognosis. Four to seven local days. He had tried not to think about that.

He nodded toward the exadons. "Why are two brightly colored?"

"It's the point in the pride's cycle. When food is plentiful, the colors come out. When living and hunting is easy, the members focus on mating, distinguishing themselves. But some conserve their power—opting not to waste it on colors. When the cycle ends, the members who were more flamboyant die out first, and those who stored up energy can out-hunt them and pick them off. There's been a recent population decline."

"So those are the survivors. The best hunters."

"Yeah. And they're probably hungry."

"Fantastic."

As the march wore on, the "water breaks" became more frequent, and they drank less and less water, most panting and massaging leg muscles, some stretching while they set their packs down for relief.

David and Sonja resumed the lead each time, setting the best pace the group could manage. They reached the tree line of the forest just as the second sun was setting.

David led them a little further into the forest, to an area where the trees were close and the underbrush was thick.

"We'll camp here."

Kate opened the first pack and laid out a black rectangular box. The familiar blue light rose from it, and Kate worked her fingers inside it.

Seconds later, the box began unfolding tile by tile, making a square floor about twelve feet by twelve feet, then a small opening that jutted out. Tiles continued unfolding, upward this time, forming walls with no windows until the walls formed a smooth circular dome at the top. The front of the... tent, David assumed, had a shimmering black portal. He stuck his head in. Amazing. He entered, and Kate followed. A queen-sized bed rose out of the floor in the upper left corner, and there was even a small desk and stool along the right-hand wall.

"Not bad," he said.

Kate laid out a tent for Milo and Sonja. David had never seen Milo move so fast.

Kate stuck her hand in to configure Paul and Mary's pop-up dwelling but hesitated. "I can configure it with two double beds or one larger."

Paul squirmed.

Mary glanced away but quickly said, "I think two beds... probably gives us..."

Kate nodded, and the tent began to take form.

David lay on the bed, which was some kind of adaptive foam similar to their bed in the lander. It felt like heaven, and he had to force himself to sit up. He couldn't let himself fall asleep. Time was running out.

Kate sat on the bed and smiled at him.

"These Atlanteans weren't exactly roughing it," David said.

"Take you back to your youth?"

"Somewhat."

"Were you a Boy Scout?"

"Tried to be. Dropped out."

"I thought you never gave up on anything you loved," she teased, using his words against him.

"Well I didn't love Boy Scouts. We didn't have Atlantean camping gear. I bailed out after Webelos."

"What's Webelos?" She took out a tin of cream and sat next to him on the bed.

"It's… not important—what is that?"

"Take your pants off."

"Hey lady, I don't know how camping works where you're from—"

"Very funny. This is a topical anti-inflammatory for your legs—"

"Wow, you are a sweet talker, but I'm gonna have to stop you right there." He sat up, grabbed his gun, and tried to sound casual. "I'll be back shortly."

"Where are you going?"

"I need to take care of something. I'll be back," he left before she could stop him, and walked quickly out of the camp. As he reached the edge of the forest, he heard someone following him, quietly.

He turned to find Sonja, her gun slung over her shoulder.

"You should head back."

"You should stop giving me orders. Let's get this over with. We both know what must be done. It's them or us."

# 19

Dorian marched down the dark metallic corridors of the Atlantean ship, his rifle pointed forward, his boot laces tied together, cutting into the back of his neck as they hung across his chest.

His four men also padded along in bare feet, careful not to make a sound that might echo in the empty corridors, which were almost pitch black.

Dorian couldn't decide if that was to his advantage or not.

David could be waiting around any corner. The fight that loomed thrilled and terrified Dorian. This was the end, his final battle with David. If he failed and Kate and David reached the beacon, his world would fall.

Dorian had tried to determine Kate and David's location, but the ship's computer was mostly offline. Dorian wasn't sure if it had been damaged or if it was a power-saving measure. If it was power-related, he didn't want to risk exposing himself by activating the ship's systems. But after he disposed of David and Kate, he certainly would. That opened another possibility, one Dorian had considered on the flight here: answers. The Atlantean ship recognized him as Ares. Perhaps it held clues about Ares' plan, or the enemy he feared so much. If Dorian could learn the full truth, maybe he could shift the balance of power and take control of the situation on Earth. It could be humanity's only hope.

Up ahead, the two soldiers at the point position halted.

They were at the entrance to Arc 1701-D, and it wasn't what Dorian expected. Mounds of black dirt covered the corridor, and where a door should have been, twisted metal snaked into the arc. It had been blown open.

Is David fighting someone down here?

Dorian motioned for his men to put their boots on and form up on him.

He crept to the arc entrance and peered in. Damp, warm air floated out, and he didn't understand what he saw: large green and purple plants. It was some sort of biosphere. Was it an aeroponics lab? A greenhouse? He had assumed the vast chamber was storage or perhaps another repository of resurrection tubes.

He selected a man to lead the way up the narrow dirt tunnel, which was likely a trap. He could lose one man; it would still be Dorian and three others to David. Good enough odds.

But there was no trap waiting on them, only a dense rainforest at sunset. David and Kate had cut a path through it. That would make it easy to catch them.

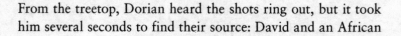

David glanced at the rock face directly ahead. He could only see the flamboyantly colored exadons now. Either the others were already in flight, or they had engaged their cloaks, preparing to hunt when the last rays of sunlight faded.

They were the perfect predators. There was no moon, and with no shadows in the dark night, they could strike when and where they chose. David hoped they were lazier than that.

"We should be quick," Sonja said.

"I agree." David adjusted his sights, marking his target.

"You think this will work?"

"We'll know soon."

Sonja spread out on the grass beside him and began firing the instant David did. Seconds later, the slow-flowing river ran red.

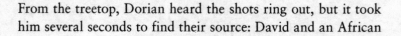

From the treetop, Dorian heard the shots ring out, but it took him several seconds to find their source: David and an African woman—almost perfectly camouflaged—at the opposite tree line, across the plain, lying flat. What were they shooting at?

Then Dorian saw it—massive beasts, not quite as big as elephants but with no snouts—rising out of the mud that bordered the plain and the river. They wailed as blood spilled out of them.

Are they out of food? Hunting? Dorian wondered. Their folly would make them the hunted now. Dorian slid down the tree.

"They're in the tree line across the plain. Hurry, we can take them by surprise," Dorian said. His men fell in behind him as they stormed up the path.

Mary sank into the bed and closed her eyes. She couldn't remember ever being this tired. Well, maybe after unpacking, when she and Paul had moved to Atlanta. Her things, combined with his, and carrying it all up and down the stairs had been thoroughly exhausting.

Why had she thought of that? Just the exhaustion? That was a time of excitement and the unknown too.

The code. They would know soon.

She reached her hand over, across the narrow space that separated the beds and put her hand inside Paul's.

He sat up slightly. "Everything okay?"

"I'm glad you came for me, got me out of Puerto Rico."

"Me too. It's probably underwater by now."

Outside the tent, they heard shots fired.

Milo was too excited to sleep or even eat. He sat cross-legged in the tent Dr. Kate had made from the case. It was yet another miracle, and he wanted to enjoy every second of the journey. He was sure he had a role to play.

Every second that passed, Kate became more convinced: she would spend her final hours with David. Here and now, at the end of her life, it all became clear, what was truly important, what mattered. Relationships. Love. How she lived her life. Who she really was. She couldn't wait for him to return.

She was asleep when the first shots were fired.

---

David began belly crawling back from the tree line, just enough to hide their position, but still in sight of the large animals thrashing in the mud, crying out in agony from the bullet wounds. Sonja joined him.

"Them or us," David said quietly.

"It usually is," she replied.

David waited, hoping the exadons would descend and devour the easy prey.

When David had seen the large animals at the river sink into the mud at sunset, he had formed his theory: the exadons hunted at night, principally via infrared, seeking heat and motion. The mud and earth served to cloak the great beasts from the exadons, balancing the ecosystem, except for when one wandered out at night, or in this case, screamed and rose out of their hiding place in pain.

David watched for any flicker of light, any moment—

The closest of the wailing beasts exploded in streaks of red, as if three massive steak knives had been drawn across its side. It rolled and threw mud in every direction—perhaps another innate defense mechanism. Patches of mud large and small flew through the air; some proceeded to fall, but many stopped and hung in the air.

Wings formed from nothingness, then long tails, and heads with a sharp spike at the end. David saw the mud-coated exadons in all their glory, ripping two of the large beasts apart. The other half of the macabre scene concerned him even more: three of the flying monsters were dragging another wounded animal away. They broke its legs and held it down, pressing their sharp talons into it. David saw it now: they were trying to lure out the remaining mud-bound animals who were forced to watch the others die.

David hoped they could resist, remain safe, stuck in the mud.

The exadons were smarter than he imagined—and more brutal.

David crawled backward on his belly, Sonja by his side.

When they couldn't see the bloody scene at the river anymore, they stood and began jogging back to the camp.

The first shot grazed David's shoulder. The second hit a skinny tree three feet away, shattering it, spraying David with splinters and throwing him to the ground. He was vaguely aware of Sonja returning fire, her hand on him, pulling him to cover.

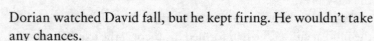

Dorian watched David fall, but he kept firing. He wouldn't take any chances.

The woman was returning fire, but she was only one; they were five.

He could easily cut the woman and David off, even lure them out. The camp had to be just down the path they had cut into the forest.

Dorian wanted to fire the final shots himself. He wanted to finish it.

He instructed two of his men to stay at the outcropping. "Keep firing on Vale and the woman. Pin them down. I'll take the camp and then their position."

Dorian led the other two men across the plain. The woman took a few shots at them, but they missed widely—she was shooting blind.

At the top of a ridge, Dorian got his first glimpse of the carnage at the river. Winged monsters coated in dirt and gore were ripping large animals to shreds in a convulsion of mud and blood that horrified even Dorian. What is this place?

He pumped his legs harder. He was almost to the opening. When he fired on the camp, David and the woman would have no choice but to attack, to come to him.

# 20

The rapid blasts of gun fire woke Kate. She listened. Two sources. Back and forth. Shooting at each other.

She leaped out of the bed, grabbed her pack, and found Milo, Paul, and Mary outside their tents.

"Pack up," Kate called to them. She ran from tent to tent, quickly entering the collapse command on the control panels.

The night was complete now, pitch black; the only sounds were gun fire, the rustling of the thick leaves and branches in the forest, and the wail of beasts in the distance. It made Kate's skin crawl.

She tried to focus. The four of them scrambled to gather their things as the tents folded in on themselves.

"What now?" Paul asked Kate.

There was only one thing they could do. "Hide," Kate said.

David was starting to get his breath back. Some of the splinters had penetrated the Atlantean suit, but it had kept a remarkable number out.

The group of rocks at their back took another barrage of bullets, showering them in pebbles and dust.

David searched his pack. What could he use?

Yes.

He pulled together some pieces of dead, dry underbrush, struck a match, and started a fire.

"Don't let this go out," he said. He took a grenade from the pack. "And cover me."

He stayed low, running as fast as he could for the exadons at the river.

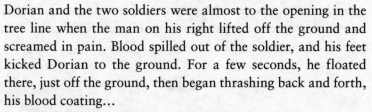

Dorian and the two soldiers were almost to the opening in the tree line when the man on his right lifted off the ground and screamed in pain. Blood spilled out of the soldier, and his feet kicked Dorian to the ground. For a few seconds, he floated there, just off the ground, then began thrashing back and forth, his blood coating...

One of the creatures.

Dorian opened fire, tearing into the monster and his own man, then swung the gun from side to side.

Two of the abominations fell to the green prairie. They flickered and popped, their scales like little mirrors. Were they machines or beasts? They bled. They were alive. And they could become invisible.

The field seemed to erupt at once.

A grenade blast at the edge of the plain. A wave of mud rose, the outlines of a half-dozen more winged creatures formed, and the massive animals that had been wallowing in the mud stormed out, catching the wrath of the mud-coated gargoyles.

Across the field, one of the men who had been firing on David from a rock outcropping cried out and flew into the air. The other turned and ran for the forest behind them, but he too was also taken, lifted, and shredded. His wails fading seconds after the beast caught him.

Dorian spun around, searching...

Where David and the woman had been, fire sprang up at the edge of the field, growing each second.

*The monsters hunt via body heat. David's trying to blind them,* Dorian thought.

Behind him, he saw his salvation. Dorian pointed. "The cave. Hurry," he said to his last soldier.

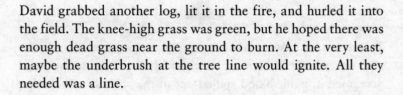

David grabbed another log, lit it in the fire, and hurled it into the field. The knee-high grass was green, but he hoped there was enough dead grass near the ground to burn. At the very least, maybe the underbrush at the tree line would ignite. All they needed was a line.

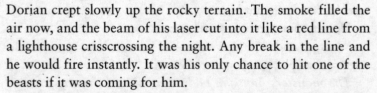

Kate could sense the jungle around her changing. It seemed to move: every leaf, branch, and tree crawled with creatures, as if they were fleeing some unseen enemy. Then Kate heard the explosion and smelled the smoke. What had happened? A new danger occurred to her. Here in this closed environment, they could suffocate. There was only one thing she wanted to do: run back toward the fire and find David. He would be furious with her if she did. She knew that, and she knew what she had to do.

She looked back at Paul, Mary, and Milo. "We need to hurry. If we don't make it to the exit…"

Paul stepped forward and took the machete from Kate's hand. "I'll take the first turn. Rest."

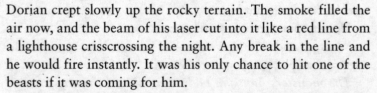

Dorian crept slowly up the rocky terrain. The smoke filled the air now, and the beam of his laser cut into it like a red line from a lighthouse crisscrossing the night. Any break in the line and he would fire instantly. It was his only chance to hit one of the beasts if it was coming for him.

But none did. They reached the mouth of the cave, which was about four feet in diameter. He poked his head inside and clicked his flashlight on quickly. Clear. And it was deep enough.

"Gather rocks," he said to the soldier. "I'll cover. We need to block the entrance so they can't see our body heat."

A few minutes later, a pile of stones lay just inside the cave. He and the man climbed in and arranged the rocks at the mouth, completely blocking it. They were safe, if they didn't suffocate.

Dorian leaned against the wall, opposite the soldier. He thought he heard the man gurgle. A snore? Dorian couldn't remember if the man had thrown up on the flight. Hopefully he was down to his best soldier. He would need one against David and his she-warrior.

Dorian's mind drifted to the cave, an unfocused thought occurring to him: what kind of beast would live here?

The man gurgled again.

"Hey, no mouth breathing."

The gurgle morphed into a wheeze.

Dorian kicked the man's leg. The muscle was hard. Too hard. Dorian felt it with his boot. Too slender as well. The leg felt no more than eight inches around. The soldier was far bigger. The skin was smooth, almost slippery.

Dorian realized the truth a second before another thick cord closed around his neck, slithered between him and the wall, and coursed all around him, pinning his arms tightly to his body and pulling him to the ground. The enormous snake squeezed him, and Dorian felt his breath go out of him.

# 21

David and Sonja marched back to back through the jungle, taking turns raking the red beam of the sight on the sniper rifle in oval circles, watching for any sign of the exadons. The smoke was closing in and so was fatigue, yet they pushed on, one foot after another.

Kate marveled at Milo. He had a well of energy she had never witnessed before. He had wrapped cloth around his hands where he gripped the machete. The blisters were the only thing slowing him down as he cut plant after plant and vines that Kate thought would never end.

Behind them, she heard rumbling in the jungle, the scattering of creatures from the trees and ground.

Paul, Mary, and Milo turned to look at her.

"Hide."

Dorian could feel the life flowing out of him. The snake had wrapped itself around him from his neck to his knees, squeezing tighter every second.

He had enough for one move. He squirmed, rolled to his side, and bent forward, pushing, crunching, and then throwing himself back against the wall of the cave.

The snake held on, but the cord of muscle spasmed, relaxing for a fraction of a second—all Dorian needed. He drew the knife from his belt and stabbed down.

The snake's mouth closed on his arm, the jaws crushing it. But the bite would be its undoing. Dorian took the knife in his other hand and stabbed again, plunging the sharp blade through the snake's head and into his own forearm. He ignored the pain as he drew the knife out, the serrated back side ripping the vile creature's head to pieces as it went. He stabbed once more with less force, and the snake went slack around him.

He reached for his pack, fumbling quickly in the dark, still holding the knife, ready for another attack.

He grasped the small cylinder and struck it. The flare illuminated the cramped space, smoke rolling off of it.

Dorian only caught a brief glimpse of the man before the smoke blotted him out, but the eyes stopped him cold. They were blank. The snake twisted, flailed, and released the man. It brushed Dorian as it retreated deeper into the cave, away from the fire and smoke.

Dorian lunged across the dead snake and felt for the man's neck. A faint pulse. He needed air.

Dorian crawled to the stack of stones they had piled at the mouth of the cave and pushed through. An inferno raged outside. The field in the middle of the freak show arena burned brightly, a sharp contrast to the dark smoke rolling off.

Dorian dragged the man out of the cave and laid him out. He would live, for how much longer, Dorian didn't know.

He picked him up and made for an indention in the rock—a place Dorian thought he could defend. He set the soldier aside, retrieved the two packs, and gathered another pile of stones.

Dorian tucked himself in the crevice and pulled the man on top of him, draping his body like a shield. If the man died, he would at least provide some camouflage. And if the gargoyles did attack, he would provide padding from their claws. Dorian stacked the rocks around them, hoping to blot out some of their heat.

He gripped his gun but didn't bother waving the laser sight back and forth. The snake had taken the last bit of energy out of him. He felt drained, almost as badly as he felt every time he spoke with Ares. The Atlantean had him—had the entire human race—like the snake had taken Dorian in the cave: silently, unseen, in the dark, seizing him, squeezing, hoping to take the last bit of life out of him and then devour the carcass.

He watched the fire consume the last of the field. As the flames subsided and the embers glowed, Dorian felt a new fire rising inside him.

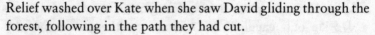

Relief washed over Kate when she saw David gliding through the forest, following in the path they had cut.

"David," she called, leaving her hiding place and running into his arms.

He grunted and turned his head slightly.

He was hurt. Her hands began searching him, finding where the blood was seeping from.

"I'm fine. Just some splinters."

David surveyed the rest of the group.

"We need to hurry," he said as he and Sonja took the lead and the others fell in.

Two hours later, the group was staring at the exit to Arc 1701-D.

There was only one problem: it was almost twenty feet from the floor.

David walked to where the last of the dark dirt met the hard composite the arc was made of. The soil was fine here. It was so bizarre.

The group focused on the two challenges at hand: getting the explosives up to the arc door then, assuming the blast broke through, getting everyone out. They exchanged ideas rapidly about how to reach the door; specifically, how to cut down a tree they could use to climb up: we use the machete; it would take too long. Use a bit of explosives; too risky—we might need all of them to get through. We come up short, we're stuck here. Shoot the tree; we need the bullets for Dorian and the exadons, and the noise could bring trouble.

Finally, they had settled on the lowest-tech, no-bullet, no-grenade, no-noise way to get the explosives up to the arc doors.

David stood at the base. On his shoulders, Sonja stood, balancing as best she could, her arms extended upward, one of Milo's feet in each hand. She shook slightly as Milo reached, attaching the explosive to the thick door and hitting the button to activate it.

Sonja let Milo fall into her cupped arms, the impact eliciting a sharp grunt from David. Then she handed him down and jumped to the floor. They all took refuge and waited, nervous about the looming result of the blast.

When the dust cleared, they saw the dim emergency lights of the corridor beyond, and a cheer went up and hugs went around. David hugged Kate, then Milo when he rushed into them. Mary found herself in Paul's arms, and David nodded sharply to Sonja, who allowed a slight smile to curl at her lips.

They reformed their human pyramid, this time hoisting the team out: Milo first, then Mary, Kate, Paul, and Sonja, who instructed the others to hold her while she gripped the straps of three backpacks and reached them down to David. He made a running go, leaped, caught the straps and pushed his feet into the wall, walking up close enough to the top to reach Sonja's hand. She pulled him close, and the others pulled them in.

The blast woke Dorian. Fear consumed him—he hadn't intended to fall asleep. The soldier's head rolled into him. "Sir?" the man whispered, his voice scratchy.

"Stay here."

Dorian raced to the edge of the rock cliff and followed the noise with the scope of his rifle.

A door. An exit—David's team had blown it open. Dorian watched that team, which actually numbered six people—none of whom Dorian had ever seen except Kate, crawl up and out.

He exhaled and surveyed the arc. It was quiet, and in the far corner, where the rainforest met the entrance, a sun peeked out. On the opposite rock face, two of the muddy birds spread out, sunning themselves.

Dorian wondered if they would stay there while the sun was out. If so, he would have a clear path to follow Kate and David.

———————————✦———————————

Kate and the team raced down the corridor, away from the arc opening and the danger beyond.

In the portal room, Kate worked the green cloud of light, and then moved to the arched door. "We're ready."

"Can you close it? Prevent Dorian from following?" David asked.

"No. The ship's in emergency protocol. This is the last evacuation route. It can't be disabled."

David nodded. One by one, Milo, the two soldiers, and the three scientists walked through the white, shimmering archway of light and onto the Atlantis beacon.

# PART II
# THE ATLANTIS BEACON

# 22

When Mary Caldwell cleared the portal, her heart almost stopped. The floor was pearl white, the walls matte gray, but it was the wide picture window spreading out dead ahead that captivated her like nothing ever had before. Earth hung there, a blue, white, and green marble against a black canvas.

This was a view only a select few humans had ever witnessed: astronauts. They were the heroes who dared to risk it all to see this, to expand human knowledge while laying their lives on the line. As a child, Mary had dreamed of this moment, of traveling into space and the great unknown, but it had always been too much risk for her. She had settled for a career in astronomy, hoping to contribute what she could while her feet were firmly planted on the ground. But this was the view and the mission she had always aspired to.

Here and now, she knew, no matter what happened next, she would die happy.

---

A single thought ran through Paul Brenner's mind: *we're screwed*. He had pretty much felt that way every day since the Atlantis Plague had first broken out, but this was different. He now felt himself coming a bit unhinged. His confrontation with Terrance North, killing the man, had almost pushed him over the edge. The race to escape the flood in Morocco, whatever just happened in that bizarre arena in the Atlantean ship, and now this: orbiting Earth, looking down on it.

He was used to trying to contain and control the uncontrollable: viruses. He knew the rules of that game: pathogens, biology, politics.

Here, he had no idea where he stood.

Almost involuntarily, he looked around, to Mary standing beside him. He hadn't seen her like that... in a very long time.

What Milo saw confirmed his belief that he was here for a reason, that he had a role to play. Seeing the world that, as a child, he had once thought so unimaginably vast, nearly limitless in size, reduced to a tiny ball, floating there, swallowed by the immensity of the universe, reminded Milo of how small he was, how minute a single life was—just a single drop in the human bucket, gone in the blink of an eye, its temporary, fading ripples the only legacy it would leave.

He believed that a person's drop could be the poison or the cure for the ails of the age—that age simply being the thin layer of water on the surface for a brief instant. Milo wasn't a fighter, a leader, or a genius. He looked around at his companions, seeing all of those qualities. But he could help them. He had a role to play. He was sure of it.

David scanned the small holding area onto which the portal opened, and then ran the length of the single round corridor, his gun raised, jerking back and forth as he searched. Empty.

The beacon's habitable area seemed to be a single level shaped like a saucer.

The portal they had just exited occupied the entire interior section, like a round elevator bank in the center of a high-rise building.

He made another circuit, beginning again at the portal opening and picture window, working clockwise. In order, the beacon contained four residential quarters similar to the crew pods on the lander (a single narrow bed, desk, and enclosed sonic sanitation bay—what he simply called "the shower" but was technically more like a waterless shower with multi-colored strobe lights); on the backside, opposite the portal, two large rooms David assumed were labs; and, in the last enclosed section, on the left-hand side of the picture window, a storage room full of silver crates and a few EVA suits.

When he reached the portal after his second trip around the beacon, the rest of the group still stood there staring out the window, mesmerized. He had to get them focused on the task at hand. They were all physically and mentally exhausted, but he wanted to grab the adults, shake them, and say, "Come on, people! Focus! Killers, chasing us, could be here any minute!"

Milo he gave a pass. David couldn't imagine himself as a teenager standing on a space station staring out at Earth. He probably would have peed his pants.

Kate had this blank expression David recognized: she was using her implant to communicate with the Atlantean vessel. The blank expression dissolved into worry as she faced him. Now he was worried. More worried.

David pointed at the portal. "Is this the only egress?"

"Yes," Kate said.

The words brought Sonja to life. "Barricade or ambush?"

In his mind, David riffled through the supplies he had seen. Not enough to completely block the portal. Not even close. "Ambush," he said. He nodded in the direction of the four residential pods. "We'll build it on that side of the portal."

He moved to the storage room, and he and Sonja moved all the silver boxes out, stacking them perpendicular to the portal so that their bullets would fire across toward the storage room, and David hoped, into Dorian and any of his remaining men. David wasn't sure if that was safe, but Dorian was likely to come through the door shooting straight on, so...

Kate grabbed his arm. "We need to talk."

"I'll take first watch," Sonja said, settling down behind the crates.

Kate was pulling David to the closest residential pod.

"There are three other quarters; everyone take one," David said. There were four of them and three rooms, but they would sort it out.

Paul collapsed on the narrow bed and began peeling the Atlantean suit off. The door opened, and Mary stepped in and set her pack down.

Paul had assumed Mary and the other woman would take a pod. "I can share with Milo."

"No. It's okay."

"You didn't want to…"

"Sorry. Sonja… she kind of scares me."

Paul nodded. "Yeah, me too."

*At least there's some good news*, Dorian thought. The soldier the snake had almost killed could walk, and he wasn't one of the regurgitators on the flight in, so maybe he was one of the better soldiers of the original six. At any rate, he was the only one left.

His name was Victor, and he wasn't very talkative. That was the balance of the good news.

Several hours into their march into the jungle, Victor finally asked, "What's the plan, sir?"

Dorian stopped, drank from his canteen and handed it to the man. They could see the peeled metal where David had exploded the exit door in the distance.

"Now we go down the rabbit hole and finish this thing."

"We have a problem," Kate said the second the door closed.

David sat at the table, weariness finally overtaking him. "Can you please never say that again, even if we're totally screwed? The phrase makes me more nervous than actual problems."

"What do you want me to say?"

"I don't know. 'We have an issue?' maybe?"

"We have an issue."

David smiled, showing Kate an exhausted look of complete surrender that softened her at once.

"Janus' message. It's not what we thought it was."

David glanced around, waiting.

Kate activated the screen above the desk and played Janus' transmission.

"That," David said, "is a very, *very* big problem."

# 23

David sat at the table built into the gray wall, trying to wrap his exhausted mind around Janus' message.

"Play it again."

From her perch on the narrow bed behind him, Kate used her neural link to play the video.

"What do you want to do?" Kate asked.

"We should share it with the group."

They had no options that David could see, and he felt they should make their decision together.

David had made the rounds, gathering everyone into the larger lab at the back of the beacon. Kate had programmed the doors to stay open, and she now stood in the open room with Milo, Mary, Paul, and Sonja. David had relieved Sonja, reasoning that she should see the footage for herself. He sat at the makeshift outpost by the portal, his rifle pointed across the entry path toward the empty storage room.

Before the video began, Paul stepped in front of the screen and addressed Kate. "I'm sorry, but can I say something first? I'm just... not sure anyone should be shooting a gun here." He specifically avoided eye contact with David.

"I agree," Mary said quietly.

Sonja stiffened.

David yelled back to them. "If Dorian Sloane walks through that door, *I am shooting him*. End of discussion."

Mary cleared her throat, "Well, it… seems to me that maybe we should stack the boxes against the portal. Then we would know when he comes through, and you could shoot into the portal—that way, at least the bullets would go back into the other ship."

"You assume," Sonja said, "that the portal would transmit bullets. If not, they would go through the portal mechanism in the center, trapping us here, which would be far worse than the quick death of decompression, which is another assumption. A craft this advanced can surely withstand impacts from outside. It's not my area, but I believe space is filled with floating rocks large and small, some moving quickly. It would stand to reason that perhaps this beacon was also built to withstand a puncture from the inside and if not, in the event of a breach, to rapidly repair itself."

"I, uh, hadn't thought of that," Mary said, her cheeks flushing.

"There's much to think about," Sonja said. "And all our minds are weary. Many unknowns." She turned to Kate. "Unless of course these unknowns are known."

"Oh, they're unknown." Kate said. Her Atlantean memories were spotty, and she had no idea what the beacon was capable of, including whether it could withstand a firefight or not.

"You said there was a movie?" Milo asked.

"Yes. Of sorts." Kate activated the large screen, the video began, and the five of them stepped back to form a semicircle around the screen.

Janus stood on the bridge of the ship he and his fellow Atlantean scientist had traveled to Earth upon and hidden on the far side of the moon, burying it below thousands of feet of lunar rock and dirt.

Janus' expression was stoic as he spoke.

"My name is Dr. Arthur Janus. I am a scientist and a citizen of a long-since fallen civilization. We made a great mistake many years ago, and we have paid dearly for it—with the lives of nearly every member of our society. The remainder of our people took refuge here, on this world, hiding, waiting. And we repeated our mistake."

The ship shook, and the panels around the bridge behind Janus flickered, popped, and went out.

"I say to you, those who destroyed our world, those we wronged, please do not continue your vengeance on the inhabitants of this planet. They are victims too."

Flames erupted across the bridge a second before the video ended.

"Yeah, so…" Paul began. "Not exactly a message to an ally."

Mary bit her lip. "How do we know the response—the message I received—is a response to this message? And do you know what the incoming message is?"

"No," Kate said. "In fact, what you received is what was in the transmission. Sometimes the beacon translates incoming signals, but it didn't in this case." The screen changed, showing an access log of incoming and outgoing messages. "Here's Janus' outgoing message, sent from the main vessel fourteen days ago. The strange part is that he routed it to a quantum comm buoy—"

"A quantum comm…"

"It's like a relay the Atlanteans used to manage communications traffic over distances. Sending information across space isn't the issue, it's folding the space, creating temporary wormholes and the power required to do so. The buoys establish those worm holes for an extremely small fraction of a second and transmit data. There are millions of them that form a redundant network."

There were blank stares all around the room, except for Mary, who was nodding.

"Why is that important?" Paul asked.

"Because it means Janus was masking the origin of his signal—he bounced it off so many buoys I can't even trace the destination from here. He clearly didn't want the recipient to know where the message came from."

"But somehow they traced it," Sonja said.

"Maybe, maybe not." Kate replied. She highlighted the next row in the communications log. "Twenty-four hours after his message went out, a response comes in. It had an Atlantean access code, so the beacon let it through. What's strange to me is that it didn't contain a message in the Atlantean format and encoding. The message is very... 'Earth-like'—the content is simplistic and far less advanced than what would be expected. The Atlantean computer can't even read it."

"As if the sender knew the Atlanteans were hiding on a less advanced world..." Paul began.

"It's bait!" David yelled from his position by the portal.

"I agree," Sonja said. "If this was a message to a great enemy, and they could not trace its origin, they could have sent a fake message to any suspected worlds, hoping to lure us out."

Paul nodded. "Hoping we would respond, reveal our location or better yet, disable the beacon so they could see exactly what's happening on Earth."

"It had our address on it," Mary said, but quickly added, "though, I guess they could have sent a customized message to every world." Kate thought the realization hit the woman hard, as if some hope she had harbored had finally died.

Paul rubbed his temples and paced away. "I'm too tired to think. We obviously can't respond, at least not yet, and we can't disable the beacon. Janus clearly believed the Atlanteans' enemy was still out there. What's left? What can we do?" He glanced toward the portal.

"I agree," Sonja said. "We're trapped."

# 24

Kate closed her eyes and massaged her eyelids. She was dead-tired and sitting at the small desk in the residential pod, staring at the screen for the last hour felt as though it were draining her even more. Yet... she couldn't help feeling as if she was missing something. Or maybe it was just wishful thinking, her desperate desire to think that there was a way out of the trap they were in.

The door opened, and David lumbered in, his eyes half closed.

Kate smiled. "How was work, honey?"

He barely made it to the end of the bed before falling into it. "I feel like an Atlantean mall cop."

She hovered over him.

"Pesky kids getting rowdy in the food court?"

"Supervisor relieved me for falling asleep on the job."

She began pulling his dirty tunic off. "Well they can't fire you," she said in a mock sympathetic tone. "This Atlantis beacon needs you too much. But you're getting dirt in the bed." She collected his pants and boots and then inserted them in the garment sanitizer in the corner.

David followed her with his eyes, not moving a muscle. "How does it work? The Atlantean laundry. Actually... don't tell me. I don't care."

She handed him a mushy bag, then uncapped the end and pushed it towards his lips.

"What's this?"

"Dinner." She squeezed some of the gel into his mouth.

David sat up and spat the orange goo on the wall. "Oh God, that's horrible! What the—What did I ever do to you, lady?"

Kate cocked her head. "Really?" She ate some of the goo. "It's just pre-digested amino acids, triglycerides—"

"It tastes like poop, Kate."

"You've never tasted—"

"I have now. It's horrid. How can you eat that?"

Kate wondered the same thing. To her, it had almost no taste. She wondered if it was because she was changing, becoming more... Atlantean. She pushed the thought from her mind.

"Well, I'm not eating that for my last meal. I'll starve first."

"So dramatic."

David reached for the pack. "What do we have left?"

Kate opened it and rifled through the MREs. "Beef stew, barbecue chicken with black beans and potatoes, chili mac..."

David fell back into the bed. "Oh, talk dirty to me now."

Kate punched him in the chest. "You're a lunatic."

He smiled. "You love it."

"I do. And that makes me a lunatic."

"I'll take whatever you don't want," he said.

"Don't think I can tell much difference anymore."

David's eyebrows knitted together for a moment, then his smile faded as he seemed to realize what she meant.

He grabbed a pack at random, tore it open, and began wolfing it down.

Kate wished he would eat slower, which would allow more digestive enzymes to release, breaking the food down better and giving him more usable calories from the meal. That had been her goal in feeding him the more nutrient-dense Atlantean pack. But... human needs.

He pinched her nose playfully, trying to lighten the mood. "No more nose bleeds."

"Nope."

He was about finished with the pack but stopped. "It was the experiments, wasn't it? The simulations."

"Yeah."

David finished the last few bites. "When Alpha said you had

four to seven days… left. It wasn't unsure of your health—the diagnosis. It was unsure how many experiments you would do on yourself. None means seven days, right?"

"Yeah."

"Good," David said. "Seven days is better than four."

"I agree," Kate said quietly.

"Okay, let's talk about the… *issue*."

Kate raised her eyebrows. "Issue?"

"Throwing the long ball."

Kate hated sports analogies. "We have a long ball?"

He pushed up on his elbow. "You know, the Hail Mary pass in the fourth quarter. That's where we are, Kate. We both know it. You said this beacon is connected to countless quantum buoys. To me, we only have one play: we send our SOS. Say… I don't know, 'our world is under attack from a superior alien occupying force.'" He paused. "Wow. I was trying to make it sound overly urgent and dramatic, but it's actually one hundred percent accurate."

Kate's mind lit up. That was it. David was still talking, losing steam with every word, the exhaustion and binge eating catching up to him fast.

"I mean, yeah, some bad guys will read it. Maybe they'll show up, but maybe some galactic good guys will give a crap, and anyway, we're screwed if we do, screwed if we don't…"

Kate pushed him into the bed. "Rest. You just gave me an idea."

"What idea?"

"I'll be back."

"Wake me up in an hour," David called to her as she left. There was no way she would wake him up in an hour. He needed rest. If Kate was right, he would need to be at the very top of his game.

Outside their room, she found Sonja and Milo manning the makeshift fortress adjacent to the glowing white portal. For perhaps the first time in her life, Milo didn't smile at Kate. He nodded solemnly, a look that said, *This is serious. We're on guard duty here.*

Kate nodded back as she passed and almost ran to the communications bay at the back of the beacon. She pulled up the transmission log she had shown the group before. This time, she entered a new date range: about thirteen thousand years ago.

The data scrolled across the screen, and Kate could hardly believe her eyes.

---

Dorian reached his hand down to Victor. "I'll pull you up. We have to hurry."

The soldier had climbed the tree leaning against the arc exit about half as fast as Dorian. The dimwit would never make the Olympics.

He jerked the man into the dark corridor, and they set out again. Dorian was glad to be out of the humid, freakish place with the snakes and flying invisible birds, and who knew what else.

He wanted to barricade the entrance, ensuring that nothing made it out, but there was no time.

The two men moved slowly through the corridor, again barefoot as they had been on the way to the arc, careful not to make a sound that might reveal their position.

Dorian had no problem facing facts: David was strong and clever. It would be just like him to send Kate to the beacon while he remained here, guarding, waiting to spring a trap.

If Kate had already sent a message or disabled the beacon, Dorian would be too late. The thought weighed on him, the proverbial weight of the world, but he couldn't rush his assault. If there was still a chance, it was up to him to stop them. If he failed, so would the world he was fighting for, had sacrificed so much for.

Ares had been right about one thing: Dorian did have a role to play.

He was adjusting to the darkness now, seeing more and more of the corridor despite the faint emergency lights.

Up ahead, the portal room loomed, waiting.

At the threshold, he and Victor paused, signaled each other, and then rushed in, sweeping the room with their rifles. Empty.

Dorian worked the green cloud of light at the panel, and the silver arched portal came to life.

Victor stepped toward it.

"Wait," Dorian commanded. "We need to be careful."

Mary and Paul were lying in the narrow bed, both staring at the ceiling.

"I'm too nervous to sleep," Paul said.

"Me too."

"For some reason, I don't want to shower either."

"Same here," Mary replied.

"Why is that? I have to think it's the fear of being in the shower the moment the invasion happens, when the shooting starts. Maybe it's the being naked part. Like you don't want to get shot when you're naked."

"Yep. Definitely the naked part."

"And the guilt. You know, after it's all over, if aliens get here, you don't want them entering it in the log:" Paul changed his voice to sound more like a computer, "this little human was butt-naked when his world fell. He was scrubbing his left thigh when the other evil human invaded and killed his team, leading to the end. He also failed to clean his back properly."

Mary laughed. "We're officially delirious." She rolled into him, tucking her face under his arm. "I can't stop thinking about the code."

"What about it?"

"Why send two parts? If it is bait, why not something straight-forward? Just the binary code."

Paul smiled.

"The complex, cryptic message just doesn't make sense as a lure."

"It's like it's a test. To see if we can solve it."

"Or encryption to make sure no one else can read it. Or can solve it."

"Interesting…" Paul said.

The door opened, revealing Milo. He grinned and raised his eyebrows. "Dr. Kate has an important update!"

When the group was assembled in the large communications room at the back of the beacon, Kate said, "I may have a solution."

"Solution for what?" Sonja asked.

"Getting off this beacon."

# 25

Kate pulled up the transmission logs on the large screen in the communications bay. Around the room, the reactions were as diverse as the group. Milo smiled. Sonja's face was unreadable. Mary squinted, focusing. Paul just looked nervous, as if the results would tell him how long he had to live.

David was guarding the portal, craning his neck around the central cylinder, trying to see the screen.

"This is the transmission log from around thirteen thousand years ago," Kate said. "This is the exact time of the fall of Atlantis—just after Ares' attack on the *Alpha Lander* off the coast of Gibraltar. During that attack, the ship was split in half, and Janus was trapped in the half closest to Morocco."

"The part we were just in," Mary said.

"Yes. We know Janus' partner was killed in the attack thirteen thousand years ago. He tried desperately to resurrect her in one of the tubes in the other half, closest to Gibraltar. In the final days of the Atlantis Plague, I learned that his attempt to resurrect his partner had partially succeeded: I have her memories. But only select memories. Janus longed to bring her back without certain memories. For the past two weeks, I've been trying to access those memories... in hopes that I could..." Kate caught David's eye.

She turned to the screen and continued. "I've been trying to access the memories, but they were erased from the *Alpha Lander* data core. That's not supposed to be possible—resurrection, especially the storage of memory data, must adhere to strict Atlantean guidelines. What I learned a few moments ago is that Janus didn't actually delete the memories. The resurrection system wouldn't let him. So he took the memories he wanted to hide from his partner and transferred them to this beacon. Then he split them in three parts and transmitted them to three other beacons, deleting them from this beacon. Copies remained on the lander, but since there were other active copies in the beacon network, he could move them to archived storage. Once there, he physically damaged the storage array, corrupting them. He also disabled the active data link with this beacon—that's why we couldn't see the message he sent and the signal Mary received from the lander: with the beacon link disabled, Janus was ensuring that copies of the memories couldn't be restored from the beacon network."

"Sonja!" David called around the hall. "Switch with me."

She walked out of the communications bay without a word, and when David rounded the curve, he focused on Kate. "No way."

"You don't even know what I'm going to say."

"I do. The answer is no."

Paul and Mary got very interested in what was happening on the floor around their feet. Milo's almost ever-present smiled faded.

"Will you let me finish?"

David crossed his arms and leaned against the door frame.

Kate pulled up a map of the beacon network on the large screen, displaying what looked like a thousand overlapping spider webs.

"The Atlanteans deployed these shrouding beacons through-out the galaxy—at emerging human worlds, research locations, and military quarantine zones—wherever there was anything they didn't want others to see or where they didn't want anyone within the beacon's range to see the outside galaxy."

"Incredible," Mary said, drifting toward the screen.

Paul looked from Kate to David. "Where's this going?"

"We can use the portal to go to any of these beacons."

Milo lit up.

Paul moved behind Mary, perhaps to catch her if she fell. "That seems…" he said, "rather uncertain."

David snorted. "It's Atlantis beacon roulette."

"It's our only option," Kate shot back.

"Do we know *anything* about the beacon destinations? You said this beacon's memory core was wiped, right? So these beacons could be damaged or even open to space. They could be in the middle of a war zone. Or they could be monitored by this great enemy. The second we step out, they take us and find Earth's location. Game over. There's a million ways this could go wrong. I can probably name a hundred right now, and my imagination sucks."

Paul interrupted Kate and David's back and forth. "Is it possible that the destination beacon is off? That the portal would take us into space? Or nothingness?"

"No," Kate replied. "If the portals establish a link, there is a viable beacon on the other end."

"Can we send some kind of probe?" Mary asked. "To get a peek at what's happening on the other end?"

Kate shook her head. "We don't have that kind of equipment here, and I think it's too risky to go back to the lander for it."

"One of us could peek our heads through," David said, "see if it gets shot off. Actually, beacon roulette is definitely the right term for this idea."

Kate ignored him. "There's reason to believe that the three beacons Janus transmitted the memories to are safe."

"Reason?" David asked, skepticism in his voice.

"Janus was a genius. Everything he did was deliberate." Kate looked at David. "You know that."

"Maybe, but he also deliberately tried to roll back seventy thousand years of human evolution. He wasn't the biggest fan of modern humanity."

"True, but we don't know *why* he wanted to do that. The answers are out there."

"And that's what this is about. Reducing seven days to four, maybe less, for a few answers."

"David, we have nowhere to go. If Janus chose these three beacons for a reason, they could be part of a backup plan—his last attempt to save us."

"Or he could have selected three beacons on the verge of being destroyed—he was trying to destroy these memories."

"I don't think he would do that."

"The bottom line is this: if we step through that beacon, it could be the end of our lives, and if we reveal Earth's location, the end of humanity. That's a lot to risk, Kate."

---

Dorian had considered several options for storming the portal: throwing a flare through, sending Victor through first, and finally, a more stealth approach.

He drew his knife from his belt, knelt at the portal and slowly inserted it into the light where the arched, glowing dome met the dark metallic floor. He ran the knife along the bottom, the entire four feet width of the portal, careful not to touch the floor or sides, aware the sound could alert his enemy.

The knife met no resistance. They hadn't barricaded the door. At least not at the bottom. He quickly continued outlining the portal, moving the knife along the sides, and stretching to reach the top, which was just over eight feet tall.

"They haven't blocked it," he said to Victor.

A few minutes later, Dorian leaned against the wall, Victor balanced on his shoulders. Victor wavered, then steadied himself with a single palm pressed into the wall.

"Careful," Dorian snapped. "Remember. Be quick."

Victor leaned his face into the light only a few inches, right at the top of the dome, and jerked it out. His eyes were wide. "They're all standing around, arguing."

"All six?"

"Yeah."

"Armed?"

"The man and the African woman."

"Perfect." This was a break—Dorian couldn't have hoped for any better. There would be no searching the beacon, no one hiding out, waiting to ambush them. He raced to his gun, which lay on the floor at the center of the room. "Hurry, Victor."

Paul thought they were getting nowhere. The group had moved the discussion—now, shouting match—to the portal area, conceivably so that David could have an ally in Sonja, who had indeed taken his side, the anti-Atlantis beacon roulette side.

"Give me a better option," Kate said. "Any option."

"The SOS," David countered.

"Is guaranteed to give away Earth's location. Guaranteed."

"And we're guaranteed to live another day."

"Not necessarily," Kate shot back. "Same-day-arrival bad guys could be listening."

"I think we're getting nowhere," Paul said.

Mary leaned closer to him. "I think I saw something."

"What?"

"In the portal."

The portal flickered at that moment.

David eyed Kate. "Did you program it?"

"Janus' first destination. I'll go and come—"

"No. If anyone is going—"

David whipped his head around. Milo was gone.

Then things happened quickly, faster than Paul could follow.

David stepped to the portal, but Kate caught his arm. He turned to her.

Sonja ran through the portal, then David threw Kate's arm off, stepped through, and Kate rushed after him, leaving Mary and Paul standing there, staring, both their mouths hanging open.

The portal's light dissolved a split second before Dorian reached it.

"What happened?" Victor asked.

The emergency protocols on the *Alpha Lander* should have kept the portal connection open, ensuring the only emergency exit remained viable. Dorian worked the control panel, which flashed the words:

```
Destination portal connection broken.
```

Dorian tried to connect again.

```
Destination portal in use.
```

*In use?* The enemy could be invading the beacon. Or... Dorian worked the panel, desperate, trying continuously to connect to the beacon's portal.

Mary took a step toward the portal.

A face broke the surface of the glowing archway, extending only a few inches.

Milo.

His eyes were closed, a look of pain across his face. "Save yourselves!"

Mary grabbed Paul's forearm, her nails digging in.

Milo opened his eyes and broke into a grin. "I'm just kidding. Come on. It's okay."

The instant the portal connection re-established, Dorian ran through and searched the small space station. Empty.

They had gone to another beacon. Fools. What dangers lurked out there? Did they know? Care?

Dorian walked to the communications bay and activated the logs. He would have their location in minutes. He hoped he could stop them in time.

# 26

To Milo, the new beacon was yet another miracle. And he had brought the team here, led the way. Instinctively, he knew that action had been his purpose all along. He felt that if he hadn't stepped through the portal at that exact second, something terrible would have happened. Perhaps he would never know. As he turned to his companions, he sensed something was wrong.

***

This beacon was different. David knew it instantly. The station that shrouded Earth was a science beacon—the floors pearl white, walls matte gray, it's every feature minimal and clinical.

This beacon felt more militaristic, dark and rugged, with black floors and walls. It seemed ancient and used, almost decrepit. Where a wide picture window lay opposite the portal door in the last beacon, a relatively small, industrial window looked out onto the black of space, where a few stars twinkled, but nothing remarkable caught his eye.

David raised his gun and began searching the space, Sonja following close behind him, covering his back.

The layout was similar to the last beacon: a saucer with the portal in the center. However, it had a staircase with two levels. There were more rooms and more equipment here. And it was empty.

David could feel a slight motion. Was this beacon rotating?

He returned to the portal, where Paul and Mary had joined them.

143

David gripped Milo's shoulders. "Never do that again."

"It had to be me."

"What?"

"I'm the most disposable," Milo said with a nod.

"You're not disposable."

"I'm not a scientist or a soldier. I—"

"You're a kid."

"No, I'm not."

"You will be the last to go through from now on."

"Why?"

"Because," David said, shaking his head. "You'll... understand when you're an adult." The words were a surreal moment for him: saying something his parents had said to him countless times, him always thinking it was a lame cop-out.

"I want to understand it now," Milo said.

"You're the last one of us we'd ever put in danger."

"Why?"

David exhaled and shook his head. "We'll talk about it later. Just... go to your room for now, Milo." David silently groaned at his own words. He saw Kate fighting a smile as Milo traipsed away toward the residential pods.

David nodded to Sonja, who began setting up to guard the portal.

He put his arm around Kate, leading her to a bedroom.

"Teenagers," she said when the door closed.

"I'm not happy with you either," he said. "You opened the door for him."

"I had no idea he would go through."

"First things first: can Sloane follow us here?"

"Yes. But he's going to have a hard time finding us."

"How hard?"

"Like one in a thousand." Kate paused. "Unless he's really, really smart."

David didn't like the sound of that. He hated Dorian Sloane. David had dedicated a large part of his life to finding and punishing Sloane, but he wouldn't lie about his enemy: he was smart.

"Then that's a problem."

The door opened, and Paul stuck his head in, cringing as he spoke. "I'm really, really sorry, but you two need to see this."

Kate and David followed him back to the portal area, where the others stood, their backs to them, staring through the small window.

David realized that this beacon was in fact rotating. Through the window, the empty view of space had been replaced.

A sun burned brightly in the center of the scene, but it was the flat expanse of debris that stretched from the beacon almost to the burning star that took David's breath away. Remnants of star ships, thousands, maybe millions of pieces spread out. David thought if a hundred Earths were destroyed in the space, that it still wouldn't have filled the area that all the shattered vessels did. The floating wreckage was mostly black or gray, but here and there, a speck of white, yellow, or blue dotted the plane. Pieces of debris collided with each other, arcs of blue and white light reaching across like lightning bolts connecting them for a fraction of a second. Taken in whole, the glistening dark debris field looked like an asphalt road in space that led to the sun.

Where the others had stood in awe of the view of Earth from the last beacon, it was David's turn. For a soldier and a historian, the view was a transcendental moment.

He felt some part of himself let go. Maybe it was the scope of it, the realization of how tiny a speck the human race was in the vastness of the universe, or perhaps it was seeing proof that there was a force this powerful in the universe, powerful enough to destroy worlds. Whatever the cause, something changed for him in that moment.

Kate had been right.

They couldn't hide. Or bide their time.

Their odds of survival were long.

They would have to take chances now. It was their only hope.

## 27

Dorian wanted to shoot the beacon's computer. And Kate Warner. During the few minutes the portal had been disconnected from the *Alpha Lander*, she had connected to a thousand other beacons. The entries were all grouped in the same time interval, preventing Dorian from discerning how long the portal had connected to each beacon. She could have connected to 999 beacons in the first second and used the remaining time to access their true destination. They could be at any one of a thousand locations in the entry.

He paced the room. How could he find them? What did he have to work with? He had checked: there was no video surveillance. Porting to another beacon was a risky move. That David and Kate had taken the leap surprised even Dorian.

How did they even choose which location? Randomly? Surely not. Did she know something? She had to—but what? What did she have to work with? Kate had the memories of one of the Atlantean scientists. Was that her clue; did she remember something that could help them? An ally? The idea struck a chord of doubt in Dorian. If they knew more than he did...

He manipulated the computer quickly. Yes. The beacon had a backup of the resurrection memories. There were three entries: those of Janus, his partner, which was identified as being deleted, and... Ares.

Dorian queried the computer, asking, *Can I see the resurrection memories?*

```
You may only access your own memories, General
Ares.
```

The beacon recognized him as Ares. He queried the computer again. *How can I view them?*

A small door at the side of the room opened.

```
The conference booth can be configured as a
resurrection memory simulator.
```

Dorian stepped into the square room. The walls and floor glowed brightly, making the box seem as though it were built out of light and virtually limitless in size. He blinked, and it was gone, replaced by a place much like a train station. A large board hung above, blank.

"Identify memory date," a computerized voice boomed.

*Memory date*, Dorian thought. Where to start? He truly had no idea. After a moment, he said, "Show me Ares' most painful memory."

The train station disappeared, and Dorian saw his reflection in curved glass—but it wasn't his face, it was Ares' face. It looked almost the same as it had in Antarctica, though the features were different somehow. Not as hardened.

At first, Dorian thought he was in yet another tube, but it was too large. He looked around. A lift. The rest of the reflection revealed his attire: a blue uniform with a rank insignia on the left chest.

As the seconds ticked by and the lift rose, Dorian felt his own thoughts and presence fade. It was only Ares standing in the lift now; Dorian was simply watching, experiencing them as they came. In this memory, he was Ares.

---

The lift trembled, and then shook violently, slamming Ares into the back wall. Words and sounds whirled around him, and he fought to stay conscious.

The blurred visions and slurred noise coalesced, and a man was shouting in his ear. "Commander, they've caught us.

Permission to port to the main fleet?"

Ares pushed up as the lift doors slid open, and the ship shuddered again. He stood on a bridge where a curved viewscreen covered the far wall. Around the room, a dozen uniformed Atlanteans were shouting and pointing at terminals.

On the screen, four large ships were fleeing hundreds of round, dark objects, which were gaining on them, shooting at them. The dark spheres converged on the tail ship, crashing through it in a ball of yellow light and blue pops.

"Port to the main fleet, sir?"

"Negative!" Ares yelled. "Deploy life rafts. Space them out."

"Sir?"

"Do it! When we've cleared the rafts, order the auxiliaries to eject their gravity mines and all ships to release their asteroid charges."

On the screen, a thousand little discs slipped out of the remaining ships in the fleet, a tiny few connecting with the round balls that swarmed the ships. The explosions ripped the spheres apart, but there were too many of them.

*We die protecting our fleet*, Ares thought as the screen filled with light and searing heat ripped the vessel open and pressed into him.

He opened his eyes. He stood in a small rectangular vessel with a single window that looked out on a surging wave of light—the remnants of the battle he had just fought.

He was on one of the life rafts—his emergency evac tag had ported him to the raft, along with nine others: the first officer from his own bridge and the captains and first officers of the other vessels in his sub-fleet. They were all standing, recessed into their medical pods. A few heads poked out, taking stock.

The wave reached them, and the flash of heat, pain, and bone-rattling force blew through Ares again.

He opened his eyes. Another life raft. The wave was farther away. The evac tag had ported them to the next raft when the wave had destroyed the last. Ares didn't bother cowering as the wave rushed forward. He watched, waited, bracing himself. The force, heat, and pain washed over him again, and he stood in the third life raft. In the fifth raft, he started dreading the wave.

At the tenth, he could no longer open his eyes. Time seemed to disappear. There was only the oscillating wave of agony and nothingness. Then the ship shook, but the heat and pain never came. He opened his eyes. The raft was twirling in space. It rotated, and he saw the gravity wave, no longer nearly as strong, rolling away, curving the tiny dots of light that were distant stars.

Ares closed his eyes. He wondered if the life raft would initiate a medical coma or simply let him die. He didn't know which he preferred. He wasn't sure what followed after that, but he experienced only nothingness, an abyss of time without feeling or thought.

Metal creaked as the raft doors opened wide. Air rushed in, and light crashed down on him, hurting his eyes.

He was inside a ship, in a large cargo bay. Dozens of officers stood around, gawking. White and blue clothed medical staff rushed onto the raft's platform, nodding to him expectantly.

He pushed out of the recessed medical pod and stepped out. His legs wobbled, and he tried with all his might to stand as he sank to the floor. He felt himself wrap his arms around his shins, curling into a ball as he fell onto his side. The med techs lifted him onto a gurney and moved him away from the raft. The other nine officers remained in their alcoves, their eyes closed. "Why aren't you extracting my officers?"

The tech pressed a device to his neck, and he was unconscious.

# 28

When Ares' memory had ended, Dorian found himself back in the shimmering room of white light inside the beacon that orbited Earth. Like Ares had been, he was curled into a ball on the floor, his body shaking. Blood ran from his nose, and nausea washed over him. His heartbeat accelerated and more blood flowed from his nose, as though his own fear would pump every last drop of blood out of his body.

He fought to stay conscious. What had the memory done to him? For weeks, Dorian had seen Ares' memories. During the Atlantis Plague, he had seen Ares' attack on the *Alpha Lander* as well as events that had shaped human evolution for the last thirteen thousand years. He knew Ares had revealed those memories to him, allowed him to see what he needed to see in order to rescue Ares.

In the weeks that had followed, the nose bleeds and night sweats had started. He awoke frequently from nightmares that faded instantly.

Dorian wondered if reliving these memories would kill him. And he wondered what choice he had. He had to know the full truth of Ares' past, and he desperately wanted to see these repressed memories that had driven his own life, the monster in his subconscious.

He glanced around. The room seemed to have no beginning or end; Dorian couldn't remember where the door was, but that didn't matter: he had no intention of leaving.

One thing about the memory was certain: there was an enemy out there. Ares hadn't lied about that.

Something didn't add up though. In the memory, Dorian had the distinct impression that Ares wasn't a soldier, at least not at that time. The battle with the hundreds of spheres had seemed improvised: asteroid charges, gravity mines—they sounded like tools of exploration, not weapons. The crews and ships hadn't been prepared or made for battle.

Dorian used the voice commands to reactivate the resurrection memory simulation. At the simulated train station, he loaded the next memory, beginning where the last had left off.

———————❀———————

Ares opened his eyes. He lay in a bed in an infirmary room.

A middle-aged doctor rose from a chair in the corner and walked to him. "How do you feel?"

"My staff?"

"We're working on them."

"Status?" Ares asked.

"Uncertain."

"Tell me," Ares commanded.

"Each of them is in a coma. Physiologically, they're fine. They should wake up, but none of them will."

"Why did I wake up?"

"We don't know. Our working theory is that your threshold for psychological pain, your mental endurance is higher."

Ares stared at the white sheet covering him.

"How do you feel?"

"Stop asking me that. I want to see my wife."

The doctor averted his eyes.

"What?"

"The fleet council needs to debrief you—"

"I'll see my wife first."

The doctor edged to the door. "The guards will escort you. I'm here if you need me."

Ares stepped out of the bed cautiously, wondering if his limbs would fail him, but they were stable this time.

The table held a folded standard service uniform. He wondered where his expeditionary fleet uniform was, with his rank and insignia. He unfolded the flimsy garment and reluctantly slipped it on.

Outside, the guards led him to an auditorium. A dozen admirals sat at a raised table at the center, just off the stage, and two hundred more citizens, wearing a variety of uniforms and insignia, filled every seat behind them. An admiral Ares didn't recognize instructed him to provide a full mission report.

"My name is Targen Ares, officer of the line, Seventh Expeditionary Fleet. Current commission…" An image of his destroyed fleet flashed through his mind. "My most recent commission was Captain of the *Helios* and sub-fleet commander of the Seventh Expeditionary Fleet's Sigma group. Our mission was to collect one of the spheres currently referred to as sentinels."

"And you were successful?"

"Yes."

"We'd like to reconcile your report with the ship's logs and telemetry we recovered from the life raft."

Behind Ares, the giant screen transformed from black to a view of Ares on the bridge of his destroyed ship. The screen showed a single sphere, floating alone.

The video showed his four ships following the sphere, then it following them.

"How did you lure it away from the sentinel line?"

"We studied the line for weeks. Our survey spanned eighty light years and confirmed the working theory that the sentinel network completely surrounds a large swath of our galaxy. The spheres are evenly spaced, like a spider web, but they're moving, collapsing in on us. It's not an immediate threat, but if the rate of movement holds, in the distant future, about a hundred thousand years, the sentinels will reach our solar system."

Murmurs went up around the room.

"How did you capture the sphere?"

"We noticed spheres occasionally breaking the line, but they quickly returned. We correlated these occurrences with errant space probes—usually ancient derelicts from extinct civilizations. Most were solar powered and emitted simplistic universal greetings. Each time, the spheres would intercept the probes, perform some analysis, and then destroy them. Our mission briefing noted that the spheres have attacked any ship attempting to cross the sentinel line. But no ship had ever been destroyed, so the sphere's destruction of the probes was curious to us. We should have taken it as a warning. We created a probe of our own that repeated a simple binary ping. We used it to lure a sphere away."

The screen showed footage of a sphere following the fleet, gaining ground on a small object floating ahead of it. It cut to a scene in the future with the ships circling the sphere, then several sequences in which spheres were destroyed.

"Several attempts to capture the sphere failed. We finally managed to capture one, though we disabled it in the process."

The screen changed to the cargo hold of Ares' ship, where a massive black sphere towered above him. The ship shook, and Ares braced against the wall.

"This is the beginning of the assault. A dozen spheres targeted the *Helios*, firing plasma charges. We were able to outrun them. The line sentinels seemed to be very simplistic. They were much slower than our ships. Our mission parameters called for comm silence, which we maintained. A few hours later, stable wormholes opened, and a new kind of sentinel arrived. Hundreds of them. They were much more... advanced. And aggressive."

The screen behind him replayed the battle.

"Why didn't you port to the fleet?"

"Fear. I feared I would lead these new sentinels to the Seventh Fleet and eventually home. I reasoned that our loss was justified. I had the same concern about transmitting our data to the fleet. I deployed the life rafts hoping the commanding officers might survive and that we could bring this intel back. I hoped the gravity mines would destroy the fleet of sentinels, and the subsequent wave would push the rafts far out of range of any sentinels late to join the battle. I spaced the rafts so that if one were destroyed, our evac tags would port us to the next raft in the chain. I wasn't sure if it would work, but I hoped that the rafts could at least carry our logs and telemetry."

"In that regard, we judge your mission to be a success, Ares. The intel you delivered may save us in this war."

"War?"

The auditorium was silent.

"Am I to be briefed on the aftermath of my mission?"

"Yes. In private. By someone who's very eager to see you."

# 29

The guards led Ares to a large stateroom that was much grander than his captain's quarters on the *Helios*. They were treating him like a member of the admiralty. He tried the data terminal, hoping for answers, but it was off. What were they hiding?

The expeditionary fleet had known about the sentinels for over a hundred years but had assumed the spheres were simply relics of a long-extinct civilization, possibly science buoys studying stellar phenomena.

They were clearly much more.

The door opened, and his wife, Myra, stepped inside, tears welling in her bloodshot eyes.

Ares ran to her but stopped short. He stared at her protruding belly, trying to comprehend.

She closed the distance between them and hugged him tightly. He hugged her back, a million questions fighting a war in his mind, with a single thought winning out: *I am alive, and she is here.*

They moved to the couch, and she spoke first.

"I found out right after you deployed. I submitted several requests to override the comm silence order, but they were denied."

"I've only been gone point one years."

She swallowed. "They wanted me to tell you. You've actually been gone for point seven years. Missing, assumed killed in the line of duty for point five. We had your funeral."

Ares stared at the floor. Gone for over half a year? What had happened to him? He should have been able to exit the medical pod in the life raft when the wave had passed, once he had stopped porting between the life rafts in the chain.

But awareness hadn't returned to him. It was as if time had disappeared, and his mind had broken from reality.

"I don't understand."

"The doctors think a part of your mind essentially shut down—it happened to all the officers. The others are still in a vegetative state, but physically, they're fine. The doctors are very concerned about you. They want me to... assess you."

"For what?"

"Any mental changes. They think the experience may have changed you—psychologically."

"How?"

"They're unsure. They think the experience may have expanded your mind's pain tolerance and even permanently altered your brain wiring, making you capable of all kinds of... I don't want to repeat it. They're worried."

"There's nothing wrong with me. I'm the same man I was."

"I see that. I'll tell them. And even if there is... an issue, we'll fix it—together."

There was something different about him. Ares felt a low simmering rage growing inside him.

His wife broke the awkward silence. "After you went missing, I transferred to the *Pylos*. They searched for point two years. The funeral followed, but I convinced the captain to allow me to take one of the survey clippers to continue searching. I used up all my leave. I think fleet medical thought if I searched long enough, until I was satisfied, it would be healthier for me and for the pregnancy."

"You found me?"

"No. I probably never would have. With the wide expanse of space and with the raft's emergency signal off..."

"I had to."

"I know. The sentinels would have found you."

"I don't understand."

"I found something else. My long-range scans showed massive changes in the sentinel line. Their alignment has broken.

They're retreating. We believe you opened a hole in the line, and someone is trying to come through. The sentinels are fighting them. The admiralty and global council think the sentinel's enemy could be an ally for us—if we could join up with them."

She took a pad out of her bag and handed it to Ares. "What I found out about the sentinel lines convinced fleet command to send all the expeditionary fleets to this side of the sentinel line. Every ship has been searching for you, deploying probes. The combined surveys revealed that the opening in the sentinel line is getting bigger." She pulled up an image. "Here's why."

Ares almost drew back when he saw it. A battlefield with the debris of thousands of ships stretched out to a massive star.

"What—"

"This battlefield, it's where our potential ally is trying to break through. And there's more. They're trying to contact us. Our probes have picked up a signal. It's simplistic. Binary followed by some cipher with four base codes. We're still working on it. We think this army has sacrificed a great deal to open this hole in the line—they concentrated on the place you first opened, where you led the spheres away from the line. The entire fleet is on their way there. We'll reach it tomorrow."

"Our mission?"

"Make contact. See if we have an ally and how we can help in the sentinel war."

"What else do we know?"

"Not much. The sentinels have destroyed every one of our probes, but we have one image." She tapped the pad, and a grainy image of a floating piece of a ship appeared. Ares stared at the round insignia, a serpent, eating its own tail.

"A serpent…"

"We're calling them the Serpentine Army."

"Are they human?"

"Based on the size of the corridors we can see in the cross section, it's possible. And their code is readable to us. We'll solve it soon."

# 30

For David, tearing his eyes away from the massive debris field that stretched from the military beacon to the burning star took an extreme act of will. The view was captivating. The mystery of what had happened here, of what could have destroyed thousands, perhaps millions of ships filled his mind with possibilities—and fear. The moment he had seen it, his entire perspective on their situation had changed, perhaps his entire perspective on life.

He turned. Paul, Mary, Milo, and Sonja waited, but he looked only at Kate, whose expression changed from dread to confusion as she tried to read him.

"Okay," David said. "Kate says we're safe here for the time being. We're going to take this opportunity to get something we need."

Haggard, defeated expressions greeted him. Not a single guess about what "they needed" was offered in the seconds that ticked by.

"Rest," David said. "Everyone is going to eat, sleep, and shower—and nothing else for the next eight hours."

Sonja glanced at the portal.

"No guard duty this time," David said. "We'll barricade the portal. We have plenty of supplies on this beacon. We'll make secondary barricades at the corridor on both sides that lead out. That will be plenty of early warning if Sloane gets through." He paused, letting the words sink in. "All right, let's go. Sonja, if you'll help me build the barricade. Milo, you too."

Milo smiled, and then grew serious as he fell in with Sonja and David, grunting as he helped them carry the heavy silver crates out of the storage rooms and up the stairs to the portal area.

When the barricade was complete and everyone had retired to the residential pods, David put a hand on Milo's shoulder. "Milo—"

"I know, I..."

"Let me finish. I told you before that you would understand when you're an adult. My parents used to say that to me all the time when I was a kid." He read Milo's expression. "I know you're not a kid, but it's something adults say to kids when there's something they can't understand yet—and there are a lot of those times. This isn't one of them. None of us wanted you to go through the portal because we would never put your life in danger before our own."

"Why?"

"Because we're adults, and we care about you. We've had a chance to grow up and become what we are. Yours is a life still to be lived, and it's more important than ours. This isn't a military decision, it's about what's right and making decisions we can live with. If we chose to put our lives before yours, none of us could live with that. Do you understand?"

"Yes," Milo said quietly.

"Can I count on you, Milo?"

"You can, Mr. David. For anything."

---

When David entered the residential pod, Kate was sitting at the small desk table, scratching her head.

"I know you're mad at me," she said.

"I'm not."

She raised her eyebrows.

"Okay, I was. But I'm not now."

"Really?"

"Seeing the debris field, this place, it's made me realize something."

Kate waited, still suspicious.

"If that signal really is from a potential enemy, and they have some idea where Earth is, we need to make a major move to find help. Assuming there's anybody left on Earth to save."

Kate looked at the floor. "I agree. What do you want to do?"

David began pulling his clothes off. "Right now, I want to rest. Then figure out a plan together. I want to start playing offense. This whole time, starting the second I found out you were sick, I've been hanging on, trying not to lose you and the remaining time we have. I've been scared. I'm still scared, but I think we need to take some risks if we have any chance of coming through this."

"You were right about one thing," Kate said.

"Yeah?"

"We should enjoy the time we have left."

Paul didn't remember going to sleep; he had been that tired. He opened his eyes and searched for the sound.

Mary stepped out of the shower and casually moved her arm up to cover her chest.

Paul shut his eyes quickly and tried to arrest his now out of control pulse.

"That shower is super weird."

"Yep," Paul said, his eyes still closed. "Like a one-person disco with no water."

Paul could hear her getting her outfit out of the hamper, slipping it on, and sitting in the chair.

"Yeah. Reminded me of a tanning bed."

He sat up and looked at her curiously.

She shrugged defensively. "I went once. In college, right before spring break. So I wouldn't burn. And probably because of peer pressure since the other girls—"

Paul raised his hands. "Not judging. I mean, from a health stand-point, it's an unsafe way to tan. But a small amount of sun daily is quite healthy. The UVB rays convert the cholesterol in your skin into a precursor for vitamin D, which is, in truth, a hormone, not a vitamin. Essential too. We depend on healthy vitamin D levels to avoid or prevent seasonal affective disorders, autoimmune conditions, and certain cancers."

"Right. Well, I was just saying that I haven't, you know, changed... I haven't started tanning or dressing differently. Not that it matters. The dating pool is abysmal in Arecibo, Puerto Rico."

"Sure. I bet. I don't think you've changed a bit."

"What does that mean?"

Paul cleared his throat. "I... you're just the way I remembered you."

Mary squinted.

"In a good way," Paul added.

Paul thought the pause that followed lasted at least three or four hours.

"You still work a lot?" Mary asked.

"All the time. Especially the past few years."

"Me too. Only place I'm happy." She propped her elbow on the table and ran a hand through her hair. "But I think I get a little less happy every year."

"I know the feeling. Few years ago, after..."

Mary nodded. "Did you ever get remarried?"

"Me? No. The other astronomer I met... is he, were you two...?"

"No. God, no. I'm not seeing anyone." She paused for a moment. "Is there a woman in your life?"

Paul tried to sound casual. "Not really." *Not really?*

"Oh." Mary looked surprised.

"I mean, I live with someone, but—"

Mary reeled back.

"No, it's not like that."

"Right."

"She just came home with me after work one day."

Mary looked away. "I figured that's how it would happen for you."

"No, that's not what I mean."

Mary began chewing the inside of her lip—one of her habits Paul knew well.

Paul cleared his throat. "It's actually quite simple. We have a kid—"

Mary's mouth fell open.

"Well, it's not my kid. Or it is now. He is. He's not an it. His name is Matthew."

"Matthew's a good name."

"Yes, of course, wonderful, wonderful name. But Matthew isn't my biological offspring—well genetically we're related, but he's—"

"I think we should get some rest."

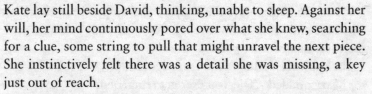

Kate lay still beside David, thinking, unable to sleep. Against her will, her mind continuously pored over what she knew, searching for a clue, some string to pull that might unravel the next piece. She instinctively felt there was a detail she was missing, a key just out of reach.

David snored a bit but stopped. Kate marveled at the man's ability to sleep—even when they were in imminent danger, as they had been for, well pretty much as long as they had known each other. To Kate, David seemed to be able to simply turn his brain off and sleep on command whenever he needed to. Was that a learned trait? From years of battling enemies in covert warfare? Or was he born that way? There was so much about him she still didn't know. Would never know. Didn't have the time to learn.

The thought made Kate slightly remorseful about what she knew was coming. Part of her wanted David to wake up, but more of her wanted him to rest.

She slipped out of bed, pulled some clothes on, and quietly shuffled out of the room, down the dark, ominous corridor of the military beacon to the communications bay.

Where to start? Janus: he had chosen this beacon for a reason. Why? What was special about it? A battle had happened here. Had Kate's Atlantean counterpart seen it?

The memory archive revealed the answer: No.

In fact, the memories Janus had stored here began thousands of years after the beacon was placed here. Kate's counterpart had never even been here.

She decided to back up. She queried the computer, seeking the historical records relating to the debris field.

```
All information related to the Serpentine
battlefield is classified according to The
Citizen Security Act.
```

*Serpentine battlefield. Classified.*

Thirty minutes of searching the computer hadn't revealed any more information. In fact, she was almost right where she had started. This beacon was devoid of any information, and there seemed to be no clues. Was it on purpose? To protect against any enemies reaching it and accessing its data core? Was that Janus' motive? Had he sent the memories here because there was nothing else to find? That would have been clever. And he was clever.

Kate was about to leave the bay when the screen faded, and a red box began flashing. White block letters read:

```
Incoming Communication
```

Kate gripped the table to keep herself from fainting.

# 31

Reliving Ares' memories had been torture for Dorian, but the Atlantean food was almost as bad.

He and Victor sat in the storage room on silver crates, consuming orange gel the Atlanteans deemed "food."

"Stuff's terrible," Victor said.

"Very astute," Dorian mumbled, finishing his bag.

"What are we gonna do?"

"Guess we'll have to rip them a new one on the comment card."

Victor looked confused. Actually, Dorian was beginning to think that was just how Victor looked.

"Where you going?" Victor asked as Dorian strode out into the corridor.

"Homework," he said, closing the doors to the communications bay.

Dorian dreaded starting the next memory, but he had no choice. Learning the truth about Ares, about the enemy beyond the beacon was his world's only hope. He had to. And he had never turned away from what had to be done. He stepped into the communications booth and began Ares' memory stream where he had left off.

Ares awoke to the standard fleet hazard alarm. He had heard it many times—most often when a team doing an experiment, either inside or outside the ship, was in trouble. The last time he had heard it, hundreds of sentinel ships had been bearing down on his sub-fleet. They had destroyed his ships and every last man and woman under his command.

He sat up and planted his feet on the cold metallic floor. He realized he was sweating, but his skin wasn't warm. Fear. Something was wrong with him.

He battled to get to his feet, his body fighting him, not wanting to respond.

The speaker system dinged, and a calm voice began repeating: "All hands to hazard stations."

*Hazard stations*. Every member of the service knew theirs. The drills came at least once every five days. Safety came first in the expeditionary fleet, and for the first time in Ares' career, he had no hazard station. No station period. He was no longer a captain of a ship or a commander of a sub-fleet or even in a chain of command. He was simply an officer with no assignment— and at the moment, no clue as to what was going on.

He donned his standard service uniform and rushed into the hall, where people from all service branches swarmed around him. He tried to ask several people what was happening, but everyone threw off his grasp and continued past him.

Ares snaked his way through the crowd, fighting to get to the lift.

At the bridge, he stopped dead when he saw the screen.

The massive battlefield that stretched to the star... it was the same scene Myra had shown him, but it wasn't dormant; it was alive with activity. The Atlantean first and second expeditionary fleets lay at the far end of it—seventy-three ships in total. But a far larger fleet loomed just above the black plane of debris. Massive ships, some the size of the entire Atlantean fleet hovered, blocking out massive swabs of the sun, throwing long shadows on the relatively small Atlantean vessels—all of which were ships of exploration.

When the Atlanteans had launched their first deep space exploration ships, they had armed them. But as the decades and centuries slipped by and no enemies had presented themselves, it grew harder and harder to justify the cost and space of arming their ships. Their primitive period of weapons-enabled ships was seen as comical to some and embarrassing to others. They had come to believe that any race sufficiently advanced to reach deep into space must be civilized.

Standing on the bridge, staring at the massive fleet that loomed above the Atlantean ships, Ares knew how wrong and foolish they had been. These were ships of war, of destruction, just as the sentinel spheres were.

"Play it again," the ship's captain called from his standing position at the high-top table in the center of the bridge. Around the bridge, officers and technicians focused on the screen. Ares stepped forward, stopping just behind the captain, his focus squarely on the viewscreen. He watched the scene reset, the timestamp in the top right reverting to an earlier time. They were watching a recording, telemetry from the fleets at the Serpentine battlefield. *We must still be en route*, Ares thought.

The First Fleet Admiral's voice played over the speaker.

"Fleet, be advised, we've received a signal from the Serpentine Army. We're working to decode it now, but we've re-transmitted the message to confirm our receipt in what we hope will be interpreted as a sign of friendship."

The screen tracked forward in time. Behind the Serpentine fleet, a wormhole opened and more ships began pouring in. They were all the same shape and size. For a moment, they paused just before the portal, then began circling, linking end-on-end with each other, forming a ring. Or a serpent? A second ring formed, just inside the other, and another until there were seven rings, all fit together, like a donut blocking out the sun. Ares saw a glimmer and realized that they were collecting sunlight. A massive solar cell, trapping energy.

The admiral's recorded voice played again. "Fleet, be advised, the first part of the signal is binary. This location in space and another region, currently uncharted. Could be the Serpentine homeworld. Second part is believed to be a DNA sequence, possibly a virus. It's not long enough to be a complete human genome."

On the screen, several small ships disembarked from a large ship deep in the Serpentine fleet and moved slowly toward the First Fleet flagship.

"Fleet, we've got incoming. Scans are negative on content. Repeat, they're either blocking our scans or there's nothing inside the vessels. Stand by. All ships hold your position."

*Fools*, Ares thought. The admiral was playing it safe, reasoning that they couldn't fight, so why run? Ares didn't see it that way. His wife was on the *Pylos*, an explorer class ship in the second fleet. He waited, hoping to hear the admiral give the order to evacuate the fleet.

The small black ships stopped halfway between the Serpentine and Atlantean fleets.

"Fleet, we're sending tugs to bring the first few ships in. This could be a peace offering or a communication of some kind. Stand by."

The tugs pulled a few of the vessels into the closest explorer class ship, and then the video log spun forward with nothing happening until it ended in a freeze frame.

Ares looked around the bridge. Everyone was tapping notes and working at their stations, some people conversing.

"Keep playing it," the captain said. "Pay attention, everyone. Any detail could be important."

"What's happened?" Ares asked him.

"We've lost contact with the first and second fleets—right after they made contact with the Serpentine ships."

"It's an attack," Ares said firmly.

"We don't know that. It could be a systems malfunction related to the communication. It could be the sentinels cutting off communication. A stellar anomaly. Anything. We're advancing all our ships to the Serpentine battlefield."

"Have you apprised the council?"

"Yes."

"Are they evacuating?"

"No. They've decided there will be no announcements until we know for sure what's happening."

"Fools. This could be the start of an invasion. We should divide our fleet, call in all the mining and freighting vessels, and evacuate as many as we can."

"And if this is simply a misunderstanding? An evacuation will cost lives too. The panic would cripple us—at the very worst time. This has been decided."

"Give me a ship," Ares said.

"Relieve a commanding officer without cause during a crisis to give you a ship? I didn't believe the psych report I read, Ares. But it's looking more accurate by the second. We'll reach the Serpentine battlefield in minutes—"

Ares stormed off the bridge, into the lift. Scenarios, options, coursed through his mind. He had to get to the *Pylos*, to his wife, and get out.

The corridors were still filled, but not as jam-packed as they had been.

Ares was twenty feet from the portal bay when the first blast rocked the ship, throwing him into the wall of the corridor. The side of his face swelled, and he thought he would lose consciousness. His ribs and wrist throbbed. He rolled onto his back and lay on the floor as the ship bounced, stabilized, and shook as the motion canceling systems recovered and failed. When the quakes subsided, he staggered to the portal bay and quickly worked the controls. If he could port to the *Pylos*, he could reach her.

He activated the link, but the screen read:

```
Portal Lockdown Protocol in Effect
```

The fleet had sealed itself off. Smart. But he was trapped.

He raced down the hallway to the shuttle bay doors. They opened, revealing a wide, deep hangar where half of the ten small crafts were overturned and some had been smashed against the bay wall. There was a lander still upright and intact. Ares boarded it and entered the launch sequence.

He donned one of the three EVA suits, hoping to save a little time. Seconds could count. As he waded back into the cockpit, he got his first view through the opening shuttle bay doors.

The creaking doors slowly revealed the horror and scale of the massacre. The entire Atlantean first and second fleets lay broken, disintegrating, floating into the debris field, joining the millions of ships that had fallen before them.

Pieces of Ares' own fleet, newly arrived to the battle, rolled by the shuttle bay, collapsing into the tempest. There was fire and light coming from the remnants of his own ship and those in its fleet, but they would grow dark soon, just like the first and second fleet. Ares watched listless ships collide, explode in flashes, then grow dark, drifting as compartments along their jagged edges decompressed, puffing air, objects, and his comrades into space.

But the spectacle of the annihilated Atlantean fleets paled in comparison to the battle that raged just above the debris field. On the far side, just before the sun, a ring of Serpentine ships rotated, a giant artificial wormhole of blue and white light stood open in the center—a feat that required unimaginable amounts of energy. A new Serpentine fleet seemed to emerge every second. The ships were all uniform in size, and at the center of the portal, a single giant column of linked ships flowed out, an enormous metallic snake emerging from a rip in space.

Pops of light flashed all around the oscillating snake. Ares enhanced the view. He could see the insignia on the side of the ships. A serpent eating itself. And he realized what was fighting it. Sentinels spheres. Thousands of them, pouring through individual wormholes that disappeared the second they dropped into the battle zone. In formation, the spheres ripped through the serpent, like buckshot into its side, ripping layer after layer of ships away, the rope of the serpent fleet unraveling, but the core never breaking. The gnawed-away sections were instantly reinforced as other Serpentine ships fell in, filling the destroyed links.

The spheres' rate of arrival was increasing; they were gaining on the Serpentine fleet, pushing the great column back. Ares saw their goal: the ring before the sun that powered the wormhole.

The scene gave him a glimmer of hope. Perhaps the winner would spare whatever was left of the Atlantean fleet. He panned the lander's viewscreen to show the fighting at the periphery. His hope slipped away. Spheres ripped into the remnants of the Atlantean ships drifting into the breach, opening any inhabited sections to space. He worked the controls, focusing the image. Serpentine ships were firing on life rafts, killing any surviving officers. The two great armies were fighting each other—and each were fighting the Atlanteans.

There was no ally to rally around here. No hope. The full truth, the weight of his hopelessness suffocated him in the EVA suit.

# 32

The blast that ripped the shuttle bay open jolted Ares back to the present. His lander was away, floating into space, into the wreckage of the fleet and the Serpentine battlefield that stretched to the sun.

Slowly, his mind took stock of his situation. There was no escape. No hope. Yet, a single desire consumed his mind. *Myra. I will see her. We will be buried here together.*

He keyed the controls. It was only a matter of time before his tiny ship would be ripped apart, becoming another grain of sand in the beach of debris that stretched to the sun.

Ares stayed focused, maneuvering the small lander, weaving through the drifting hulks, slowly making his way to the *Pylos*. It lay in three large pieces and no doubt thousands of smaller ones. Ares debated about where to look. Communications, her duty station? Or her quarters? The wreckage made the decision for him: the communications bay was gone.

He docked the lander at a section of wreckage that contained half the residential floors. He was vaguely aware of how irrational he was being as he cleared the airlock. His logical mind had shut down; it stood aside, watching, pitying Ares as he sailed through the dark corridors, the lights from his helmet illuminating the floating objects that drifted past him. The ship's power was completely gone; not even the emergency lights or artificial gravity was working. Life support would be off. Even if he found her in her quarters...

He decided he would stay there for the duration, floating with her, surrounded by her things, and the blank screens that would have shown their pictures.

The door to her quarters opened. A single EVA suit rotated in the air, listless. It turned, and Ares saw the face inside. Her face. He pushed through the door, colliding with his wife, hugging her.

Her voice whispered in his helmet. It was faint but controlled. "Ares…"

He hugged her tight. "You were smart. You put your suit on." She didn't hug him back. Was she almost out of air? Semiconscious? "We're getting out of here."

Her hands clamped around his arms, her strength shocking him. "We must stay."

He dragged her out of the room, and then pushed her through the corridor. She was in shock. She fought him as they flew through, dodging bodies, boxes, and items that crossed their path. At the airlock, he pushed her through first. She lay on her side in the lander's decompression chamber. She was completely exhausted, spent.

Ares rushed to her and began trying to pull her suit off.

The lander's decon alarm went off, and the door began closing.

Ares got out just before it slammed shut. He rushed to the door and peered through the small window that looked into the chamber. The screen beside it flashed the words:

```
Biohazard Quarantine Initiated
```

He activated the comm.

"Myra."

She rose slowly and turned to him. In the bright white light of the chamber, he could see her face clearly for the first time. Her skin was ashen, almost gray. Tiny blue blood vessels snaked across her skin, and Ares thought he saw something crawling underneath it.

On the screen a full body scan appeared.

```
Xenobiological pathogen identified.
Classification unknown.
```

Two buttons appeared below it: Disable Quarantine and Sterilize Chamber.

Ares felt himself take a step back.

"Open the chamber, Ares. It's okay. It's not what you think it is. The ring will save us."

Ares' eyes drifted to the scan. *She's not pregnant anymore.*

"They removed the growth, Ares. Open the door. You'll see. They're doing this to save us."

Ares took a step away, then another. He was numb. The ship shook. Why would it shake?

He was on the floor, looking up. Quarantine. Ship under fire.

He staggered to the cockpit and saw three sentinel ships targeting his lander. They were firing on the aft compartment.

Where Myra was.

He had to save her. He—

The next wave of blasts sliced the ship in half. The screens scrolled emergency procedures, listing bulkheads that were closed, systems that were offline. As the front of the lander spun around, he saw the sentinels tearing apart the severed tail section, including the decontamination chamber that held the only thing he loved in the universe.

The sentinels ignored him. They destroyed her mercilessly.

He slumped into the chair, not able to tear his eyes away. And then he waited, ready for it all to end.

# 33

To Dorian, the bright light of the conference booth was a scorching sun, boring into him, never relenting. It seemed to seep straight through his eye lids, pounding into his head. The memory of Ares' loss at the Serpentine battlefield had left a deep well in him, and Dorian felt lost at the bottom.

He rolled onto his belly and pushed up, staring at the growing pool of blood that dripped onto the glowing white floor. The memories were poisoning him. Or was he already dying?

Dorian had felt the slow creep of disease grabbing hold of him weeks ago, but now the danger was more urgent.

He tried to focus. Again, Ares' memory had raised more questions than answers. The Serpentine Army had clearly infected Ares' wife with something, and the sentinels had been attacking the Serpentine Army—and the infected Atlanteans.

Was one side—either the Serpents or the Sentinels—the great enemy that had finally sacked the Atlantean homeworld? Dorian was about to activate the next memory, but he hesitated. Was there a better way to find out? Perhaps a way that didn't kill him a little bit every time he peeked? That would be ideal. He didn't know how many more trips into Ares' past he could survive. And he had a place to start now.

He exited into the communications bay and accessed the computer, requesting information about the Serpentine battlefield. At every query, the screen flashed a red warning message:

```
Information classified by The Citizen Security
Act
```

The Atlanteans had been careful to erase all information related to both the Sentinels and the Serpentine Army.

In fact, even all the telemetry and data from deep space survey probes passing by that area had been erased. But... there was a beacon orbiting the battlefield. Dorian's mouth almost dropped open when the entry appeared. Kate had connected the portal here to that beacon twenty hours ago. It had been one of a thousand beacons in Kate's frantic rotation, but... it was quite a coincidence.

Dorian paced the room, his mind rifling through the facts. Kate and David knew about the signal to Earth—the transmission Ares was terrified of. And they had come here to the beacon to respond to it or even to disable the beacon, allowing the sender to find Earth.

But something here had given them pause, caused them to reassess. They had sent no transmissions nor disabled the beacon. Had they learned of the enemy? Had they gone to the beacon at the Serpentine battlefield to learn more, or possibly try to conference with an ally away from Earth, where a wrong guess would have less consequences?

The carnage of Ares' memory had been real to Dorian. The Atlantean was justified in fearing either the Serpentine Army or the Sentinels.

He selected the entry for the beacon at the Serpentine battlefield. The log contained only two entries: a portal connection yesterday, and a data transmission approximately thirteen thousand years ago.

*Interesting.* What was significant about that date? Janus. He had been trapped around that time—during Ares' attack on the scientists' lander off the coast of Gibraltar. Had Janus sent a message to a potential ally? A call for help? It was possible.

Dorian queried the date. There had been three transmissions from this beacon on that date. Was Janus increasing his chances of reaching help?

Kate had come here, seen something that scared her, and

then had the courage to step through the portal—to a beacon anywhere in the universe, which could be in any condition imaginable. The payoff on the other side had to be huge. And she had to be somewhat certain there wasn't an immediate danger waiting there.

Janus' breadcrumbs. Dorian realized what they were: memories. Kate was playing the same game he was: trying to unravel the past of the Atlanteans and learn the truth about their enemies and allies. Her team had gone to one of the three beacons. And they were likely still there. Dorian burned the beacon addresses into his mind. It was only a matter of time now.

***

"Slow down," David said. He looked around the communications bay at everyone assembled. He was right: Kate was laying down the revelations too fast for everyone, except maybe for Mary, who looked almost hypnotized.

"It's a transmission—coming from the battlefield," Kate said.

"How?" David asked.

"It must be from the wreckage." Kate activated the screen, scrolling the message quickly, as if anyone could actually read it. "It's just like the one Mary received on Earth—a binary number sequence at the start and a body with four base codes."

"Is it the same message?" Mary asked quickly.

"I don't know," Kate said. "It's the same format though."

"So at the very least, the sender could be the same," Paul said. Kate nodded.

"What do we know?" David asked. "I mean, you said information about this place is classified."

"Yes," Kate said, focusing on David. "And I checked: the scientist, Janus' partner, never visited this place. In fact, she has no recollection of the Serpentine Army at all."

"Yet Janus sent a transmission to someone in his final seconds, and then sends his partner's memories here—to a battlefield she never visited, where a signal strangely like the response to his message has been transmitted on repeat for thousands of years." David scratched his head. It didn't add up to him. What was he missing? There was something wrong here. "They put these beacons in places they didn't want anyone to find, right?"

"Right," Kate confirmed. "Or to keep what's inside from seeing out."

Yes, that was it. David was sure of it.

A mechanical sound on the top floor, just above them broke the silence.

David's eyes snapped to Kate. "The portal."

"It's not me," she shot back.

"Keep this door locked," David said, as he ran out of the communications bay, Sonja close on his heels.

A single stairwell led from the bottom floor to the top floor, which held the portal, large storage bays, and the residential pods. The bottom floor housed the communications bay and a series of small storage rooms.

David's options were bad and worse: climb the stairwell and face Dorian and whatever men he had left on the second floor or wait here, hoping to ambush them when they descended.

He quickly decided on the ambush. He motioned for Sonja to take up position inside one small storage room; he moved quickly to another. They would fire on Dorian from those two positions, waiting until he reached the bottom of the stairway to open fire.

David heard a metallic clang coming down the stairway, like tin cans rolling. Surely Sloane wasn't stupid enough to... Across the way, David saw Sonja peek out from her doorway. Three black round cylinders bounced from the stairs into the narrow corridor. Flash grenades.

David spun, hiding behind the door frame, covering his ears, closing his eyes tightly. A split second later, the flash and boom consumed his sight and hearing. Everything moved in slow motion. David pushed against the wall, opened his jaw, and blinked, trying to regain his senses.

He glanced out. Sonja. The blast had caught her full on. She staggered forward, into the corridor.

A figure barreled down the stairwell, taking the stairs three at a time. He began firing at Sonja before he reached the bottom.

David raised his rifle, firing on the man, but it was too late.

Sonja fell, blood pouring out of her. The man rolled on the floor across from her, convulsing, still pulling the trigger, spraying bullets in every direction, including back into the stair well.

A small object ricocheted off the stairwell wall, then another. They bounced and rolled. David's eyes grew wide. Grenades.

He stepped back and tripped over a crate. He sat up just enough to see out of the narrow doorway, into the blood-filled corridor, where Sonja and Dorian's soldier lay lifeless. For a moment, there was no sound. Then… an orange wall of light formed, crackling, glistening, containing the grenade blast. A forcefield.

The small door of the storage room closed, and the force of motion threw David against the back wall. The artificial gravity in the room released its grip, and he slowly floated upward, joining the silver boxes.

It was all like a bizarre dream with no sound. David rotated, staring out the window at the military beacon. The room wasn't for storage. They had just used it for storage. It was an emergency escape pod. And it was floating into the vast debris field, joining the millions of other pieces of wreckage from battles fought and lost. He simply stared out the window, the view and silence feeling bizarre and unsettling. Sadness. Sloane would reach Kate and the others. He had failed. His final defeat. And he would never see Kate again.

## 34

Kate waited in the communications bay with Milo, Paul, and Mary, listening as the gunfire gave way to explosions. The wall screen erupted, a red dialog covering it.

```
Decompression Imminent
Containment Protocols Initiated
```

A single word blinked.

```
Evacuate
```

Kate surveyed the state of the beacon. It had been ripped in half. Forcefields were holding the vacuum of space at bay, but the beacon couldn't power them much longer. All the escape pods had been on the other side of the forcefield, and the beacon had deployed them.

She had no choice. She quickly keyed the portal to the next beacon location Janus had sent memories to. She downloaded the memories from the current beacon onto a portable memory core and moved to the door.

"Come on," she said, trying to fake as much bravery as she could. "Stay behind me."

The doors slid open. Sonja and another soldier lay dead on the black floor. Sorrow and joy filled Kate. David wasn't there. Still a chance.

A glowing orange forcefield obscured the view of space and the debris field beyond.

Kate glanced around. One way out. The stairwell. She stepped through the blood, over the bodies, and onto the first stair.

She hesitated, wondering if she should grab a gun. Paul's eyes lingered on the fallen soldier's rifle a second before he tore it free from the man, and then moved forward, taking position in front of Kate.

"You know how to use that?" she whispered.

He shrugged. "Not really. You?"

"Not really."

They stood for a second. There was no sound above. At the back of her mind, Kate kept hoping David would round the corner, peek his head into the stairwell and say, "Coast is clear. Let's go."

But he never came. She crept up the metallic stairwell, the others following her, Paul at her side.

The blast of sound from the emergency evacuation message almost threw her off her feet and back down the stairway.

At the top of the steps, she could see the glowing portal, and through the reflection of the small glass window opposite it, a soldier lying in the corridor on the other side of the portal. It wasn't David. She glanced out the window, at the now growing debris field. Pieces of the beacon slowly floated past.

She couldn't move.

She felt Paul's hand around her arm.

"We need to go, Kate," he said.

Her mind was moving in slow motion now, but she forced herself to trudge through the portal.

The portal's destination wasn't a beacon. Kate knew it instantly. The place was expansive, huge, so unlike the cramped, utilitarian beacons.

She, Paul, Mary, and Milo stood in a massive room with a window that stretched at least a hundred feet wide and fifty feet tall.

The scene beyond left the entire group speechless, utterly spellbound. Horrified. For Kate, the view of Earth had been awe-inspiring. The Serpentine battlefield had been terrifying but distant, a danger long-since extinct. This place was very much alive.

Row after row of black spheres stretched out, unmoving, small lights hovering just above, like cars lined up in a parking lot at night.

In the middle row, above the stacks of stationary spheres, a long cylinder stretched out into space with no end that Kate could see. Spheres were moving through it, coming out the other side larger, more complete. This was an assembly line for the spheres, and it was producing thousands per second. Maybe millions, depending on how far the manufacturing cylinders stretched. Large ships moved across the lines, docking with the cylinders. Supply ships? Emptying minerals and raw materials for the manufacturing process?

This wasn't a beacon. It was a factory in space. A factory making an army of spheres.

The scale was unimaginable.

Kate tried to focus. They couldn't stay here.

She was fairly certain the soldier lying in the corridor at the last beacon had been Dorian. She thought he was dead. Hoped. But she couldn't help thinking about David, whether they could go back, save him somehow. She would be risking all their lives. And David might already be dead. She had to focus. *What do I know?*

Dorian had found the last beacon—out of a thousand in her diversionary rotation. He could easily find this one if he had discovered Janus' transmission.

They had to move, get to safety somehow. Maybe the third beacon would offer some refuge.

She activated the portable data core and downloaded the memories Janus had transmitted here.

She programmed the portal to the final destination.

She stepped through, and the others followed without a word.

The moment Kate stepped into the third and final beacon Janus had transmitted memories to, she knew they were in trouble. Heat. The place was burning up. And it was another military beacon.

She peered out the window, which seemed tiny compared to the view from the factory.

A dead world, red and rocky, loomed below. Black burn marks pocked the surface. Kate knew this place. Yes. She had seen it before—in the last memory she had accessed in the *Alpha Lander*, when David had saved her. The thought of that brought a new pang of sadness, but she pushed it out of her mind. Janus had tried to erase the memory of what had happened to this world. In the memory, this world had been under a military quarantine. Janus' partner had taken the *Beta Lander* to the surface to investigate...

"I think we should get out of here," Paul said.

Everyone was sweating now, and no one strayed far from the portal, hoping, thinking there was another destination.

Kate interfaced with the beacon. Yes. It had an address, local, close. The *Beta Lander* was still on the surface. She programmed another sequence of beacon connections—ten thousand this time—just in case Sloane made his way here. If she was right and Sloane didn't know about the *Beta Lander* on the surface, they would be safe. It was their only move.

She stepped through the portal, followed by Paul, Mary, and Milo.

Around them, the beady floor and ceiling lights of the *Beta Lander* grew brighter, the ship around them waking up.

"Are we safe here?" Paul asked.

"I think so." Kate looked around. The ship seemed intact. Her neural link told her its systems were all online now. She focused on the memory. It had ended with her outside, a burning impact. "Don't go outside though."

She walked away from them without another word, wandering lifelessly into the crew quarters section. She picked a residential pod at random and sat on the bed, staring for a moment. It was exactly like the one she and David had shared on the *Alpha Lander*.

She curled up on the bed, but sleep wouldn't come.

---

Dorian rolled onto his back, wishing the beacon's emergency voice would shut up. It was quite apparent to him that he needed to evacuate.

The "assault" hadn't gone as planned. He blamed two things. First, Victor had continued shooting as he had died, not necessarily in any direction. The imbecile couldn't even die properly. Dorian had him and his errant gunfire to thank for pushing Dorian back, away from the assault, forcing him to throw the grenades in a desperate attempt to finish off his enemy. It hadn't worked. The beacon and its forcefields had repelled the impact of the blast back up through the stairwell, into the small space on the first floor, throwing Dorian into a wall. He didn't remember anything after that, but he knew this: he was okay, he had his gun, and Kate and company were gone.

But... he knew where they were going. She had only two options. He stepped to the portal, working the panel. A break: she hadn't done a random portal rotation before they had stepped off. *Haste makes waste, Kate*, Dorian thought. He could follow them now.

He glanced back, seeing the Serpentine battlefield for the first time. Incredible. How had Ares survived? The mystery would have to wait. Dorian stepped through the portal.

The sentinel assembly line that stretched out instantly struck fear into him. He raised his gun instinctively, and then paused, realization dawning on him. This was an Atlantean portal—at the sentinel assembly line. Were they manufacturing sentinels to fight the sentinels he had seen? Or had the Atlanteans conquered the sentinel army? Was it their army now? Or had it turned on them, destroying their homeworld?

*Focus on the task at hand*, he thought. He quickly searched the factory. Empty. Kate and her friends couldn't go back to the Serpentine battlefield. Dorian had them. He keyed the portal for the final destination and stepped through.

The heat greeted him, and the view from the window confirmed that the beacon was falling into the planet's atmosphere. And it was accelerating.

Dorian raced through the dark metallic corridors of the military beacon, quickly searching both floors. Empty.

The screen in the communications bay flashed a red warning message.

```
Orbit Decaying. Atmospheric Entry Imminent.
Evacuate
```

Dorian checked the computer. Kate had been more careful this time. Ten thousand portal entries. Ten thousand possibilities. The portal connections had sapped the beacon's last bit of power. It was falling faster now. Dorian had to move.

He stepped through the portal again, back to the only place he thought was safe.

He stared at the sentinel assembly line. He was trapped, but perhaps there were answers here, something he could use.

Kate simply stared at the wall opposite the narrow bed, for how long she didn't know.

The door opened, and Paul stepped in. "You should see this."

He led her back to the bridge, a cramped space with several workstations and room for about five people. The small screen showed a glowing ember moving through the clouds.

"Is it the beacon?" Paul asked.

"Yes," Kate said.

As the beacon burned in the sky, she realized that they were truly trapped now. The *Beta Lander* had been designed for moving between ships and planetary surfaces. So had its portal. They couldn't leave this world.

"What are you thinking, Kate?" Mary asked.

"I think we have to throw the long ball."

# PART III
# A TALE OF TWO WORLDS

# 35

Dorian had searched the sentinel factory again. It was truly empty and had been for some time. To him, the massive base floating in space felt like a hospital except it wasn't clinical or clean; it was industrial and rugged, utilitarian, yet precise. A symmetrical grid of wide hallways led through the four-story complex, opening onto rooms with strange equipment and mechanical pieces he assumed belonged to prototype sentinels. It was like a workshop. That's what it was: a place where they tweaked the sentinels, revising the formula for distribution to the assembly line for "the next version." A research lab.

All the terminals recognized him as General Ares, and the entire facility opened for him without restrictions.

Dorian had been over his options. They amounted to porting back to the beacon around Earth and returning to Ares for help or sorting through the rest of the memories. He felt as though death awaited him down either path, but one held answers, and possibly an opportunity to unravel the mystery behind Ares and change Earth's fate. It was an easy decision.

He loaded the data core with Ares' memories into the conference booth and stepped inside.

---

For Ares, time was like a river: flowing, unstoppable, washing away the last grains of his emotional core. He felt less every second, every minute, every hour.

He watched the Serpentine Army battle the sentinels, which swarmed into the breach. The black sentinel spheres seemed to multiply exponentially. But the serpent grew faster. The black ring of Serpentine ships that harnessed the power of the star formed a blue and white portal in its interior, almost blotting out the sun, except for a thin ring of yellow and orange fire peeking around its edges like a solar eclipse. The great serpent that poured through the portal shed its outer layer as its pieces—ships—sheared off, engaging the sentinels. The spheres dug into the main cord of the serpent and the ships that separated, shredding them, ripping them into tiny specks of black and gray which drifted down to the enormous debris field like ash falling on a highway.

The momentum of the battle coursed back and forth, the serpent growing wide, extending then receding as a new wave of spheres devoured its sides and forced it to collapse back and regain its size. Finally, the serpent pushed through. Its head formed another ring on the other side of the battlefield, and another portal took shape. The great snake flowed through the battlefield, an endless procession of ships moving between the two portals. The remaining spheres winked away, the battle apparently lost.

Ares ignored his hunger. The desire to quench it never rose inside him.

He watched a small group of Serpentine ships prowl the wreckage. Were they searching for Atlantean survivors to assimilate? Or their own kind, now converted Atlanteans? What had Myra called them? The ring. Thinking of her, what they had done to her and his unborn child made Ares ache, reminded him that not all feeling had left. He glanced away from the Serpentine ships, refusing to watch.

Ares had thought all the sentinels were gone, but he realized one was hovering close to his ship, seeming to stare at him, reading his soul.

Ares stared back with no emotion, only a single thought, *Do it*.

A slot in the sphere opened, and it moved forward, swallowing Ares' ship.

The darkness was complete. Ares floated in his EVA suit. There was only a vague curiosity about his fate.

---

The light that breached the darkness was blinding. Ares raised his arm to cover his eyes. The shard of the lander that held him floated free as the sphere backed away.

Ares' eyes adjusted a little, and through the ship's cockpit window, he could just make out a fleet of sentinel spheres, but it was the enormous ship that took his breath away. Three distant stars shone enough light for him to make out its shape but not its features. It was elongated, and Ares wondered if it was the control ship for the sentinels or perhaps a carrier or factory.

Several small spheres attached to his derelict ship and ushered him toward the waiting super ship. A bay opened, and the sentinels deposited his ship inside.

When the bay door closed, the rush of artificial gravity threw Ares into the ship's floor. For a moment, he thought the impact would knock him out, but the EVA suit had cushioned the blow.

He pushed up and wandered out of the ship, into the vast, empty chamber. It was illuminated, and the artificial gravity seemed to be Atlantean standard, which Ares found to be a bizarre, slightly unnerving coincidence. His EVA suit told him the air was breathable, but he decided not to remove the suit.

Double doors opened at the end of the bay, and Ares exited into a corridor that was narrow, with gray-metallic walls, and beady lights at the floor and ceiling.

He hesitated for a moment, not sure whether to push forward or retreat back to his ship. Curiosity got the better of him. He wandered deeper into the corridor, which ended in a large intersection where two other corridors split off to the left and right, and a set of large double doors stood dead ahead. The doors opened, revealing a cavern in the interior of the ship, much larger than the bay his ship had landed in.

Ares proceeded slowly, half-wondering if he were wading deeper into some trap. The contents of the chamber puzzled him. Glass tubes, row after row, stacked from the floor into the darkness above and as far as he could see into the chamber. Each tube looked large enough to hold a single Atlantean.

"You can remove your suit."

Ares turned, getting his first look at his captor.

# 36

Ares glanced from his captor to the endless rows of glass tubes. The man, or at least Ares thought he was a man, stood at the entrance of the chamber, just inside the double doors, the glow of the lights from the corridor forming a halo behind him.

"What is this?" Ares asked, not daring to remove his suit.

"You already know."

Ares glanced back at the tubes. *Stasis chambers. For deep space travel. A colony ship?*

"Yes."

Ares stepped backwards involuntarily. *It can read my thoughts.*

"Yes, it can. Your body emits radiation this vessel can read, allowing me to see it as an organized data feed."

"What are you?"

"I'm the same as you, except I've been dead for millions of years."

Ares tried to organize his thoughts. He said the first question that popped into his head. "You're not... here? Not alive?"

"No. What you see is my avatar, a reflection of what I used to be. My race has been extinct for a long time. All that remains of us is the Serpentine Army."

"You're one of them?"

"No. I never was. I am merely one of the ones they slaughtered in their march across time. Long ago, my world made a great mistake. We sought the ultimate answer, the truth about our origins and the destiny of the universe. We chose the wrong tools to find it: science and technology. Methods beyond your comprehension. In our pursuit for the ultimate knowledge, the technologies we created eventually enslaved us, taking the last of our humanity before we even knew it was slipping away. Our civilization fractured. Those who resisted were assimilated. The Serpentine Army is what's left. The members call themselves the ring. They believe that they are the fate of this universe and the beginning of a new one, a ring that runs through space and time.

"They believe their ring will one day circle all human worlds, binding every last human life, and in doing so, harness a force they call the Origin Entity, enabling them to create a new universe, with new laws, where they can never be destroyed."

Ares exhaled and pulled his suit off. He was in way over his head, and he figured if this ghost of humanity's past wanted him dead, he wouldn't even be here.

"What do you want from me?" Ares said flatly.

"Salvation. An opportunity to right the wrong my people are committing against yours right now."

A holographic image rose in the dark space between them. Ares' homeworld hung there, a ring of black ships forming a portal before it. A thick rope of Serpentine ships poured out. The end of the rope frayed, spraying ships onto the surface like dark tear drops falling on Ares' world.

Thousands of sentinel ships fought the serpent, but just as they had at the Serpentine battlefield, they were losing. The Atlantean homeworld was falling.

"In our final days, when we realized our folly, we created what you call the sentinels, hoping to save the other human worlds from our mistake. As you've seen, the sentinels are greatly outmatched in the Serpentine war. As a last resort, we shifted our strategy to hiding the human worlds."

"The sentinel line."

"Yes. It forms a barrier, a sort of beacon network that cloaks your space, preventing the Serpentine Army from seeing worlds that harbor human life. The line also prevents hyperspace tunnels from crossing it."

Comprehension dawned on Ares. "I created a hole in the sentinel line that allowed the Serpentine Army to come through."

"Yes. But that is the way of the cycle."

Anger rose within Ares. "You could have warned us."

"We've tried that. Many times, for many years. Warnings of disaster are far less effective than memories of disaster."

"Memories?"

The avatar walked to the tubes. "You will take this ark to your world. The radiation that transmits your thoughts can also be used to transmit a cellular blueprint of your bodies. The sentinel fleet surrounding this ship will get you into orbit. The Serpentine virus, the biological technology they use to assimilate human life has one limitation: the subject must submit. Their techniques are overwhelming, but in large populations, a few brave souls can resist. Those who will not submit, the serpent slaughters. This ship will capture their radiation signatures, resurrecting them. They will be your people. You will rebuild your civilization upon them. They will have seen the Serpentine horror. They will know the danger. You must see the darkness to appreciate the light."

---

In the resurrection ark's bridge, Ares watched the blue and white waves of hyperspace dissolve, and his world take form on the screen.

The ship shook as it took fire. The Serpentine siege of Ares' world was nearly complete. Large dark ships covered large swaths of every continent. The sentinels battled them, but they were slowly losing.

Ares watched the ark push through the immense battlefield, taking fire, but never returning it. Each time a phalanx of Serpentine ships broke through the sentinel battle line, more spherical ships appeared, repelling it.

The avatar led Ares out of the bridge, back into the chamber, and they both stood silently as the tubes filled with Atlanteans.

The turbulence grew by the second, and finally, the figure turned to Ares. "It's time."

Ares stepped into the closest tube, and the fog slowly consumed him. His people's Exodus would be complete soon, and they would land at their new home. The avatar had told him that the ship dilated time as well. The passage here would be nothing compared to the time outside.

Finally, the avatar returned, and the tube opened. Ares stepped out and followed him back to the bridge. The viewscreen showed an untouched world, green, blue, and white.

"What if the serpent finds us?"

"We've established a new sentinel line and placed a beacon in orbit around this world. It will shroud you. We've also placed a beacon at the Serpentine battlefield, in hopes that it will keep any other sentient species from stumbling across the wreckage and the Serpentine signal the ships transmit. It is connected to the beacon network, which the Serpentine members can't access, but I urge you to stay away. The serpent has left the battlefield, but they could return at any time. Stay behind your new sentinel line—it's your best hope of survival. We're at the end of what we can give you. We've shown you the danger, and we have saved you. I can offer you one last gift: the human code. It will ensure you don't repeat our mistake."

The avatar talked at length, sharing his people's philosophy, a blueprint for a peaceful existence. "A simple life according to the code is all we ask in return for saving the last of your people. There are many human worlds within the new sentinel line, all less developed than yours. Someday they too will venture out, seeking answers, disturbing the new sentinel line. Your people can bear witness to the danger beyond, saving countless lives on countless worlds. Spread the human code, and you can all live here in safety. It is the key to your shared survival."

Ares thought of his last moments with his wife, what they had done to her, and of his world, the black ships covering it, the slaughter of billions. He tried but failed to calm the rage inside him. "The beast you created massacres my people, and you make demands?"

"We offer guidance, a path to serenity and peace. An opportunity to prevent others from repeating your mistake, from suffering the same fate."

Ares focused on the small group of sentinels that floated next to the ark.

*We're not going to hide and pray and try to wish away our enemy. We're going to fight.* A second too late, he remembered that the avatar could read his thoughts.

"You contemplate your own great mistake."

"Says the dead man who's been watching human worlds get massacred for millions of years."

"Your fear and hatred betray you."

Ares ignored the avatar. A plan began to form in his mind.

The avatar stepped closer to him. "Remember our story. The technology we built enslaved us. Beware, Ares: the cost of your security could be your freedom. Possibly your survival."

"You know what I think: you've been losing this war for so long, it's all you know. And you can't even remember what it feels like to be human—that's the only way you would allow so many to be murdered on my world. It's all a big math problem to you. But they were lives to me, people who mattered. We've had enough of your *help*. We'll fend for ourselves now."

"So be it, Ares." The avatar slowly faded, a sad expression on his face.

For a long moment, Ares stood alone in the dark chamber, gazing at the endless rows of tubes that held the last of his people. They would awaken soon. They were all Ares had left, and he would ensure their survival at any cost.

From the escape pod, David watched the forcefields in the beacon at the Serpentine battlefield flicker and dissolve. The atmosphere vented to space in a burst that sent the beacon crashing into the debris field. The pieces tumbled and collided as they settled into empty pockets in the field. David felt the mass of the field pulling his own escape pod, and he knew his body would soon be a permanent fixture here.

He thought about Kate. How would she spend her last days? He had only one wish: to see her again, if only for a second. His last vision of her ran through his mind: her standing in front of the screen, explaining some science thing he could barely understand. What were his last words to her? "Lock the door." He smiled. It was somehow extremely fitting. Their last interaction had been like most of their time together. Time was a precious thing. Now both of theirs was short, measured in hours.

He realized something then: that he had actually been scared of living without her. Knowing he wouldn't have to face that provided a strange sense of calm.

Above the debris field, a rift opened, like a jagged blue and white rip in the black fabric of space. A single ship slipped out and quickly moved across the debris field, making a direct path for David's escape pod.

Had the destruction of the beacon enabled the ship to see what was happening here, realize he was stranded?

As the ship grew closer, David could make out an insignia on the front: a ring. No, a serpent swallowing its tail.

# 37

Dorian lay on the floor, sweat pouring off of him. The last memory had been the worst. But he couldn't stop. He was close. He felt it. The ship—the ark—was the same Ares had buried under Antarctica. Had the Serpentine Army found the Atlanteans again? Were they the great enemy Ares feared?

Dorian walked into the enormous factory and looked at the lines that produced sentinels by the thousands. Or had the sentinels betrayed him?

Dorian ate and steeled himself to see the final truth.

---

In the days after the ark had landed on the new Atlantean homeworld, Ares' people had confirmed everything the avatar had said. The reborn who emerged from the resurrection vessel had been filled with purpose and fire, a unity Ares had never seen before. They were one people with one purpose: the fall of the Serpentine Army. They had dedicated every ounce of their energy to it. And the technology on the ark and sentinels had provided the rest.

Around the ark, first settlements, then cities, then civilization had risen. The cornerstone of their laws derived from the avatar's story, his warning about the dangers of runaway technology. Ares had rejected the avatar's demands, but he knew his people would be foolish to ignore the truth: an advanced civilization with no limits on technology would always grow into a Serpentine world, whether assimilated or not. The anti-Serpentine laws banned any innovation that could lead to a singularity, and the battle against uncontrollable technology became a shared mantra.

At the ratification ceremony, Ares stood on a stage, shouting to the crowd, "We are the greatest enemy we face. The serpent lurks inside of us. We must guard against ourselves as we guard against our enemy beyond the sentinel line."

The memories came in flashes after that. Ares stood on a ship in orbit, staring at a sentinel construction facility that floated beyond the new Atlantean homeworld. "We need more."

He stood in another factory, staring at a new sentinel assembly line which stretched so far into space he couldn't see the end.

"More."

The memories flowed by. Other factories. New sentinels. The pace of innovation slowing. Him standing in a room, pleading his case for more research and technology staff. But he himself didn't believe it anymore. His own fire was gone. Using the time dilation and healing properties of the tubes, he had leap-frogged through the ages, to a point when the automated mining ships and robotic factories were producing more sentinels than the Atlanteans could even count.

The members of the Exodus, who had been reborn in the tubes, had all lived long lives, opting like Ares to use the tubes to return to optimum health. But they were all gone, having long-since lost the will to go on. Some had made it to their eight hundredth birthday, a few to their thousandth, but ultimately, all but him had met the true death, far out of range of the resurrection tubes, never to return.

He found himself utterly alone, the last of the founders, the last of his kind, the tribe that had seen the carnage of the Serpentine Army firsthand, the hardworking citizens who had built their new world.

For millennia after the fall of the old world, vigils were held every year at the ark. Then the ceremonies came every ten years, every century, and finally, they stopped.

Each time Ares awoke from his tube to attend the council meetings, he felt more like a stranger in his own world. His people had settled into a life of leisure and comfort, focusing on art, science, and entertainment. The sentinel factories were all empty, left to be tended by the robots. The Serpentine threat had turned into the proverbial boogeyman, a scary nighttime tale that might not even be true.

He was regarded as a relic, a figurehead from a dark chapter in the distant past, an era of intense paranoia and war-mongering.

He had announced to the council that he would meet the true death, and they had reluctantly agreed.

The betrayal came in the form of a public announcement the following day: the council had voted to archive him, honoring his service and forever remembering the sacrifice he and the other members of the Exodus had made.

Guards had appeared at his residence, news cameras crowding behind them.

People lined the path to the ark shrine, children and adults alike maneuvering to get a glimpse of him. The inscription in the stone facade read, *Here lies our last soldier.*

Ares stopped before the threshold and spoke to the chairman of the council. "Every man deserves the right to die."

"Legends never die."

He wanted to reach out and wrap his fingers around her neck and squeeze. Instead, he walked inside, down the corridors he had first seen the day of the fall of the old world and stepped into a tube.

The time dilation saved him the agony of the flow of time, but nothing could treat the emptiness and solitude Ares felt.

Figures appeared at the entrance to the vast chamber and ran to his tube.

Ares stepped out and followed them without a word. Perhaps they had reconsidered. Hope—an almost foreign feeling, rose inside him.

They exited the shrine that held the ark and walked silently into the night. A city unlike any Ares had ever seen loomed in the distance. Skyscrapers reached into the clouds, catwalks crossed between them, and holographic ads marched through the night sky like demons dancing in front of the moon.

A blast severed a catwalk. Another reached between the buildings, setting fire to both. The fire leaped from tower to tower, desperately trying to outrun the fire suppression systems. Another blast went up.

"What is this?" Ares asked.

"We have a new enemy, General."

# 38

Ares barely recognized the world he had brought his dying people to and helped build. It was clean and sparkling but crowded, its people angry. They lined the streets, pushing, shoving, holding signs and shouting.

"Serpentine Restrictions = Slavery"

"Evolution = Freedom"

"Ares is the True Serpent"

At the council chamber, a group of imbeciles detailed the plight of Ares' beloved world. Intellectual discrimination had segmented Atlantean society, fracturing it into two factions: intellectuals and laborers. The intellectuals represented nearly 80% of the entire population, and as best Ares could tell, spent their days making things with their minds: art, inventions, research, and activities Ares didn't understand and didn't care to ask about. The remaining 20% of the population, the laborers, made their living with their hands, and they were tired of it, tired of the subsidized wages and welfare state that kept them in a perpetual second-class existence.

The core of the issue was that education had reached the limits of how much it could elevate raw intelligence. On both sides, the two classes realized that intellectuals would always be intellectuals, and so would their children, and likewise for laborers. Marriage between the classes had become increasingly rare as no intellectuals dared risk their descendants slipping into the lower class, never to return.

The economic and social rift had grown increasingly tense. Accommodations and deals had been made, keeping the peace.

But compromise had finally failed, and violence had become the laborers' only means of negotiation.

The screen detailed the labor faction's growing unrest, the escalation from protests to riots, to random attacks, to organized terrorism that claimed thousands of lives.

Ares turned the problem over in his mind, barely listening to Nomos, the chairman of the council. "The crux of the issue is our police force."

"What about it?" Ares asked.

"We haven't had one for three hundred years. There's simply been very little crime, and citizen enforcement, coupled with mass surveillance, has meant that any perpetrators were always apprehended. This is different. These people are willing to lay down their lives for their cause—to ensure that their children don't suffer as they have."

Another councilman spoke up. "The bigger issue is that the new police force will have to be drawn from the laborers—and we could never trust them. They could overthrow the government and completely take over. And I think that's what we're all scared of, even if I'm the only one willing to say it."

Silence followed.

Finally, Nomos spoke. "Ares, the solution we've come to, that we've awoken you to... consult on, is relaxing the Serpentine Restrictions."

Ares failed to suppress his anger. "Those laws were created for a reason—to save us from ourselves."

Nomos held up a hand. "We're only considering slight relaxations in two of the three restrictions: removing the ban on genetic engineering—just once, for a single treatment to bring the laborers to intellectual parity. Secondly, we would lift the ban on robotics, allowing simple service droids to handle all physical labor. These changes will create a single sustainable society—"

Ares stood. "If you fools open the box of genetic engineering and robotics on this world, you guarantee that we become a Serpentine world at some point—without even being invaded.

It's inevitable. This is how the Serpentine blight emerged in the first place. We'll be repeating our predecessors' mistakes. I won't stand for it. Put me back to sleep, or better yet, allow me the true death. I can't watch this."

"What would you do?"

"Our problem is very simple," Ares said. "Twenty percent of our people are killing the rest. They've got to go."

---

Ares looked around at his army in training. If the beacon weren't floating in orbit, hiding his world's light from the universe beyond, they would be the laughing stock of the cosmos.

The council had been right: recruiting a security force from the labor class was certain folly. Ares had settled for intellectuals who might fit the bill: models—chiseled, muscular, and well-trained at the art of looking fearless regardless of their actual ability; dancers and acrobats—they moved with grace and precision but couldn't fight to save their lives; and athletes—they had great aim and comfort in raging crowds but would no doubt melt when people started dying.

Ares watched them train. An army they were not and never would be. But with their uniforms and practiced movements, they looked the part, and that was all he needed.

Ares longed for the days of the expeditionary fleet, but it had been yet another casualty of the Serpentine Restrictions. Space exploration could lead to unknown dangers, or the greatest risk of all: rediscovery by the Serpentine Army.

The thought of it reminded him of his own role in the mission that had led to the end: his capture of a sentinel sphere that opened a break in the line, allowing the great serpent to flow across and port to the Atlanteans' first homeworld. He would never see that mistake repeated.

The Atlantean dream was a single society on a single world, safe behind the beacon and the immense sentinel army that formed a wall in space around it; an Atlantean world of peace and plenty, stretching into eternity. The dream was built on forsaking three temptations: the easy labor of robotics, the false advancement of genetic engineering, and the fascination of deep space exploration.

Ares realized Nomos was at his side, but he said nothing, hoping the moron would reciprocate. As usual, Ares was disappointed.

"They look more like an army every day," Nomos said, further lowering Ares' opinion of his intelligence.

"Yes, they'll play their role nicely."

Ares didn't know when the next attack would come, but it didn't much matter. The future was a foregone conclusion for him, an equation working its way to a known end.

He rarely slept, and when sleep did come, it was fitful. He sat at the desk in the apartment they had given him, flipping through the letters his wife had written him, watching videos of her, and replaying endless scenarios in his mind, debating about how things might have been different. But the truth was that he had simply played his role, as many had before him and would after him. The avatar had been right. Ares knew it now. Ares wondered how many worlds he had seen rise and fall. A thousand? A million? More?

The avatar had advocated a simple existence, living by a shared code. Ares imagined that on those worlds, every citizen was an intellectual and a laborer, and every life was respected. They had it right.

Ares mused at his own words back then: *We're going to fight.*

But there had been no great enemy to fight, only a few helpless victims. There had been no harrowing threat at their door, bonding his people together. The Serpentine Army had never come, and in the absence of a threat, his people had lost the very will to fight. In fact, confronted with the first taste of violence in thousands of years, their solution had been to dig him out of hibernation: a fossil of an almost forgotten past, back to vanquish the barbarian threat.

No, they didn't want to fight. This was the dark side of the human reality: with no conflict, no challenge, the fire within winks out and without the flame, society stagnates, slipping into a slow decline. There was only one solution to his world's problems: cutting out the cancer.

Ares dreaded it. But it was a conflict, a challenge, a reason for him to exist. He wondered if it was the only thing keeping him alive.

He walked to the window and marveled at the city they had built—one of thousands that covered almost every inch of the globe. They were meticulously planned. Unlike the cities of the old world he had grown up on, these metropolises blended nature with steel and glass in a canvas of art and function.

From his 147th floor apartment, Ares looked down at the green and brown forests, fields, and gardens that covered the tops of the buildings. Below the tops, catwalks connected the buildings like a spider web. People and pods moved across the catwalks, like a colony of insects snaking through a maze of metal and glass that twinkled, every light regulated to optimize beauty and function. Massive greenhouses topped some buildings, the lush plant life illuminated by the grow lights and city lights at night.

How could a civilization so advanced be so flawed—all the way down to its very core?

Across the city, explosions erupted. Catwalks shook and fell. Buildings crumbled.

Entire swaths were bathed in flame and smoke spread across, blotting out the canvas of light, glass, and steel.

The door behind Ares opened. "Blasts in sectors four and six, General."

Ares dressed quickly and marched at the head of his newly formed army. He stopped just shy of the battle zone. Another blast went up, and a wave of screams and fleeing citizens coursed toward them.

The soldier beside Ares cleared his throat and spoke quietly. "Should we begin, sir?"

"No. Let it go for a while. Let's show the world the type of people we're fighting."

# 39

Kate was sore and drenched with sweat when she woke up, but the worst hurt wasn't from her body. Every movement was a struggle, as if her body were made of lead. She dragged herself out of bed and pulled her clothes on.

Outside her room, the mood among the others wasn't much different. For the first time since she had met him, Kate saw true sadness in Milo. He stared constantly at the floor. Paul and Mary seemed overwhelmed, much the way they had been after their desperate run up the mountain in Morocco, when they had first seen the *Alpha Lander* a few days ago.

Seeing the three of them actually changed Kate, steeled her. They needed her. She needed to be strong for them, and knowing that gave her a new sense of strength.

"This isn't over," she began. "I have a plan."

"You do?" Paul asked, probably not intending to sound so surprised.

"I do." Kate led them out of the common area into the ship's bridge. She activated the screen and panned the image to the view outside: the ruins of a burned out city. "I said before that we can't go outside. I saw this world in one of the Atlantean scientist's memories. She landed here—in this ship, and then ventured out. I think she was killed here by some group that guarded the planet. She could have been resurrected. That could be one of the reasons Janus erased the memory, and possibly why viewing it made me…"

"Sick," Milo said, fear in his voice. "You can't, Dr. Kate."

"I have to." Kate adjusted the screen to show the atmosphere where the beacon had entered, the streak of white the only remaining evidence. "With the beacon gone, *we are trapped here*. That's the bad news. But we have a few options. This lander's communications array is still intact. And it's still fully operational—we can lift off and get into orbit."

"How far can we travel?" Paul asked.

"Not far, unfortunately. The lander has no ability to generate a wormhole, no hyperspace travel ability. But we could send a communication—try to get help. With the beacon gone, this world is exposed."

"And apparently well-guarded," Paul said. "At least in the past."

"Exactly," Kate said. "And that's where I'm going to start. There's an adaptive research lab on this ship, just like the *Alpha Lander*. I used the portable data core to retrieve all the memories Janus wanted to keep from his partner. I'm going to look for any clues as to what this world is, who's guarding it, and how we might be able to get help." She motioned to Paul and Mary. "I've programmed these terminals to teach you the Atlantean systems. It won't take you long to learn—David and Milo got up to speed in less than a few days." That hadn't come out the way Kate intended, but she pressed on. "When you can work the ship, I want you to start comparing the two signals—the one Mary received on Earth and the one from the Serpentine battlefield. That's our other hope: figuring out what it is."

"What about me?" Milo asked.

"You're going to help me. You'll monitor my vitals while I'm in the resurrection chamber. If anything goes wrong, you're to get Paul and help him navigate the ship's medical systems."

Milo shook his head. "I don't like this. David wouldn't like this."

"David and I talked right before... we came here. After seeing the Serpentine battlefield, he realized our situation was dire, that we had to take chances to have any hope. This is one of the chances. The other is the signal. This is our plan."

Kate led Milo out of the bridge, and although the teenager didn't protest further, she could tell he dreaded what might result from Kate's trip into the giant yellow vat similar to the one he and David had found her in several days ago. Putting on a brave face had prepared Kate for entering the vat once again, but once inside, standing in the virtual train station, staring at the board that was now full with a complete listing of all the Atlantean scientist's memories, fear started to set in. What would happen inside the memories? What would it do to her outside? She had no choice.

She selected the first memory, the earliest entry Janus had deleted, and loaded it.

The train station disappeared, and she stood in a science lab. Janus stood before her, talking excitedly and pointing to a projection of a world on the wall. The wall of windows on her left revealed a vast city, twinkling in the night. A network of catwalks connected the buildings, and the city teemed with life. Momentarily, Kate was captivated by it, but the feeling faded quickly. In its place, comprehension rose. She instinctively knew where she was: the new Atlantean homeworld. She knew things about herself. Her job. Her desires. This memory was different. In the others, Kate had possessed some control over her thoughts, though the actions were those of the scientist. Not so here.

Here she had complete access to the Atlantean scientist's thoughts, and they joined her own, crowding them out. Kate was gone, simply a spectator, seeing, feeling, and reliving the Atlantean scientist's past. The woman's name was Isis, and her life began unfolding, out of Kate's control. Kate's last thought was wondering what would happen to her when Isis died in the memory, as Kate knew she had on Earth thirteen thousand years ago.

Janus clicked through the images of the worlds again. "All these worlds hold hominid life."

"Or did," Isis shot back.

"True, these surveys are as old as the Exodus, but assuming there haven't been any population collapses, these worlds still hold human life. In fact, some could have grown into advanced civilizations or even evolved in ways we can't imagine. Think about it. For an evolutionary geneticist, this is the opportunity of a lifetime."

Janus paused for effect. "There's no one I would rather have by my side, Isis."

She turned from him and faced the window that looked out onto the city. "I appreciate that, Janus. And it's an incredible opportunity, but it's hard for me to trek off into space when our world is in this kind of shape."

"I know your feelings on the labor debate."

"The equality debate," Isis corrected.

"Quite right," Janus said, nodding. "The equality debate," he said, repeating the mantra of the labor supporters, the words he and the other pro-intellectuals never uttered in private.

When Isis said nothing, he pressed on. "The equality debate will work itself out with or without us. We can make history, advance the Atlantean cause. We're calling it the Origin Project."

"It'll never get past the Serpentine Restrictions."

"That may change."

"What have you heard?"

"Just rumors but there's talk of relaxing the restrictions to resolve the labor revolt." He quickly corrected himself. "Equality debate."

"Interesting."

"All the pieces are in place, Isis. We're already retrofitting the survey fleet."

"You can't be serious."

"I am. I know the ships are old—"

"And they haven't been used since they mapped the new sentinel line just after the Exodus."

"They'll do just fine. We've tested them. And in time, we could build new ones."

Isis shook her head, still uncertain.

"Can we talk tomorrow, after your speech in the forum?"

"Sure."

---

In truth, Isis had found Janus' proposal fascinating. It was the opportunity of a lifetime; that much was true. But turning her back on the equality debate that raged on their world was unconscionable to her.

She thought about her speech the next day—the research she would present that she hoped would turn the tide in the great debate, altering the course of their society. The stakes were high, and she could already feel her nerves as she exited the building onto the skyway. She loved moving between the buildings at night. The glass corridors gave the sense of flying over the city, and sometimes she couldn't help but stare out as she walked.

In the distance, a plume of fire rose, and a split second later, a building sank, then another. Skyways in the distance released, and the web of walkways seemed to ripple as the cascade of explosions rolled toward her like a wave. The ground loomed over a thousand feet below her.

She glanced between the entrance and exit. She was closer to the end, and she bound toward it, her feet pounding the floor. The building ahead shook, and the walkway swayed, the floor cracked, and tiles from the ceiling rained down.

She held her arms up, covering her head as she cleared the skyway. The building's lifts were inoperable, and Isis crammed into the stairwells, flowing with the masses trying desperately to escape.

At the bottom floor, masked, armed troops corralled them into a dark holding area, occasionally shouting for them to move faster and pushing anyone who got out of line.

When the trickle of people ended, one of their captors stepped forward and said, "You are no longer citizens. You are no longer members of the elite who perpetuate the intellectual feudalism that has oppressed us for thousands of years. You are instruments; tools of the revolution. You will be given a number. You are now a hostage of the equality movement."

# 40

For the last three hours, Ares had been touring the hospital, talking with the citizens undergoing treatment for burns, broken bones, and shrapnel wounds. The small facility was overwhelmed. The halls were chaotic, with people darting in all directions. Ares was a beacon of calm in the storm. Seeing the carnage readied him for what he had to do, confirmed he was making the right choice.

A staffer led him out of the main hospital into an adjacent building, which had been used as office space but now served as a makeshift psychological hospital.

The citizens in every room looked the same to Ares: vegetables.

"They're suffering from resurrection syndrome," the doctor said.

Ares had never heard of the condition. His tour guide read his expression.

"It was never diagnosed in your time. Possibly never even seen. Mentally, the patient is unable to cope with life after resurrection, or more specifically, their brains are unable to integrate certain memories, in this case, those of their violent death. The syndrome has become more prevalent as our lifestyle has changed. We think the shifting emotional range of our citizenry is partly to blame. Repeated resurrection is also a risk factor. Some of these patients died in the first wave of terror attacks with no symptoms or a very mild case of resurrection syndrome. This time around, they've been reborn in almost a catatonic state. Either way, this could become a pandemic in itself."

Ares nodded, wondering if, in another few thousand years, any of his people would be able to survive resurrection.

Ares' ear piece activated, and his second in command said, "Sir, we have a new development. The terrorists have taken hostages."

Ares smiled. *Now we're getting somewhere.*

Isis was scared, but not nearly as frightened as the people around her. *This will turn the whole world against the labor faction*, she thought. This would truly be the end of the revolt, the last straw that steeled the citizenry to take drastic action. Isis could only imagine what that action would be. She pushed the scenarios out of her mind as she stepped forward in the line.

"Your number is 29383," the man said. "What is your number?"

"29383," Isis answered.

Beyond the line, two men were arguing.

"You've dug our grave."

"I've saved us, Lykos. I've done what you didn't have the guts to do."

The other man, Lykos, caught Isis' eye. He stopped, as if he had recognized her.

The masked man issuing numbers motioned for the next person in line and said to Isis, "Move on, 29383."

Isis shuffled forward, joining the group in front of her, but Lykos stopped her, pulling her over to join the other man he'd been arguing with. "This is what I'm talking about," he said, pointing to her. "Do you know who this is?"

"Of course. A hostage. What's your number, hostage?"

Isis opened her mouth, but Lykos cut her off. "Don't answer that. Her name is Dr. Triteia Isis. She's an evolutionary geneticist—"

Lykos' adversary raised his hands. "Forgive me, I don't know too many evolutionary geneticists—"

"She's created a genetic therapy that would enable our people to do anything the intellectuals can."

The rebel leader paused, and Lykos continued. "She's presenting her research to the full forum tomorrow, or she had planned to before we took her hostage. She was a supporter of our cause." Lykos focused on her. "And I hope she still will be, and that she accepts our apology for the barbaric methods of some members of our cause." He waited for her response.

"I... am. I do."

"Now we're going to release you," Lykos said. "And I hope you'll still give that speech tomorrow."

Isis nodded. "I will."

Lykos led her away.

The other man called to them, "If they listen, it's because of what we did here."

Lykos led her through the corridors, not speaking to the guards who simply nodded and let him pass. When they were alone outside the building, past the last checkpoint, he said, "I'm very sorry for what happened to you. We've lost control of the situation. Please tell them that, whether you give your presentation or not. Something has to be done. These methods only represent a minority of our people. We're ready to make whatever sacrifices we need to."

---

The council was in full panic now, and that pleased Ares greatly. He had them right where he wanted them.

Nomos was speaking, and Ares sat at the head of the table, barely listening.

"The revolutionaries are running all over that army of yours."

"They can't fight," another councilman said.

"Quite right," Ares answered, standing.

"What's your solution, General?" a woman asked.

"You'll hear it tomorrow in the forum."

Another council member slammed his fist into the conference table. "I want to hear it now. We might not make it to tomorrow. All options, ladies and gentlemen. Can we create a pathogen that would only target labor? Cut our losses and have the sentinels bombard the occupied zones?"

The room erupted in shouting. Ares slipped out the door. Strangely, the night before he knew the battle would begin, he slept well.

# 41

In the forum the following day, Ares sat in the chairman's box and watched silently as speaker after speaker took the central stage and shouted at the three thousand attendees in the auditorium and the tens of billions around the world watching. This was the moment every politician had always dreamed of: the issue that would shape generations to come. A single vote that would ensure that they were remembered, that their pitiful name and face would be put down in the history logs, immortalized. They scrambled for the spotlight, practically tripping over each other, grasping desperately for every second of fame. Half the time was spent arguing about time itself—how much the current speaker had left, how much the previous speaker had run over, and how much would be allotted to the current time-waster. The spectacle left no doubt about why compromise had broken down.

But the urgency of the situation had inspired attention on all sides, and from many, radical solutions.

The debate raged all day, and still Ares stayed silent. He wanted his solution to be the last presented. It would be the final solution.

At the opening of the evening session, a scientist took the podium. She had been scheduled for earlier in the day but had never shown. The council had counted her among the many labor advocates who had backed out in light of yesterday's escalation of violence, but the scientist, Isis, had apparently had a change of heart. Several representatives had yielded their time to her, and she used that time to describe a global research project, which had sequenced the genomes of every Atlantean. Isis detailed how she had isolated the genes that powered evolution, setting the Atlantean species apart from the other hominid genome samples that had been collected by Ares' own expeditionary fleet during what had become known as the age of exploration, before the fall of their first homeworld.

Isis insisted that this basic Atlantis Gene could be manipulated to bring all Atlanteans to a state of cognitive equality. Her proposal came down to a simple genetic therapy, and to Ares' dismay, the representatives in the forum began rallying around it.

Ares rose and approached the lectern in his box. All the other voices faded, and the light on his microphone turned green. It felt as though the lights had dimmed, that it was only him and Isis below, standing on the stage. The DNA diagram filled the massive screen behind her, and seeing it steeled Ares, convinced him he was right.

"What you're describing would be a cataclysm," Ares said. "A singularity. We know of only one world, one race who ever pursued such an endeavor. All that's left of them is a great serpent that seeks to circle the universe and strangle every last human life to death."

"We can control this. We're talking about a slight modification," Isis said.

"Then what? Even if you succeed, there will always be some people who are smarter than others. There will always be some who can run faster than others. Some more attractive than their neighbors. To whom will you deny genetic equality? Who will decide it? Who will make the final decision about whether I'm genetically inferior and need to be fixed? Perhaps when I wake up in another ten thousand years, I will require an update, but I want to remain the way I am. What are my genetic rights?"

"My solution is voluntary."

The auditorium erupted, and Ares smiled. He had cornered her. These people wanted the issue dealt with permanently. A voluntary solution for some people felt like kicking the can down the road, delaying the inevitable.

"My solution is not voluntary," Ares said.

Shouts went up from boxes and balconies across the hall, people yelling in unison into disabled microphones, "What is your solution?"

"I brought our people to this world. With the other founders of the Exodus, I set forth our dream of one people on one world, stretching into eternity. The anti-Serpentine laws were written to protect us from ourselves, and they cannot be broken. Must not." Ares ignored the smattering of voices. "But our dream of one people on one world cannot be realized in peace. And I refuse to see a war within our own people. I won't fight it, and it's clear to me that no one else can. Ours will become a tale of two worlds. We have the means to solve our strife tomorrow, to give equality and opportunity to every citizen. The fleet of ships we built in the years after the Exodus still exists. They are science ships and transports and mining vessels. As you know, we mapped every world within the new sentinel line. There are many that can become the new home of the labor class. They can create their own world there, so long as they adhere to the Serpentine Restrictions. We cannot allow them to become a danger to themselves or us."

Questions came quickly and so did Ares' answers. The mining ships could be configured for terraforming, transforming the new world into a haven, free of natural disasters and safe from cosmic dangers. The transport ships that carried the staff and parts to the sentinel assembly line would take the colonists to their new world. The debate quickly devolved into how to label the exiting Atlanteans, with one contingent insisting that "exiles" was the correct term since it was a forced removal. The term separatists was entertained but deemed too confrontational. Finally colonists was ratified, though the rules made it clear that one of the conditions the colonists adhere to would be the Serpentine Restriction of never leaving their world for exploration or colonization.

When the major questions were answered, and the debate descended into small details, like which districts would be evacuated first and what each person would be allowed to bring, Ares slipped away.

"I'll leave the vote to you," he said to Nomos.

They awoke him in the middle of the night, which Ares felt was ironic for someone they let sleep through a ten-thousand-year period in which they had thoroughly ruined his planet.

"We're close on the vote," Nomos said. "We need a compromise. A large voting bloc wants to ease the exploration restrictions. They request use of some of the science ships for deep space exploration."

"To what end?"

"They're calling it The Origin Project. Just a simple study of primitive hominids."

Ares turned the idea over. It could be problematic. "Okay. Two conditions. One: there are military beacons orbiting some worlds. They can't go near them. They perish if they do. Second: they only get one ship. We can't risk having hundreds of ships parading around the galaxy."

They again woke Ares several hours later. The second Exodus, what was called the Atlantean Equality Act, had been formally approved by a narrow margin.

# 42

The day the Exile Order was signed was the worst in Isis' thirty-five years. In her mind, she debated how she might have been more persuasive, presented the data differently, how she might have bested Ares in the forum.

Around her, the world changed and not for the better. In the aftermath of the vote, the greatest fear had been retribution from the labor population, but none had come, at least not against the intellectuals. Ares' strategy had been sound. The leaders of the labor revolution promptly released their hostages and actually turned their focus inward, persecuting any laborers who protested the forced relocation. Their methods were brutal and the news coverage relentless. Political leaders ignored it. A small group of intellectuals continued their protests, holding out hope for a single society. The voices mostly came from citizens in cities that hadn't been touched by the riots or terrorists blasts. The victims who had lived through the carnage counted the days until the exile in silence.

A week after the vote, Lykos had visited Isis at her lab, and to her surprise, thanked her. They had seen each other regularly after that, and each time, she looked forward to it a little more.

She always provided an update from her side. The restrictions on automated technology had been relaxed a bit, easing the post-exile transition for the intellectuals.

With every visit, there was less to talk about, but Isis still looked forward to the meetings. She dreaded the day when the ships would come, load the laborers, and leave forever.

It was during one of their conversations, when Lykos was describing how the labor leaders were codifying the criteria of a laborer, that Isis formed her plan.

"They're using income, job type, and even what your parents do," Lykos said.

"Are they considering a genetic definition?"

"No."

"Have they identified the relocation world?"

"Yes. General Ares and the teams are already terraforming it. But I don't know where it is," Lykos replied.

"Can you find out?"

"Maybe."

Isis shared her plan, and when she was finished, Lykos was silent for a long time.

"Just think about it," Isis said.

The following day, she visited Janus.

"I've reconsidered. I'd love to join The Origin Project."

She felt slightly guilty that the enthusiasm she shared with him was for different motivations, but that was something to work out later.

Ares stared out the window of his survey ship at the blue, green, and red planet below. Massive machines crawled across the surface, turning dirt and sending plumes of red dust into the atmosphere. The terraforming machines were moving mountains, creating a paradise for the Atlantean Exiles.

"The geological survey is in, General Ares. The tectonic plates in the northern hemisphere won't be a problem for four thousand years. Should we leave them?"

"No. They may not be able to fix them in four thousand years. Make accommodations now." The struggle of a global disaster could ignite their evolution. That would be dangerous. Ares wanted life to be easy for them here. That was essential to his plan.

On relocation day, Ares watched the fleet of transport ships from the lunar observation deck. The ships reached to the burning white star beyond, and the sight of the full fleet took his breath away. He felt the hair on his arms stand on end. A single thought dominated his mind: *I have won.*

---

The Origin Project launched a week after the fleet returned from transporting the last of the Exiles. The launch ceremony was lavish. Pundits and politicians hyped the expedition as the opening of a new age of Atlantean exploration—under the strict guidance of the anti-Serpentine laws. The team of scientists would study human life throughout its galaxy, on the worlds within the new sentinel line, finally unraveling the secrets of evolution and the Origin Mystery itself. Many believed that the breakthroughs could yield new clues about how the Serpentine ring accessed the Origin Entity, and how it might be defeated. The team was given the opportunity to conduct research that had been banned, never even talked about for thousands of years. Janus had been right about one thing: the project was the perfect place for Isis to continue her research. But that wasn't her true motivation.

The first time Isis toured the massive science ship, she was blown away. The scale of the ancient vessel was staggering. It contained hundreds of science labs, and at the center, two giant arcs capable of harvesting entire ecosystems from a world. The ship had been built in the years after the Exodus and used to complete a full survey of the stars and planets within the sentinel line. Probes and survey drones had done most of the legwork, but a large science team had followed up on the ship, studying worlds that might have an impact on Atlantean safety. They had used the massive arcs to bring back entire samples of worlds for study by specialists on the new Atlantean homeworld.

Whereas the arcs had been used for science in the distant past, they would serve as entertainment in Isis and Janus' time.

Citizens clamored at the opportunity to visit other worlds without ever leaving. Each time The Origin Project disembarked, a new wave of speculation rose about what they would bring back. The attention served to rally support and funding for the project, and Isis knew that was a large motivation for the arc component. The other, she felt, was Ares and the council's desire to periodically check in on the scientists. Each time they returned home, a team of two dozen specialists from fields including infectious diseases, nanotechnology, and psychology performed a rigorous battery of tests on each scientist. But they never brought home anything harmful. And interest in the arcs they brought back waned with every return visit. Eventually the worlds started to look the same, and Janus and the team began seeking more exotic specimens with every trip, a desperate attempt to reignite the public's interest. It was a losing battle. The crowds lining up to see the arcs were smaller each time they returned.

Over the years, the data began to look the same as well, and the differences in each new hominid species delivered less excitement at every world.

Public disinterest eventually infected the science team.

They had begun with fifty scientists, carefully chosen from thousands of applicants. Janus had enlisted Isis to help him select their team, and she had felt truly lucky—many of the candidates had much more experience than she did and more right to be on the expedition. But her motivation was stronger than theirs... and very different.

The team that started as fifty dwindled to twenty, then to ten, five, and finally two: Janus and Isis. She couldn't blame them. The scientists had grown up on a crowded world, in a dense social environment. The abject isolation of deep space exploration, hibernating for years at a time and repeating the same experiments over and over wore on the scientists. And those who weren't bored with the research longed to return to the Atlantean homeworld where a new intellectual renaissance was happening. The new era of a single united society was a lure none but Janus and Isis could resist. They found themselves alone, and they were both glad for it, albeit for different reasons.

"It feels like we're the last two people in the universe," Janus said. On the viewscreen behind him, world 1632 emerged, a marble of purple, red, and white. It grew as the ship approached it.

"Yes," Isis replied. "It's the perfect way to do our research."

Janus had collected his samples alone on 1632, barely speaking to her during their three-week survey. Isis knew that she had hurt him, but lying was worse. She was saving the lying for when she absolutely had to, and she would very soon.

As they entered their stasis chambers, Janus finally broke the ice. "See you at the next world, Isis."

She nodded as the tube closed, and the fog surrounded her.

The next world, 1701, was the one she had been waiting for. It was just in range.

Janus was his old self again when he emerged from the tube. For each of them, only a few seconds had passed, but two years had gone by outside. The time-dilation bells at each end of the ship, coupled with the stasis chambers, made leap-frogging through time and space as easy as taking a nap.

"Some exotic species have evolved since the initial survey," Janus said. "Let's take the *Alpha Lander*. Could be an arc opportunity."

"I agree," Isis said. She activated her own terminal and scrolled through, searching for an excuse to escape. "The advance probes also found signs of fossilized life on one of the moons of the seventh planet. I'd like to take the *Delta Lander* to retrieve some samples."

Janus agreed reluctantly, and then said, "Let's maintain periodic radio contact."

"Of course."

Isis had selected the *Delta Lander* for two reasons: it was the only lander capable of short-range hyperspace travel, and it had a resurrection raft.

At the edge of the solar system, she made the jump she had waited twenty-three years for: to the Exile colony.

The viewscreen inside the *Delta Lander* revealed a civilization taking its first tentative steps. The settlements were still too small to see from orbit, but under the viewscreen's magnification, she saw farms on the outskirts of simple towns. The Exiles were slowly creating their own utopia, one very different from their homeworld.

Isis made radio contact, arranged the rendezvous, and landed on the surface. She ejected the resurrection raft just before she put down, then stood outside the lander and waited.

The location was a rocky terrain several miles outside a small settlement. After a few minutes, Lykos emerged from an outcropping. His boyish face was more chiseled and weathered, but his features still radiated a charm Isis found irresistible.

Without thinking or saying a word, she closed the distance between them and hugged him, almost bowling him over.

"Hey," he said, holding her back to look at her. "You haven't aged a day."

Isis nodded to the rectangular structure a few feet away. "The stasis chambers do wonders. You'll see."

Lykos studied the structure skeptically. "What is it?"

"A resurrection raft. The larger vessels eject them if they're in danger. If the crew dies, they resurrect there and can be rescued."

Lykos shook his head. "It reminds me of the old world. Life here is a little more simple."

Isis sensed something in his tone. Hesitation? Fear? "Are you having second thoughts about our plan?"

"No… It's just. We're building something good here. When we talked… back then I thought exile would be our ruin. But we've come together here. There's a unity and purpose."

"That won't go away."

"It's been over twenty years for me. Tell me again."

Isis took out a canister. "It's a retrovirus. You simply release it anywhere. Ideally a populated area."

He took the silver cylinder. "Sounds like something from the revolt."

"There won't be any terror or sickness. This virus will reunify our people, Lykos. We can live together on the same world—any of us can. One world. One people."

"How does it work?" He raised his eyebrows. "The simple explanation."

"My research isolated the genes that pull the levers of evolution. I call it the Atlantis Gene. It's actually a set of genes and gene activation is a crucial part. The therapy will modify the Atlantis Gene for everyone on this world."

"We'll change?"

"Slowly. I'll take periodic readings and make adjustments if anything goes wrong. The changes won't be noticeable. It's a slight change in brain wiring, specifically in the areas of information processing, communication, and problem solving. This therapy will expand the potential of everyone on this world. Someday this will be seen as the act that brought our people back together." Isis waited, but Lykos said nothing. "Do you trust me?"

"Completely," Lykos said, without hesitation.

"Then I'll see you in a few minutes." She smiled. "Ten thousand years, local time."

In orbit, Isis couldn't help but watch as Lykos journeyed back to the small village with the silver cylinder. Just before the shadow of night reached across the world, covering the rocky area that hid the resurrection raft, Lykos ventured back to it empty-handed and stepped inside.

Isis exhaled. Anticipation filled her. She opened a wormhole and returned to world 1701 and the main ship.

Janus instantly recognized her renewed energy and reflected it. "You must have had a good trip."

"I did."

"Me too. I loaded the D arc. You won't believe it." He brought up a series of images on the screen. "They're flying reptiles with a photosynthetic dermal layer. They actually become invisible at night when they hunt."

"Impressive."

They talked about the exhibit on the homeworld, how the tours would have to be guarded, and how it might reignite excitement for the project, and even inspire a new group of scientists to venture out with them.

Finally, Janus said, "Ready for world 1723?"

Isis nodded, and they again entered their glass tubes, the fog floated up, and time slipped away.

# 43

The sound of the alarm was Isis' first indication that something was wrong. The tube opened, and the fog cleared. As usual, she was out of her tube before Janus. She hobbled across the cold metallic floor to the control panel and worked the green cloud of light that emerged, trying to determine what had gone wrong.

"Did the hyperspace tunnel collapse?" Janus asked. He rubbed his eyes and staggered out to join Isis.

"No. We've reached world 1723."

A message over the speaker echoed in the small space. "This world is under a military quarantine. Evacuate immediately."

Isis and Janus raced to the ship's bridge. The viewscreen showed the planet below, which looked nothing like it had in the probe's survey thousands of years ago. Where a lush green, brown, and white world had been, a wasteland lay. Black craters dotted the surface. The oceans were too green, the clouds too yellow, the land only red, brown and light tan.

The ship's voice boomed in the bridge. "Evacuation course configured. Execute?"

"Negative," Isis said. "Sigma, silence notifications from military buoys and maintain geosynchronous orbit."

"This is reckless," Janus said.

"This world was attacked."

"That's not certain."

"We have to investigate this."

"It could have been a natural occurrence," Janus said. "A series of comets or an asteroid field."

"It wasn't."

"You don't—"

"It wasn't." Isis zoomed the viewscreen to one of the impact craters. "A series of roads lead to each crater. There were cities there. This was an attack. Maybe they carved up an asteroid field and used the pieces for the kinetic bombardment." The viewscreen changed again. A ruined city in a desert landscape took shape, its skyscrapers crumbling. "They let the environmental fallout take care of anyone outside the major cities. There could be answers there." Isis' voice was final.

Janus lowered his head. "Take the *Beta Lander*. It will give you better maneuverability without the arcs."

Isis set the *Beta Lander* down just outside the city, reasoning that there could be leftover explosives or any number of dangers inside the ruin. If the lander were destroyed, she would have nowhere to resurrect, and her life would permanently come to an end. Setting down outside was the only safe bet.

She donned her EVA suit and exited the lander, making a direct path for the ruins of the city.

Along the way, she turned the mystery of 1723 over in her mind. The initial survey had shown two hominid subspecies, both closely related. Their evolutionary progress was in line with the other hominids within the Atlantean swath of space, and they had been deemed unremarkable.

But something had happened here. Progress, evolution had ignited. They had made a great leap forward, and an advanced civilization had risen, only to be bombarded, bombed away in an apocalypse. The thought saddened her. This world could have been what the new Atlantean homeworld had longed for: a peer world. Its discovery could reignite interest in space exploration. But clearly someone already knew about the world or had discovered it after the collapse: they had placed an Atlantean military beacon in orbit.

There were only two possibilities. The first was that the initial survey results had been incorrect, that the world was already destroyed when it was initially probed. The alternative was that world 1723's civilization had risen and fallen in the interval, and some Atlantean organization had found it and opted to hide the truth.

Isis had been hiking for almost two hours when Janus's voice came over her comm, urgent and nervous. "Incoming ship." He paused. "It's a sentinel sphere."

Isis waited. She stared at the sky, as if expecting the sentinel to break the cloud cover.

"It just scanned our ship," Janus said. "It's moving on. Isis, I think you should get out of there."

"Copy." Isis started for the lander.

"The sphere is releasing something. The object is entering the atmosphere. It's a kinetic bombardment—"

The comm signal turned to static, and then cut off. Isis saw the burning object break the clouds above her, a burning hot poker streaking through the sky. Isis began to run but stopped. It was no use. She stood there, waiting, wondering why the sentinel would fire on either this world or her.

The heat grew, and she dropped to the ground and curled into a ball. The pain beat down on her, and sweat poured out of her skin for a few seconds, and then evaporated in the baking heat of the suit. The end came quickly after that, and in the next instant, she opened her eyes, staring out of the round resurrection tube in the *Beta Lander*.

Kate opened her eyes. She too was in the *Beta Lander*, on the same world, thousands of years after the memory. She also stared out of a round glass tube, this one a vat of yellow light in the research bay.

She lay on the floor, her head in Milo's lap. The vat where

she had floated, watching, experiencing the memories of Isis lay open, a pool of blood in the floor. Her blood. Isis' death on the world outside thousands of years ago had felt real, and it had done damage, Kate knew it instinctively. She could barely move.

Paul and Mary stood over her, and the fear on their faces confirmed her assessment.

# 44

When Kate opened her eyes again, she was on her back on a flat metallic table. She recognized it. It was the same type of surgical table she had awoken upon in the *Alpha Lander*, just after the surgery there.

Paul looked down at her, worry on his face. "That was close, Kate. Beta says your life expectancy is now less than one day."

Kate sat up. "I saw what happened here." She realized Mary and Milo were also in the room. She spoke to the three of them, recounting what she had seen on the Atlantean homeworld, how their society had fractured.

"Why did the sentinel attack Isis on this world?" Mary asked.

"I don't know," Kate replied. "I think the next memory will reveal that." She read the apprehensiveness on their faces. "I have to. We've been over this." She decided to change the subject. "Any progress on the code?"

"If you want to call it that." Paul walked to the wall panel and pulled up an image that looked like a single frame of TV static but in color. Kate was amazed at how well Paul worked the panel. She wondered how long she had been in the vat. Either way, she elevated her opinion of his intelligence.

"This image is a translation of the four base codes to CMYK. We tried RGB—red, green, blue—with a null terminator, but it was even worse. We've also ruled out a video and several other scenarios."

"The running joke," Mary said, "is that it might be like one of those pictures where you stare at it long enough and it transforms into some image."

"But we've been staring at it awhile, and it hasn't changed." Paul said, completing her thought. "Our working theory is that it's a genome sequence. My guess is a retrovirus."

"I bet you're right," Kate said. "It could be some sort of therapy that changes brain wiring, even allows for communication over distance. Or it could work like a quantum beacon in subspace."

"Creating a quantum entanglement," Mary said.

"Yes," Kate agreed. "We inject the virus, and a return signal comes in for whoever sent it."

"Do you know what it is?" Paul asked.

"No. But..." Kate thought about the retrovirus Isis had administered to the Exiles and about the sentinels and the Serpentine war with the Atlanteans. "I think I'm close. It could be in the next memory."

Before anyone could object, Kate ushered them out of the adaptive research lab, down the corridor and into a medical lab. She explained the genome synthesis systems and again was impressed at how quickly Paul learned.

When the sequence was loaded, Beta began counting down the construction phase. In a little less than three hours, they would have the retrovirus in the signal, and Kate hoped she would know the full truth of the Atlantis world.

She returned to the vat, donned the silver helmet, and delved back into the memories Janus had tried to erase.

The *Beta Lander* shook violently from the earthquakes after the impact, but to Isis' relief, it remained intact. When the tremors subsided, the doors to the resurrection bay slid open and Janus ran in. *He must have ported to the lander right after the impact,* Isis thought. It wasn't like him to take such a risk.

The tube opened, and Isis staggered out. Janus held his arms out to catch her, but she waved him away with her hand. "I'm okay."

"We need to go."

He led her to the portal, and they stepped out onto their main ship. Janus quickly keyed the next destination and opened a hyperspace window before they could reach their stasis chambers.

"Why did the sentinel attack me?" Isis asked.

"I don't know. Maybe the world was invaded by the Serpentine Army."

"Impossible," Isis said. "They would have had to break the sentinel line. If so, they would have reached our homeworld a long time ago. The ruins on 1723 were old."

"We need to report this."

"Too risky. Besides, we were told not to approach any world quarantined by a military beacon." *By Ares*, Isis thought. She mulled that over for a moment.

"What if the sentinels are malfunctioning?" Janus asked.

"Unlikely. I think someone programmed the sentinels to annihilate the inhabitants of 1723."

"That's a big accusation."

"It was a big civilization."

Neither said anything after that. Isis' thoughts drifted to the Exile world and to Lykos, lying in the stasis chamber in the resurrection raft. She decided to alter her plan, to get back there sooner than she had promised, just in case. "Let's take some time to think about this. And let's move on while we do. What's our destination?"

"2319"

Isis pulled up the survey details, focusing on 2319's location. It was too far away from the Exile world; she couldn't reach it in the *Delta Lander*. She searched the database of planets that would work.

"What about 1918? It had three hominid species during the initial survey. It could be interesting to do a comparative evolutionary study."

Janus thought for a moment. "Yes. I agree."

When 1918 came into view, Isis knew she had made a good choice. The world was the third planet in its solar system, had a single, uninhabited, rocky moon, and had recently undergone a significant global climate change. A small isthmus had risen between two of the minor continents in the northern and southern hemisphere, dividing the planet's massive ocean into two smaller bodies of water, altering sea currents and the habitats of several species of primates on the central continent. Several hominids were venturing out of their ancestral jungle habitats onto the plains. The environmental and dietary changes were causing permanent changes to their genomes.

"I'm now reading four genetically distinct hominid populations," Janus said. "Assigning catalog numbers. They'll be subspecies 8468, 8469, 8470, and 8471."

They spent a few more hours conducting their pre-landing surveys. The beacon that hid the world was fully functional and passed all its system checks. Per protocol, they began making arrangements to bury their primary ship deep under the dark side of the world's moon.

"I'd like to take the *Alpha Lander* down," Janus said. "It's overkill, but the C arc is empty, and I think there might be an opportunity."

Isis agreed; she only needed the *Delta Lander* for her purposes.

On the surface, they took DNA samples and conducted a series of experiments, comparing the data with the initial survey.

"The progress is amazing," Janus said. "And the diversity."

"Indeed. I'd like to do a longitudinal study." She tried not to appear nervous while she waited for Janus' answer. "I don't think anyone on the homeworld would mind. They haven't seemed to miss us lately."

"I agree. And a longer-term comparison would be interesting. Suggested sample interval?"

"Ten thousand years?"

Janus compared the recent data and the initial survey. "That should work well." He smiled. "I'll advise the science council not to expect us anytime soon.

The two scientists prepped and retired to their stasis chambers. Just before she stepped in, Isis set her own countdown for five thousand years. When she awoke, she would port back to the main ship, then take the *Delta Lander* to check in on the Exile world, just to make sure.

But the five thousand years awakening sequence never came.

Isis once again awoke to an alarm—an urgent encrypted communication. She checked the hibernation log. Only 3482 years had passed. She and Janus raced to the *Alpha Lander's* communications bay.

The first message was an urgent advisory that their home-world was under attack. Immediately, the memory of the sentinel attack that had killed her on world 1723 ran through Isis' mind.

"Look," Janus said. "There's a sentinel directive here, commanding all sentinels not on the line to rally to the homeworld."

Isis paced the room.

"It must be a Serpentine invasion," Janus whispered.

"Then we're not safe here."

"True. But we can't leave either."

They ate after that, neither saying much. Isis' thoughts drifted from her own world to the Exile world.

The comm alert went off again, and they rushed back to the communications bay.

The new message was even shorter. Their world had fallen. They were ordered to simply hide and await further instructions.

"We're marooned then," Janus said.

Where sadness should have been, Isis sensed only contentment from Janus.

## 45

Dorian had almost regained his strength. The hours in the conference booth reliving Ares' past were taking an increasing toll on him. He sat, staring out at the sentinel assembly line that stretched into the blackness of space. He was close to unraveling the full truth behind Ares, including his motivations and why he had come to Earth, what he wanted with humanity.

Dorian had been impressed with how Ares had handled the revolt on his own world. It hadn't been as dramatic as Ares' flood of Earth and the plague before it, but nevertheless, Ares had proved a proficient soldier.

Dorian stepped into the conference booth and loaded Ares' final memories.

After the Exile, the deep sense of emptiness had returned for Ares. He once again found himself in a world where he had no place. He was an outsider in a world he had created. The irony wasn't lost on him, but he knew that he had done what had to be done. That was the thread that ran through his entire disjointed existence. Around him, the intellectual utopia his world had always longed to become rapidly took shape.

While the world around him was changing, Ares was staying the same. He was truly a relic, a man out of time and out of touch.

There were no battles left for him to fight, no great campaign, no reason to exist.

He once again requested to be allowed to die, and once again, his request was denied. He once more took the long walk to the tomb that held the ancient resurrection ship, the celebration even larger this time, the crowd packed to the brim, the noise deafening, the camera flashes blinding.

Nothingness followed. Only the curve of glass and wisps of fog within the tube, and the faint tickle of the turning of time.

Around him, the ship shook. *An earthquake?* Ares wondered. Impossible. Any tectonic anomalies would never be allowed to progress.

His tube opened, and Ares ran out of the ancient ark. The sky was dark except for flashes in the distance and large, triangular ships descending. Blasts erupted in the city before him. The skywalks severed and buildings collapsed. The entire metropolis was coming down.

Heat issued forth, and the cacophony engulfed him, disorienting him. It was as if time were standing still, as if he were in a dream, a nightmare. The world Ares had sacrificed so much for was falling, crumbling before his very eyes in a wave of heat and light and thunder. The roar rattled him to his core, and he staggered backwards involuntarily. This was not a situation he could *handle*. In that moment, he felt utterly powerless, alone against an unknown force, an enemy with no equal he had ever seen.

A ship landed just outside the ark and masked soldiers poured out, surrounding him.

*Soldiers. Here.*

Ares' tried to process it. It was impossible. The sentinels...

One of the soldiers stepped forward and projected a hologram into the area between him and Ares. A violent battle raged in the space around the Atlantean homeworld. Tens of thousands of sentinel spheres fought a losing campaign, just as they had around the first Atlantean homeworld. For Ares, history was repeating itself. The wreckage of the sentinel spheres was slowly forming a new debris field that stretched to the sun.

Ares didn't recognize the other ships. They weren't Serpentine; they were much smaller and better-adapted to fighting the sentinel spheres, as if they had been built for that purpose.

The man removed his helmet. Lykos.

Ares recognized the rebel leader. Ares had negotiated with him during the revolt, and considered him the most reasonable man in an utterly unreasonable, barbaric faction.

"You betrayed us," Lykos said.

"We have not," Ares shot back. "Why are you attacking us?"

"You struck first, Ares. Call off the sentinels. That's all we want."

Ares rifled through possibilities, discarding move after move, searching for any way out. "I will," he said, a plan taking shape in his mind. "The sentinel control systems are located inside the ark. I'll disable the sentinels, and then we can talk about making this right."

Lykos eyed him. "I'll accompany you—to keep you to your word."

The two men walked in silence past the stone edifice that housed the ark. As they passed the vast chamber, Ares realized the flaw in his plan. The tubes were filling with prominent citizens who had just been killed. The resurrection ship had been keyed to resurrect critical citizens in the event of an extinction-level catastrophe. It was the fallback point for Atlantean civilization.

More tubes filled. Some opened, and bodies poured out, falling lifeless on the floor. *Resurrection syndrome*, Ares thought. The trauma of their death had been too much, just as it had been for a few during the labor revolts. How much time had passed? Thousands of years? The Atlanteans had slipped so far into a utopian existence that the experience of a violent death was too much for any citizen's psyche. They were ruined, all of them.

The tubes continued to fill and open, body after body of unmoving Atlanteans spilling out.

He had to stop the resurrection sequence, had to end their purgatory. They could never wake up. But he could make them safe. He was a soldier. It was his job... his duty.

The realization filled him with fire, purpose. Focus.

Ares rushed forward, killing Lykos in a single blow. He ran through the corridors to the ark's bridge, where he disabled the resurrection cycle, ensuring that his people remained in stasis but didn't emerge from the tubes.

He accessed the sentinel control program and instructed the spheres fighting the Exile ships to aid in his escape.

# 46

For a long while, Ares stood on the ark's bridge, watching the blue and white waves of hyperspace form and flow by on the viewscreen. The ancient relic had performed admirably, jumping out of the planet's gravity well and in the next split second, slipping into hyperspace, away from the battlefield of the Atlantean homeworld.

Ares had wondered if the ancient ship would still function. Their benefactors had built it to last, and Ares wondered if the avatar who had provided the ark to him so long ago had known this would happen, somehow planned for it.

Ares hadn't seen the avatar since the Exodus, when he had condemned Ares' actions, what he called his great betrayal. Ares had ignored the words, charging ahead with his own plan to secure his people. And now that plan had backfired. He was partly responsible for the destruction of his world, and the thought haunted him.

He stomped down the dark metallic corridors, deep in thought. He replayed the conversation with the avatar, specific phrases jumping out.

*We allowed our society to fracture. The Serpentine Army is all that remains in your time.*

Ares knew that his people had repeated the same mistake. Atlantean society had divided, but Ares had made accommodations: the anti-Serpentine laws. In the chamber that held the thousands of tubes that stretched into the darkness, Ares stopped at the tube that held Lykos. The rebel's eyes were hard. Ares would soon know the secrets his mind held. The resurrection process had captured his memories, and Ares could watch them.

At one of the adaptive research labs, Ares stepped into the yellow light inside the large glass vat and watched Lykos' memories flash by.

He saw Lykos board a vessel in the Exile fleet and leave the Atlantean homeworld for the colony world, where he and his people set about building a humble, yet robust society with farming and hard work at its core. Years passed, the settlements grew, leaders were selected, and Lykos became a beacon to his people.

Ares watched him hike into the hills one day. A lander, one of the Atlantean science vessels, lay in wait, and a scientist Ares recognized stood before it: Isis.

Ares saw their conversation and Lykos take the container. After it was deployed, Lykos slipped into the tube in the resurrection raft and time flowed by, interrupted at regular intervals.

The Exiles had formed a cabal of leaders who knew the truth about the accelerated evolution, and they apprised Lykos periodically. Where settlements had been, villages emerged, morphed into towns, cities, and finally into sprawling metropolises that rivaled those on the Atlantean homeworld.

To Ares, the march of civilization was like watching the time-lapse photography of a green plant spreading out and blooming into an intricate, multicolored flower.

In the next memory, Lykos charged out of the tube in the resurrection raft, past the rock outcroppings, to the side of the mountain, where he watched glowing embers streak across the sky and crash into the cities. Ash and fire consumed the horizon.

Though he could barely admit it, Ares knew the slaughter was partly his fault. In the years after the Exodus, he had programmed the sentinel drones to attack any species that advanced across a threshold, any species that didn't contain the pure form of the Atlantis Gene. Isis hadn't been the first to isolate what made the Atlanteans genetically distinct; the science teams in the years after the Exodus had taken samples from countless hominid species, isolating the genes that controlled Atlantean evolution. Ares had used the blueprint to distinguish any potential enemies.

The avatar had warned Ares the moment the plan had formed in his mind, condemning it as a betrayal, but Ares had thought it justified: it was merely the way of survival. Any advanced civilization would become a danger to the Atlanteans. They could break the sentinel line, just as the Atlanteans had as they ventured out, or worse, attack the new Atlantean homeworld directly. Or they could repeat the Serpentine mistake, allowing their technology to overrun them and take control of their civilization. There was room for exactly one advanced race within the new sentinel line, and Ares had programmed the sentinels to annihilate any emerging species without the Atlantis Gene—any advanced civilization that wasn't Atlantean.

In Lykos' memories, Ares watched the sentinels execute their programming, dropping kinetic bombardments on the Exile world as they had on many others, obliterating the cities and altering the planet's climate, which would no doubt do in any survivors.

But Lykos' memories revealed that the Exiles had battled hard for survival on their ruined world. The race Isis had helped create was resilient, determined. They retreated underground, building cities that receded below the surface with as much sophistication as the metropolises that previously towered above. Isis' therapy had created a race with a runaway intellect and something far more dangerous: an uncompromising drive to survive. They overcame challenge after challenge. They replicated the Atlantean resurrection technology, and their leaders used it to leapfrog through the ages as they prepared their escape from the wasteland of their world. And they had. Thousands of ships sprang from beneath the surface, engaging the sentinels that appeared in space, eventually winning the conflict and jumping away.

The sentinels had hunted them relentlessly, and the Exile-sentinel war had ebbed and flowed for several thousands of years. The Exile fleet had eventually turned the tide enough to make a mad dash for the Atlantean homeworld, hoping to force their former persecutors to call off the sentinels that had tortured and massacred them for years.

Ares watched Lykos land his triangular ship just beyond the ancient shrine that held the ark, where he and his soldiers found Ares and the two men's memories joined.

Ares stepped out of the yellow vat. He was only partly to blame for the fall of his world. The remainder of the fault lay with Isis, and she was the key to turning the tide.

At the chamber that held the resurrection tubes, Ares stood before the double doors. It was a great irony: the harsh measures the Atlanteans had undertaken to protect themselves had eventually grown an enemy that brought about their downfall. And in their march to a peaceful, advanced civilization, they had become psychologically unable to even fight back.

Ares wondered how he would cure his people, if they even could be fixed. But he had larger issues to deal with first. The Exile fleet was capable and growing. It would soon overwhelm the sentinels, and then find the ark. Time was short. And when the sentinels were gone, the Serpentine Army would pour through, wiping out the Exiles and Atlanteans alike.

His options were limited. He needed a new weapon, a technology that would strike the final blow.

Isis. She was the key.

# 47

Kate stared out of the yellow vat, steeling herself for one final journey into Isis' past. The next memories would reveal the truth of the Atlantean presence on Earth, and she hoped, the key to stopping Ares.

---

Isis felt that the years after the distress call from home seemed to drag on. Every time she and Janus awoke from their tubes, there was no update waiting. The only clue of the march of time was the readings from the hominid subspecies they had come here to study. They had watched their initial groups spread out across the world, rise, adapt, die out, and rebound countless times. Their logs charted the progress, and they settled into the only routine they knew: analyzing the data, designing new experiments, and periodically venturing out to conduct them. Janus remained detached, clinical, his only emotion directed at Isis. Even with their circumstances, she didn't reciprocate. But she was changing, growing more connected to the emerging species on the planet. Perhaps it had been the drama on the Atlantean homeworld or her time with Lykos, but something had broken loose inside her, an emotional cataclysm that couldn't be stopped. But there was no outlet for it. She focused on the science and bided her time, hoping for an update.

A new group of hominids evolved on the central continent, and they assigned a new catalog number: subspecies 8472. They were advancing rapidly, developing remarkable tool making and communication abilities.

"They're one to watch," Janus said.

"I agree."

Like the others, they tagged the new subspecies and checked their population levels each time she and Janus awoke from their hibernation cycles.

An alarm woke them, and Isis quickly saw the source: a super-volcano on an island near the planet's equator had thrown ash into the atmosphere, lowering temperatures on several continents. The volcanic winter had decimated the new subspecies' population. They were on the brink of extinction.

When Isis ventured out to take a sample from the last two survivors, she made a fateful decision. In a cave, staring at the survivors, she was unable to simply watch them die. She could save them. For all she knew, the strike on the Atlantean homeworld could have been part of a series of attacks on hundreds of human populations on worlds across the new sentinel line. She wouldn't watch this species slip into extinction, especially when her research could save them.

She brought the survivors back to the *Alpha Lander* and administered a modified version of the Atlantis Gene therapy she had treated the Exiles with.

She turned to find Janus in the research lab.

"What are you doing?"

"I'm... conducting an experiment."

"What kind?"

"Modifying a few genes that control brain wiring. I think I can give them a greater chance at survival. It's my research—"

"You can't."

"We have to," Isis said. "They could be the last of our kind. We can't watch them go extinct."

Janus continued his protests but had finally agreed, provided they monitored the experiment closely.

Several hibernation cycles passed without incident. Isis and

Janus watched the subspecies' population rebound and venture out of the central continent, advancing geographically and intellectually. Their progress was breathtaking, and Isis felt a sense of pride that matched Janus' growing apprehensiveness.

"This could slip out of our hands," Janus said.

"It won't."

"We need to consolidate and control the genome. Mutations could occur during the hibernation intervals. We could awaken to a hostile, advanced civilization."

This time Isis relented. They placed a radiation beacon in the Alpha's bones and ensured that the first tribe kept it close.

Several cycles later, they awoke to another alarm: an incoming ship.

"It's General Ares," Janus said. "The ark."

Ares buried the ship under the thick ice cap that covered the continent at the southern pole, and Janus and Isis ported to his ship.

Ares stood waiting for them in the portal room and spoke without preamble, his enraged eyes boring into Isis. "You massacred our people."

"We've been here the entire time," Janus shot back.

Ares activated a wall panel, and a hologram emerged, replaying the memories from Lykos. The three of them watched Isis land on the Exile world and provide the genetic therapy. The Exile civilization advanced rapidly after that, until its near annihilation by the sentinels. Years after the massacre, the Exiles rose from the ashes, into space, where they bested the sentinels lying in wait. The final sequences were of the Exiles laying siege to the new Atlantean homeworld, killing countless inhabitants.

Isis felt her legs go weak. Her attempt to reunite the Atlantean race had led to its downfall, a war beyond imagination.

No words came. She felt listless.

Janus' voice was harsh. "It's a fake."

"It's not. I have Lykos in a tube. He'll verify it."

Isis tried but failed to hide her response. Awareness came back to her in a crash, and she desperately wanted to charge out of the communications bay. Janus read her expression, and his reaction was the most emotion Isis had ever seen him display. His hurt was almost as crushing as seeing the holomovie.

"The memories are accurate," Isis said quietly.

"If so," Janus said, focusing on Ares, "it means *you* unleashed the sentinels on our own people. You caused the downfall."

"The sentinels were built to protect us from any threats."

"The Exiles were no threat. Just an advanced civilization. We saw another, on another world. Also bombarded. Will you deny it?"

"I will not," Ares said. "I've protected us from countless threats. We'd be long extinct if it weren't for me. Her therapy made them a threat. Had she not altered their genome, they would have been left alone."

Isis stood there, still stunned.

"What do you want from us?" Janus asked.

"I read your research logs. You've performed a similar genetic alteration on a human species here."

"Yes," Janus said. "To prevent their extinction."

"Well, your last science experiment almost caused *our extinction*. I'm joining your little expedition to make sure history doesn't repeat itself."

Ares and Janus had argued for what felt to Isis like hours. Ultimately, Janus had yielded. Before they left the ark, Isis turned to Ares. "I'd like to see Lykos."

"I think you two have seen enough of each other. And besides, we don't allow visitation for prisoners of war."

# 48

In the weeks after Ares arrived, life almost went back to normal for Isis and Janus. They conducted their experiments as they had, except now Ares was constantly present, always looking over their shoulders, rarely saying a word. And neither did Janus. When he did speak, it was only about the task at hand, and there was no excitement, no passion for the work he had dedicated his life to. That, along with the knowledge of what she had done to her own people, drove Isis into a well of darkness. With each passing day, the walls of the lander and the small world they could never leave seemed to collapse in on her. She felt trapped, truly alone.

She often turned to find Ares' cold eyes staring at her, but he never approached her or said anything.

One day, when Janus was in the field, Ares sent for her. She reluctantly ported to the resurrection ark. In the back of her mind, a hope lingered: *he's reconsidered. He's going to let me see Lykos.* She followed the ship's directive to report to the auxiliary stasis bay. It made sense to keep Lykos there, separate from the primary stasis bay. Her hope grew.

The doors parted, and Isis's mouth fell open. A dozen tubes stood in a semicircle, and each held a different hominid.

"Just wanted to get your attention. I know you have an affinity for barbarians."

Isis spun around. "You had no right to take them."

"They're in danger. In fact, thanks to you, they're the most endangered species in the universe. The Serpentine Army will assimilate them one day. Unless the sentinels find this world and obliterate them first. Assuming, of course, the Exiles don't find us all—"

"You're wrong—"

"You weren't there, Isis. You should have seen the Exile fleet sacking our world. They're savages. Savages with incredible abilities but no control. Monsters, created by your therapy. Victims of your experiments. Just like subspecies 8472."

"What do you want from me?"

"I want to give you a chance, Isis. A chance to redeem yourself."

When Isis said nothing, Ares continued. "We have an opportunity to right all the wrongs, to bring our people back together and save these humans."

"How?"

"We can guide their evolution. We can create something that will end this war."

Isis wanted desperately to resist, to run out of the room and never return, but the lure of righting the wrongs she had committed was irresistible. She decided that she would hear Ares out. There was no harm in that. Quietly, she said, "I'm listening."

"I've taken genetic samples, but I don't have the skill to engineer the species I need. You can. And I have the knowledge you need—information about how the sentinels target DNA and the Serpentine virus, information that I've kept from our people since the Exodus." On the screen at the other end of the room, a DNA sequence appeared. "This is the Serpentine virus that was used on the Atlantean expeditionary fleet before the Exodus. It's the key. With my information, and your knowledge of genetic engineering, we can change the course of the universe." Ares stepped closer to her. "The species we create will restore our people. If you refuse, you truly have killed us all."

Ares seemed to know where every one of her buttons was, and he played them like a musical instrument. He held the one thing Isis would do anything for: redemption. A chance to reunify their people and make the Exiles safe again. Isis told herself that to do good things, sometimes it was necessary to work with bad people. But in the back of her mind, she wondered if she was rationalizing.

In the years that followed, Isis worked with Ares in secret, again keeping her work from Janus, who Ares rightly predicted would have objected. Isis knew that Ares was withholding information, giving her just enough to complete the experiments that he needed. His mantra was always that the sentinel and Serpentine information was need-to-know, that revealing the full details to Isis would compromise the safety of countless worlds.

Isis knew she was a pawn, but she felt she had no way out, no alternatives. As the years went on, she couldn't bring herself to come clean with Janus. She couldn't betray him again.

Cycle after cycle, she retreated to her hibernation chamber, hoping that Ares would honor his word, that at the next awakening, Ares would announce that subspecies 8472 was ready, and that Atlantean reunification was at hand.

She instead awoke to an alarm. As the screen outside the hibernation chamber lit up with population alerts, Isis grasped the magnitude of Ares' betrayal. Around the globe, human subspecies were dying out—three of them at once, all but subspecies 8472, his weapon.

If Janus realized the truth, he refused to say it. He did what Isis expected: rushed to save the species he could, subspecies 8470, which would later be called Neanderthals. The *Alpha Lander* touched down just off the coast of an area that would later be called Gibraltar, and Janus and Isis suited up, disembarked, and carried back the last living Neanderthal.

As they reached the ship, explosions rocked it, tearing the vessel in half, tossing Janus and Isis about wildly. They placed the Neanderthal in a hibernation tube and made their way to the bridge.

"Ares betrayed us," Janus finally said.

Isis couldn't bring herself to speak. As the seconds ticked by, she thought Janus realized the full truth, but he didn't say a word to her. He focused on the control panel. He locked down the lander, then activated the intrusion protocols on their space vessel, ensuring that Ares would be trapped if he tried to use it. Another blast rocked the lander, throwing Isis into the wall. She looked up, semi-conscious. Janus moved across the room and knelt over her, staring into her face. Through his transparent visor, she could see the faintest hint of emotion. Pain. Hurt. Betrayal. Isis desperately wanted to confess, to tell him everything, to ask for his forgiveness. But no words came. He lifted her up, his suit's exoskeleton easily supporting her weight. He raced through the lander's corridors and charged through the portal, exiting into the ark. Isis' last memory was seeing Ares fire a shot at her, a blast that killed her as she slipped from Janus' arms.

---

Kate was drenched in sweat. Every breath felt as though she were drowning. She had seen all the memories now—the ones she was born with and those Janus had tried to hide from her. And she knew the rest. Ares had shot Janus that day in the resurrection ark, but he hadn't killed him. Janus had made it back though the portal to the *Alpha Lander* that lay buried, wrecked off the coast of Gibraltar. Janus had been trapped in a section close to Morocco. He had desperately tried to resurrect his partner in the other section of the *Alpha Lander*, but without her death signal, the ship wouldn't comply. He had tried for years, testing countless methods on the stasis chambers.

When he had finally given up, he programmed the ship's time dilation device to emit radiation that would roll back Ares' and Isis' genetic changes, hoping to revert humanity to a genome that would be safe from the sentinels, Exiles, and Ares.

Then Janus had waited. The lander had lain buried for thirteen thousand years, until a group called Immari International began excavating the area under the Bay of Gibraltar, hoping to find Plato's fabled city of Atlantis. They hired a miner named Patrick Pierce, who had been wounded during the First World War. When his team reached the time dilation device, which they would later call the Bell, it unleashed a pandemic, the Spanish flu, killing millions. Pierce had placed his dying wife in one of the tubes he had found, and the fetus inside her was born in 1978. He named her Kate Warner, and for thirty-five years, until the final outbreak of the Atlantis Plague, she had harbored some of Isis' memories. The fragments in her subconscious had driven her entire life. She had become a geneticist focused on brain wiring, dedicating her life to creating a therapy that addressed cognitive differences. For her entire life, Kate had been trying to fix the Atlantis Gene, trying to complete Isis' work and fulfill her desire to correct her mistake. Now Kate finally had the knowledge she needed to do that.

She opened her eyes.

She felt the cold floor of the bottom of the vat on her back and Milo's arms around her shoulders. Blood dripped from her nose into the pool below.

"You're hurt, Dr. Kate."

"It's okay. I know what we have to do."

## 49

Dorian felt his life slipping away. He lay on his back in the conference booth, staring at the ceiling. In his mind, he rifled through the memories and what he knew, hoping for a clue about Ares' next move.

Ares had killed Isis the day he had attacked the *Alpha Lander*, but he had failed to kill Janus. For years, Janus had tried to resurrect Isis, and in his desperation, he had sent all the resurrection data except his own to the tubes in the section off the coast of Gibraltar. When the Bell attached to the *Alpha Lander* had unleashed the Spanish flu, Dorian's father, a leading member of the Immari, had placed him inside one of the tubes, where he had remained until 1978. Dorian had awoken changed, unaware that Ares' memories lay buried in his subconscious, driving him. All Ares' hate, his resentment of Isis, was there, deep within Dorian's mind. All his life, Dorian had feared an unseen enemy, a great threat he believed the human race was genetically unprepared to face. Now he knew it was true. The Serpentine Army, the Exiles, the sentinels—they were all threats. And so was Ares. He wanted to use humanity for his own ends; they were the key to his plan, which still wasn't clear to Dorian.

After Ares' attack on the ship in Gibraltar, he had deployed the retrovirus Isis had helped him develop, using a supervolcano in Indonesia as his delivery vehicle. Then he had ported to the scientists' ship, but Janus' countermeasures had trapped him there. Ares had used his link to the ark buried under Antarctica to appear as an avatar, making contact with Dorian when he had finally entered over thirty years after his rebirth in the tubes and thirteen thousand years after Ares' attack on the science team. Dorian had carried a case out of the resurrection ark in Antarctica. Its radiation had completed humanity's genetic transformation in the final days of the Atlantis Plague, and the portal the case had formed led Dorian to the scientists' primary ship, where he had rescued Ares.

In the weeks that followed, Ares had wrecked the planet, flooding it, collapsing nations into civil wars. Dorian was sure of one thing: it was no way to build an army. Ares was weakening humanity. But why? As bait of some sort? Or was the plan longer range? It didn't make sense.

Dorian struggled to his feet and staggered out of the glowing white conference booth. He stopped in the open area with the tall glass windows looking out on the massive assembly line. The cylinder that produced the sentinel spheres stretched into the blackness of space with no end in sight. The line that had produced thousands of sentinels each minute had stopped, but there were more sentinels than ever. Dorian walked closer to the window. Small pops of blue and white light flickered across the sky, like thousands of fireflies blinking in the night. Wormholes opened and closed, each delivering a sentinel, which were arriving by the thousands each second. The entire sky was filling with the black objects. They blotted out almost every star, the pops of light heralding their arrival the only shred of light in sight.

Something was happening. They were gathering here, waiting.

Dorian moved to the communications bay and interfaced the sentinel positioning database. All the systems recognized him as General Ares, and no information was withheld from him. Dorian studied the map. The sentinel line that protected this region of space from the Serpentine fleet was collapsing. Large groups of sentinels were leaving the line, rallying to the factory. On the edge of the old line, where the military beacon had been, at the Serpentine battlefield, a Serpentine fleet massed, establishing a staging area. The ships were simply a swarm of dots on the screen, but Dorian felt his mouth run dry. Blood ran down his nose, and he wiped it away. He wondered how long he had left. And if he could do anything to save his world.

***

Natalie woke to the sound of doors slamming. She slipped out from under the quilt and crept to the window, the cabin's cold wood floor creaking under her feet.

Three of the four Humvees cranked, their lights flashing through the window for a moment as they backed down the pine tree-lined, dirt driveway that led to the country road in the mountains of North Carolina. She glanced back at the bed. Matthew was still asleep, snuggled under the heavy quilts.

She started for the bedroom door, but her feet were freezing. She pulled on her shoes and a sweater and ventured out.

Major Thomas sat by the fire, sipping coffee, listening to the radio.

"What's going on?"

"Supply concerns," he said. "Coffee?"

She nodded and sat in the rustic chair across from him, facing the fire. "Are we out of supplies?"

"No. Not yet. But the government is." He pointed to the radio, and Natalie listened for a moment while he poured her a cup of coffee.

*This broadcast is a service of the United States government. All able-bodied citizens are now required to report to your closest fire station. Our government and our food supplies are under attack from insurgent militias. If you have military training, you are especially needed to defend the American homeland. Report immediately to your nearest fire station for further instructions. You will be fed, and you will help save lives...*

Thomas turned the dial down on the antique radio. "The calls have gotten more urgent since last night. The fighting must be getting more intense. My guess is that the Immari militias have scored some victories."

"You're not going?"

"No. It's just a matter of time before someone shows up here."

Natalie took a deep breath, unable to speak.

"And besides, there's nowhere else I'd rather be."

On the bridge of the resurrection ark, Ares watched the last pieces of ice slip off the ancient ship, falling back to Antarctica as it lifted off.

The vessel rose through the atmosphere, and Ares surveyed the planet he had ruined. Massive storms raged, and the coastlines were toxic marshes of submerged cities.

It would be irresistible to his enemy. His time on the tiny world hadn't gone exactly as planned, but he was back on track now. Nothing could stop him.

The ancient ark cleared the atmosphere, and Ares targeted the floating beacon. He fired a single shot, destroying it. Now the vulnerable little world would be exposed for the serpent to see. It would be here soon, and then the final war would begin.

Ares keyed his destination into the ark and opened a hyperspace tunnel. For a second, he stood on the ship's bridge, watching the blue, white, and green waves flow by on the screen. They were like a countdown to his destiny.

Finally, he marched out of the bridge, through the dark, metal corridors to the chamber where he had spent most of his time during the last few weeks.

Lykos hung from the straps on the wall. Dried blood was caked on his face and chest. He didn't look up at Ares.

"I want to thank you for your help." Ares said.

Lykos stared straight forward, making no reaction.

Ares activated the wall screen and played the video he had

tortured Lykos into making—a false distress signal to the Exile fleet.

Lykos lifted his head just enough to see it.

"It's fitting," Ares said. "You and Isis unwittingly destroyed both our civilizations. Now you'll help me make it right. It won't be long now."

Ares moved to the door, but Lykos stopped him. "You underestimate us."

"No. I underestimated you once. It will be the last time. I should have annihilated you on our homeworld when your kind began killing our own citizens. That was our mistake: making peace, resettling you. We left you alone, and you repaid us by returning home and slaughtering us."

"We had no choice. We only wanted to stop the sentinels."

Ares changed the screen to show the hyperspace window, which disappeared a few seconds later. A massive factory in space and a fleet of sentinels took its place.

Lykos couldn't hide his horror.

"I haven't underestimated your people. I've been building a new sentinel army for forty thousand years. The new sentinels are adapted to fight your ships. And I've pulled everything from the sentinel line. Every sentinel in existence will soon descend on the Exile fleet. You won't win. I just transmitted your distress signal."

On the screen, large groups of sentinel ships jumped away.

"This will be over in a matter of hours," Ares said.

"The Serpentine Army—"

"I've made plans for them. I just wanted you to know what was happening. I've kept you alive so you can watch. I'm going to show you the wreckage when it's done."

Ares walked out, ignoring Lykos' screams. The hour he had planned for was at hand. He had anticipated an overwhelming sense of victory, of fulfillment. But he felt as dark and cold as the corridors he marched through.

In the chamber that held the tubes and the last of his people, he paused. For years, he had blamed Isis and Lykos, but Ares had killed Isis and taken his revenge on Lykos. Soon he would complete his retribution on all Lykos' people. Yet the emptiness remained.

When the docking procedure was complete, Ares exited the ark and began moving through the ancient sentinel factory. At the observation deck, he paused, instantly alert. Someone had been here. Was here. Wrappers from Atlantean rations lay strewn across the floor. Blood stains, dry.

Ares stepped around the corner, following the blood trail. It ended at the communications bay. He opened it.

Dorian lay in the corner, his eyes half open. Blood was caked on his face just like Lykos. Ares glanced at the conference booth. Dorian had accessed the memories. Had he seen it all? It didn't matter. He had kept Kate Warner from contacting the Serpentine Army before Ares could make his escape. He had performed his role one last time. Now he truly was useless.

"You lied to me," Dorian said, his voice faint. "Betrayed me. All of us."

"Well, what are you going to do about it, Dorian?"

Dorian opened his palm. A metallic device rolled out, stopping under the table, out of Ares' sight. He stepped forward and realized what it was a second before it went off. A grenade.

# 50

The last thing David remembered was the ship with the serpent insignia arriving at the battlefield in space and it pulling in his escape pod from the military beacon. He must have passed out after that. Or they had gassed him.

He awoke in a soft bed, in a well-lit room with bare white walls. He wasn't sure if it was a prison cell or a hospital room, but it felt somewhere in between. The room's only feature was a small picture window that looked out onto space. The scene stopped him cold. Ring after ring of ships spread out to the horizon. It reminded him of Saturn's rings, but these circles were made of linked ships. Serpentine ships. How many were there? Millions? Billions? He stood in the ship at the center of the rings, in the belly of the beast so to speak.

The door slid open, and to David's surprise, someone who looked human glided in, a mild expression on his face. His hair was blond, and he wore it in a tight ponytail. His features were youthful, and David put his age at around forty.

"You're up," his visitor said.

"I am." David hesitated, not sure where to start. Had they rescued him? Or captured him? He would start with a neutral question and go from there. "Where am I?"

"Inside the first ring."

"First ring?"

"We'll get to that. Our understanding of your communication customs is limited, but you're probably wondering what to call me."

"Yeah…"

"247." The man held out his hand, and David shook it reluctantly. "Yes, it's a weird name, but we don't need names, so we just have to make something up when we come across someone like you. I was link number 247 in the first ring, and now it's about all I have, uh, name-wise."

"Right. Well, I'm David Vale."

247 reeled back, holding his hands up. "I know. I know all about you. And your people. You've caused quite a stir around here."

David squinted, unsure what to say.

"You see, we found you at an ancient battlefield, where we once came into contact with the race you call the Atlanteans. The bizarre part is that you have some of their DNA, some of our DNA, *and* you also have some new DNA, some very exotic genetic components, sequences we've never seen before." 247 smiled. "And we thought we had seen it all."

David remained silent, but inside him, alarm bells went off. Something was very wrong here. This creature wasn't what it seemed. David's training kicked in. He knew what this was: an interrogation.

247 raised his eyebrows. "Oh, don't think that way. I'm not interrogating you—Oh, right, let me explain. Your body emits radiation we can read, so I'm not reading your mind per se. Your mind is broadcasting to me." He smiled again. "I can't help it."

"What do you want from me?"

"Nothing. Absolutely nothing. We actually want to help *you*."

"Help me do what?"

"Join the ring."

"I'm not a joiner."

"I know," 247 said brightly. "Again, I know all about you. I've seen your memories. But you don't know anything about the ring. We're offering you a chance to save millions, maybe billions of your people." 247 paused. "But let's face it, you only really care about *one* person."

The opposite wall transformed into a video, seen from David's perspective. It showed a bedroom with French doors that opened onto a small veranda overlooking the sea. Gibraltar. Kate lay in the bed, looking up at him, her eyes soft, inviting, staring up at him.

"We can save her," 247 said.

David heard himself ask how, the words almost an involuntary reaction.

"Her body is broken, but it doesn't matter in the ring. The ring exists outside of space and time. Every link is eternal. We've transcended primitive biology and so can she. So can you. You can be together forever, living a never-ending life. And you can be even more. We created the ring to access a quantum fabric that we call the Origin Entity. We believe that when we've harnessed every life form in the universe, every link to the Origin Entity, we will have full control of the entity, making us truly eternal, all powerful. We are the ring that circles space and time, and we are unstoppable. Join us."

"You need me."

"We want you. We want to help you."

The opposite wall transformed again, showing the Serpentine battlefield where the last shards of the beacon were crashing into the plane of debris. Rings of ships rotated before the sun, generating portals of blue and white. An endless flow of ships moved between them.

"This fleet of ships is heading to your world. It's one of many hidden worlds we've been trying to find for a very long time. Similar ships are headed for every world inside the sentinel line. The line itself is an artifact from my own civilization, the world that created the first ring. Our world fractured. Some people clung to the past, to their primitive, mortal existence, just as you do now. They created the sentinels to buy time for the other human worlds, but the sentinels are obsolete now. They're retreating. They've been retreating for a long time now. Each time they form a new sentinel line, smaller than the last, and each time we break through."

"Your fleet intends to attack my world?"

"We prefer the term liberate."

David studied the man, or thing, or whatever it was. "What will happen to my people?"

"That depends on you. You can't fight us. Your world is in shambles. Look at the suffering, what your people have done to themselves. Their suffering. We can end all that. Think about your life."

The wall changed again. David saw a montage of scenes from his life form and fade, a march of memories, most of them sad. He was a child, at his father's funeral, running to his room and the peace of isolation in that dark time. A graduate student running toward the buildings on 9/11; them falling, burying him. His agonizing recovery. Joining the CIA. Almost being killed and setting out again, joining Clocktower. His battles with Dorian. His takeover of the Immari base in Ceuta. The flooding of Earth. And finally, his retreat into the lander and his journey to the beacon.

"You've always been on the losing side, David. You've always fought a futile battle based on your heart. Use your head for once. Join us. Kate needs you."

"And you need me?"

"We don't. We don't need anyone. The ring is inevitable. But if you join, it will help us assimilate your people. As I said, we've never seen anything like you. Yours is a completely new species, and we believe you have some sort of special connection to the Origin Entity. We think it could even change how we do business around here." 247 grinned. "Let me explain. Your body is composed of atoms that are quantum entangled with the atoms of everyone you've ever come into contact with. All of those atoms are also tied to the quantum force we call the Origin Entity. Our technology is past your understanding, but if you accept your role as a link in the ring, we can access your connection to the Origin Entity, and then we can access those you're connected to. Kate. The rest of your people. It's a domino effect. If our theory is correct, the ring will spread instantly via your quantum entanglements."

"That's what you're after: my connection to this universal entity? My soul."

247 looked disgusted. "Your terminology is crude—"

"But it's the truth."

"Yes."

"And if I refuse?"

"We always try it the easy way, David. We've been doing this a very long time. If you refuse, we'll try to assimilate you anyway. If we can't, we'll kill you. Then, when our ships arrive at your world, they'll kill everyone else. We kill anything we can't assimilate. There's only room for one advanced species in this universe, and the ring is that race. Be smart, David. Think about Kate. What she would want. If you join the ring, those ships will be picking up links when they arrive. Otherwise, it will be a massacre. Kate will die too. So will you."

"So it's join or be killed?"

"That's the way of this universe, David. Whether you can admit it or not. Now what's it going to be?"

David glanced out the window at the almost endless rows of rings. There was no escape from this place. For David, the decision was a reflection of the beliefs that had driven his whole life. He believed every person deserved the freedom to be different. Freedom, in a word, was what he had been fighting for his whole life. On one hand lay freedom and death, on the other lay Kate and assimilation, and on both, the fate of his entire world. But David believed his world had fought too hard to accept assimilation. Humanity hadn't fought so hard just to become a few links in an endless chain. The decision was easy. "My answer is no."

The room's white walls dissolved to black. The comfortable bed morphed into a hard metal table. David was strapped in. 247's human exterior faded to gray skin that crawled with tiny machines under the surface.

"So be it."

David felt a needle jab into his neck.

# 51

Mary was pacing the dark metallic floors of the medical lab on the *Beta Lander*, deep in thought, when the wall screen flashed a notification in red block letters.

"It's ready," she mumbled. She realized then that she had been dreading the moment the ship finished building the retrovirus from the signal she had received a few days ago. Why? This was the crowning achievement of her career. If the virus was a means of communication with an alien civilization, this breakthrough would validate her entire career, her every choice.

Paul lifted his head up from his arm. He had been somewhere between sleep and daydreaming. Mary grinned at him, seeing what he couldn't.

"What?"

She licked her thumb and rubbed his forehead. "You were marking on your face."

Paul tossed the pen on the table. "Oh. Thanks." He focused on the screen. "So it's ready."

"How does this work?" Mary asked.

"You enter the medical pod, and Beta administers the therapy. It's similar to the way the other bay operated on Kate. If something goes wrong, it will try to save you."

"You're not taking the therapy?" Mary asked.

"No. Well, I hadn't planned to. It's your discovery. I assumed you'd want to be the first."

"I would have—a few days ago. I would have leaped at the opportunity. First contact, the culmination of all my work. But I've realized something. I threw myself into my work after we…

went our separate ways. I was obsessed with my work because it was all I had left. I've been looking for something, and it has nothing to do with aliens or signals on radio telescopes."

"I know exactly what you mean. But if Kate doesn't wake up from that vat, this is our only option for getting out of here. We'll be trapped otherwise."

"I know. What do you think? Talk to me, Paul. What do your instincts tell you about this?"

Paul looked away. "I know what this signal represents to you, Mary, how much you've sacrificed over the years for your career. If you ask me what my gut instinct is, I just don't believe a friendly species would beam a retrovirus into space. I know we're out of options, but I think we should wait."

Mary smiled. She was worn out, scared out of her mind, and strangely, the happiest she had been in a very long time. "I agree. And there's no one I would rather wait with."

Paul's eyes met hers. "Same here."

"I'm sure we can find something to do while we wait."

---

Paul didn't know how long he and Mary had been in their room, and he didn't care. He had figured out how to lock the door and turn the lights out, and that's all that mattered.

Mary was sleeping beside him, the sheet hanging halfway off of her. He stared at the ceiling, his usually busy mind blank, a feeling of complete contentment.

A knock on the metallic door echoed in the dark, and Paul sat up. Mary was awake a few seconds later, and they dressed quickly and opened the door, where Milo stood.

"Dr. Kate. She's awake. She's sick."

In the adaptive research lab, Kate again lay on the stiff table that stuck out of the oval medical pod. The screen on the adjacent wall revealed her vitals.

She didn't have long. Paul scanned the surgical log. Milo had put her in the pod after her last session in the vat. The ship had done all it could, but it was hopeless. She had an hour at most.

"Paul…" Her voice was faint.

Paul moved to her bedside.

"The retrovirus."

"What is it?"

"The Serpentine virus."

Mary and Paul shared an expression that said, *That was close.*

Kate closed her eyes, and the screen changed to show the communications log. She had sent a message to a planet, apparently using her neural link with the ship. Paul wondered if she had learned the location in the memory simulations.

"The Exiles," Kate said. "They're our only hope. I can save them."

*Exiles?* Paul was about to ask what she was talking about, but Kate explained quickly, her voice still a whisper. She described the fracturing of the Atlantean civilization, how the scientist, Isis, had genetically altered the Exiles, making them a target for the sentinel's anti-Serpentine programming.

"They'll be here soon," Kate said. "I hope. If I'm gone, you have to complete my work, Paul."

Paul glanced at the DNA sequences on the screen, trying to catch up. "Kate, I… there's no way. I can't understand half of this."

The ship shook, and the screen changed to show the scene outside. A hundred sentinel spheres hung in orbit. They were firing on the planet. On the *Beta Lander*.

# 52

Paul felt Mary's hand slide inside of his. On the viewscreen in the *Beta Lander*'s adaptive research lab, they watched the falling objects burn in the atmosphere as they crashed down toward them.

The strange calm he had felt in the bedroom came again. There was nothing he could do, but there was also a feeling of utter peace, of having fixed something broken inside of him.

The first kinetic bombardment hit about a mile away from the lander. The shockwave a second later threw Paul, Mary, Milo, and Kate into the far wall. On the screen, an eruption of dust and debris, some from the ruined city, rose into the air.

Through the cloud, Paul saw a new fleet of ships arrive. They were triangular, and the second they cleared the blue and white portal, they broke apart and attacked the sentinels, thousands of triangles darting to and through the spheres, firing, shattering the black objects, sending wreckage into the atmosphere.

Even through the distortion of the dust, the battle was the most awesome thing Paul had ever seen. He almost forgot about the kinetic bombardments barreling down on them.

From the outer corridor, he heard the thunder of footsteps.

He turned to face the door, crowding Mary and Milo behind him. Kate was several feet away, unconscious.

He braced as the flood of intruders broke across the threshold of the communications bay. Soldiers, in battle armor head to toe. Helmets hid their faces, but they were humanoid. They rushed forward, injecting each person with something. Paul tried to struggle with them, but his limbs went limp. Darkness closed from the sides of his vision, then consumed him.

---

Paul awoke in a different place; a comfortable bed in a bright room. He surveyed it quickly: pictures of landscapes on the wall, plants, a round table with a pitcher of water, a sitting area, a desk with a wood top and metal legs. It was like a hotel suite. He got up and walked out of the bedroom and into the sitting area. A series of windows revealed a fleet of triangular ships, thousands of them, in formation.

The double doors slid open with a hiss, and a man strode in, his footfalls silent on the thin carpet. He was taller than Paul, his features chiseled, his skin smooth, his black hair close-cropped, like a military haircut. The doors closed, and the man tapped something on his forearm. Had he just locked the door?

"I'm Perseus."

Paul was surprised: the man spoke English.

"The injection we gave you enables you to understand our language."

"I see. I'm Paul Brenner. Thank you for rescuing us."

"Welcome. We received your signal."

"I didn't send it."

Perseus' demeanor changed. "You didn't?"

"Well, *I* didn't. The woman I was with, the sick one, did."

Perseus nodded. "We're working on her. There was some debate about whether the signal was another trap, another false distress call. That's what took us so long."

"I understand." Paul had no idea what he was talking about. The fact that he was talking to an alien on an alien space vessel was just starting to dawn on him. His nervousness grew by the second. He tried to sound casual. "The woman's name is Dr. Kate Warner. She can help you."

"How?"

"She's a scientist, and she's seen the memories of an Atlantean scientist. Isis. She can make you safe from the sentinels."

Skepticism spread across Perseus' face. "Impossible."

"It's true. She's designed a gene therapy that will make the sentinels ignore you. This therapy will save you."

Perseus smiled, but there was no warmth. "A scientist told the Exiles that once before, a long time ago. And we were much better off then. The timing is also very curious. A few hours ago, a new fleet of sentinels attacked our ships. We live in space now. We've tried to settle dozens of worlds, but the sentinels always find us. We've become nomads, constantly running. The new fleet of sentinels that appeared today is relentless, and their numbers seem limitless. They know how to fight us. It's as if they were built to fight us, not the Serpentine Army. They've defeated us at every battle. We believe this is the final offensive that will annihilate us. You can understand my suspicion. A scientist offers a genetic therapy that can save us? On the day of our demise?"

Paul swallowed hard. "I can't prove anything I've said. I can't keep you from killing me, but what I've said is true. You can trust me, and we can all have a chance at surviving, or you can turn away, and we'll all die. Either way, there's another woman in my group. She's not sick. She and I... I'd like to see her before I die."

Perseus studied him for a moment. "You're either a great liar or superb agent. Follow me."

Paul followed the man through the corridors, which were the utter opposite of the Atlantean ships. They were well-lit and teaming with people scurrying from one door to another. Some carried pads they studied, others talked hurriedly. To Paul, the feeling was of the CDC on an outbreak day. A crisis situation.

"This is the second fleet flagship. We're coordinating the civilian fleet defense."

Perseus led Paul into what he thought was a clinic or a research lab. Through a wide glass window, he saw Kate, lying on a table, several robotic arms hovering around her cranial area.

"She has resurrection syndrome," Perseus said.

"Yes. She risked her life to see the Atlantean scientist's memories. That's how she found out about your people and the gene therapy." Paul stepped forward and peered through the window. "Can you save her?"

"We don't know. We've been studying resurrection syndrome for tens of thousands of years, since the siege of our homeworld. When we attacked, we assumed that anyone we killed would simply resurrect after the battle. Our goal was to find the sentinel control station, disable the sentinels, then help rebuild our former world with the citizens returning from the resurrection tubes. During the invasion, we learned that resurrection syndrome was occurring for one hundred percent of those we killed. None of them could come back. With the sentinels battling us, we couldn't rescue anyone on our homeworld. We left empty-handed, but we've been studying resurrection syndrome ever since. Our hope has been that we could one day rejoin our fellow citizens and heal them. We've been working on a therapy based on the data we downloaded during the siege and our computer models. We have no idea if it will work." He nodded to the window and Kate on the operating table beyond. "She's the alpha for our therapy."

"Then all our hopes rest on her."

# 53

When the needle punctured David's neck, the room on the Serpentine ship faded. He found himself at the bottom of a dirt pit. *This is an illusion.* The thought brought a downpour of rain, flooding into the earth pit, soaking the ground, which grew soft, swallowing his legs, pulling him into the mud. The water was gathering, forming a pool that rose by the second.

David waded to the wall, straining to pull his feet from the heavy, black mud. *This isn't real.*

He dug his hand into the wall. It was dry. Dry enough. His hand held, and he climbed, one hand after the other, ascending to the surface. He climbed for hours, how long he didn't know. A faint sun peeked through the clouds. Slowly, it crept across the pit until it was out of sight, the shadows of its rays its only remnants. Still David climbed. The pit must have been a hundred feet deep, but he pushed himself, a deep well of energy powering him.

The rain never stopped, but neither did he. The sides he dug his hands into were growing soggy. It was taking him longer to make his hand-holds. He threw hand after hand of mud into the pit until he struck solid dirt, then he climbed. The water was coming, but he was climbing faster. Hand over hand, he dug and climbed. He had almost reached the surface when the sides began to slide. Globs of mud dripped, rolled, and dropped onto him, and then the mudslide consumed him, covering him, pulling him down into the water. He was completely coated in black mud, and he struggled under the water, the added weight pulling him into the abyss. He worked his arms, brushing the mud from his body, trying to free himself. His arms and legs burned, and then his lungs burned. He was drowning.

He fought, punching and kicking. Finally he broke the surface of the water, just long enough to take a breath before sinking again. He felt that if he allowed himself to sink, that if he gave up, allowed his will to break, the ring would have him, his soul, and every person he knew and loved. Kate. The thought gave him a new burst of energy, and his head breached the surface again. He sucked air in, waving his arms violently. The mud flew off, but the rain kept coming.

He put his arms and legs straight out, and he floated to the surface, the rain falling on his face.

He understood now. He couldn't escape. Submission was the only way to survive. But he wouldn't. They would have to drown him.

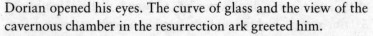

Dorian opened his eyes. The curve of glass and the view of the cavernous chamber in the resurrection ark greeted him.

The resurrection had restored him physically, but he was still sick, Dorian felt it at his core. *How long do I have? A few hours?*

Directly across from him, Ares stared out of another tube, his eyes cold.

Their tubes opened at the same time, and they walked out and stood across from each other, neither flinching. The echoes of their footsteps carried deep into the cavern, brushing past the miles of tubes stacked from the floor to the ceiling. When the last sound faded, Ares spoke, his voice hard.

"That was a very stupid thing to do, Dorian."

"Killing you? I actually think it's the smartest thing I've done in a very long time."

"You haven't thought this through. Take a look around you. You can't kill me here."

"Sure I can." Dorian rushed forward and struck Ares, killing him in one blow. The Atlantean hadn't expected it, and Dorian fought like a feral animal with nothing to lose. Ares' limp body fell to the black metallic floor, blood oozing out.

Dorian backed away and into the tube. It would reset the clock, correcting all his ailments except for resurrection syndrome, the only affliction the resurrection tubes couldn't fix.

He watched the white clouds fill the tube across the way. Time passed, how much he didn't know, but when the clouds cleared, a new Ares stood in the tube.

It opened, and Dorian rushed forward, killing Ares again.

The cycle repeated twelve times, and twelve dead bodies, all Ares, lay before the tube. Dorian fought like a man with nothing to lose, and he instinctively knew Ares' every move—thanks to the memories that would soon take Dorian's life.

On the thirteenth resurrection, Ares stepped out, kneeled and held his hands up.

Dorian stopped.

"I can fix you, Dorian." Ares looked up. When he realized Dorian had halted, he rose and continued. "You're suffering from resurrection syndrome—memories your mind can't process." He pointed into the chamber, at the thousands of tubes. "So are they. Fixing them is my goal. It's why I've sacrificed so much. You've seen those sacrifices, and the memories made you sick. I'll fix you, Dorian. You're like my son, the closest thing I have. I've waited thousands of years for someone to prove himself to me the way you have. You can kill me, or we can both live—together."

In the area just beyond the stack of dead bodies, a hologram rose. A space battle raged; thousands, perhaps millions of spheres zoomed into the breach, tearing through triangular ships.

"Our sentinels are battling the Exiles, Dorian. They will win. I've been preparing for this war for a very long time. When the Exiles are gone, we will inherit this universe. It will be over in a single day. My revenge. Our revenge. We can share it."

Dorian paced to the hologram. The spheres were winning.

They consumed fleet after fleet of the triangular Exile ships, each time jumping away to a new fleet.

"How would you fix me?" Dorian asked, his voice soft.

"You go back into the tube. I need time to find a cure. But I will fix you."

"What about Earth?"

"That's the past, Dorian. Earth is but a pebble in our sea."

"Show me. Show me my world."

"It's not your world anymore."

Dorian rushed forward and again killed Ares.

When the Atlantean emerged from the tube the fourteenth time, he instantly activated a hologram that showed Earth surrounded by Serpentine ships. Triangular ships fought a battle with them, but they were losing.

"The Exiles are fighting the Serpentine Army?" Dorian asked.

"Yes. Fools. They fight for all the human worlds. The ring has poured through, as I knew they would when I withdrew the sentinel line. This is part of my plan, Dorian."

"We're a weapon."

"Yes. The scientist you saw, Isis. I shared the Serpentine genetic information with her. She created a sort of anti-virus. That's what the Atlantis Gene that humanity received really is. It's the most sophisticated survival technology the universe has ever known. Look at what it has done to your world. No civilization has ever advanced so quickly. I combined what Isis created, what she gave to the Exiles, with the Serpentine virus. That's the Atlantis Gene you know. That's what you are. Your desire to assimilate, your drive to create a single unified society marching to a common goal, accessing some universal power. It's your fatal flaw and the salvation of our people. When the serpent bites, your people will poison it."

"What does that mean?"

"They assimilate, Dorian. They assimilated my wife, all of my people before the fall of our world and our Exodus. Someone will resist, and when they do, the serpent will bore deep, trying to access their link to the Origin Entity. They will offer the fruit, something the person desperately desires. Then they will engulf them in fire, filling them with fear. At each point, they offer a false salvation. If the person can resist, the serpent will initiate a forced assimilation. Their DNA will flow into the serpent, destroying it from the inside out. It only takes one."

"That's what you were doing. Your army."

"Yes. I was looking for a single soul with the will to resist. Adversity breeds strength. I destroyed your world in hopes of creating a single soul with the will to survive Serpentine assimilation. And I wanted to make your world look like easy prey for the Serpentine Army; a world full of souls on the brink of ruin. Defenseless. Irresistible."

Dorian felt listless. The enormity of the situation was closing in on him.

"Go back to your tube, Dorian. Await my next move. I will fix you, as I will every person in this chamber. Everything I've done has been for you and them. I will protect you. I will save you."

Dorian desperately wanted to retreat to the tube to wait for Ares, the father he had never had, whom he had longed for, to come and rescue him, to fix him. He stepped back. The bodies lay to his left, a mound obscuring the expanse of tubes.

"Do it, Dorian. I will come back for you."

Dorian took another step back.

Ares nodded.

Dorian stopped. "You lied to me before." As the seconds ticked by, he felt his fear closing in on him. Paranoia. The raw wounds. Images flashed before his eyes. His father, whipping him as a young child, chastising him, leaving, returning when Dorian was sick with the Spanish flu, placing him in the tube. Dorian saw himself awakening in the tube, changed. His hatred, his longing, his quest to find the resurrection ark. He had found his father there, but again he had slipped through his hands, killed by the Atlantean device, the Bell. At every turn, Ares had betrayed him.

Ares saw his hesitation and spoke quickly. "You were

uneducated before. You didn't know the scope of what we faced. You wouldn't have understood."

Hatred filled Dorian. "Your greatest fear was that you would spend eternity in this tomb, never able to die, relegated to purgatory."

Ares clenched his jaws.

"You've betrayed me too many times."

Dorian rushed forward and killed his enemy again.

When the bodies reached one hundred, Dorian waited, but the tube never filled with the gray fog. Ares never reappeared.

Dorian marched down the corridors to the ship's bridge. The panels revealed his suspicion: Ares had disabled his own resurrection. In the few seconds before his hundredth death, Ares had used his neural link with the ship to ensure he never returned, never had to face death at Dorian's hands again. He was gone forever.

Dorian had won. For a long moment, he felt a thrill. He had bested his nemesis. He was the better man. Then reality set in. He had a few short hours. At the wide windows of the sentinel factory, he watched the last of the spheres jump away.

He had been a pawn; he had played his role. He had killed his enemy, Ares. Now he was empty. No one would come for him; no one would fix him. No one loved him. And deep within his own heart, he knew that was right. He deserved no love, had earned none. He had lived a wretched life, full of hate, and with his last enemy gone, that was all that remained. The hate was poisonous; like the bite of a snake, it coursed through him, unseen, flowing in his veins, killing him from the inside out. There was only one way to get rid of it.

He walked back into the ark. In the chamber that held the tubes, he gazed at the tall mound of bodies. At the bridge, he disabled his own resurrection, and then he trudged to the airlock. The decontamination chamber rang alert after alert: no environmental suit detected.

He disabled it.

The three triangular shards that made up the door twisted open for him, as they once had in Antarctica. Then, he had thought they were welcoming him to his destiny. He had the same thought as the vacuum of space sucked him out, and he took his last breath. His dead body floated across the empty sentinel yard.

# 54

David floated in the water, unmoving. The sun rose and fell. Rain came and receded, and the water level rose and dropped. Each time, when he felt the ground upon his back, he stood, walked to the wall, and climbed, hand over hand, until the rain came again and the walls turned to mud and washed him down into the pool, where he fought to free himself, struggling for every breath. But he never gave up. His body burned with agony, his muscles, his lungs, every inch of him. But he refused to relent.

Then the sun disappeared forever, and nothingness followed.

When he opened his eyes again, he lay on the metal table he had seen after 247's charade. The straps had been released, and he sat up. Through the window, he saw the rings of ships, but they were different now. Before, they had rotated in formation. Now the links were broken. A cluster of ships floated listlessly, colliding into each other, no connection between them.

David was alone in the drab room.

He walked to the door, which stood open. The corridor was empty. He paced down the dreary hall. All the doors were open, as if some evacuation protocol had been initiated.

At the third door, he saw bodies, stacked in the corner. They were like 247: gray skin with glassy, oval, reptilian eyes. But the tiny beads that had crawled under 247's skin were gone. The bodies were utterly without life. *What happened here? And how can I escape?*

Kate instantly knew she wasn't in the *Beta Lander*. The robotic arms that hung before her and the lighted surgery room was very... Un-Atlantean. Somehow more human or Earth-like. Well-lit and bright.

She sat up. Behind her, several people stood behind a glass wall. "How do you feel?" a voice called over the speaker.

"Alive." But she felt more than that. She felt cured.

The Exile scientists led her to a conference room where they debriefed her on the procedure they had performed. Their years of studying resurrection syndrome had paid off, and she hoped she could reward them.

Kate felt a new vitality, a confidence. But behind it was a certain sadness. David. She pushed him out of her mind. She had Isis' memories; all of them. They were the key. With the Exile scientists and fleet commanders assembled in the large conference room, Kate stood before a screen that covered the far wall and presented the research—both what she had done in her own time and that which she had seen in Isis' time. She described a gene therapy, a retrovirus that would make the Exiles invisible to the sentinel fleet.

"After the therapy, you'll appear like Atlanteans to them," Kate said.

"We've heard this before," Perseus said.

"I know. I've seen. This is different. I know both sides now. I know the full truth—the genes that control the Atlantis Gene and the radiation it emits. The sentinels hone in on that radiation. If it doesn't match the expected Atlantean norm, they attack. Isis didn't know that. She never would have modified you if she had. She was very, very remorseful about what happened."

The committee dismissed her, and Kate waited outside, pacing nervously. After a few minutes, Paul, Mary, and Milo rounded the corner. Milo's hug almost squeezed the life out of Kate, but she gave no complaint. The nods from Paul and Mary told her how relieved they were that she was well again. And Kate sensed something else about the two of them, something that made her both happy for them and a little sad for herself.

"What was the vibe?" Paul asked.

"I'm not sure," Kate said. "But I know one thing: their decision will spell their fate. And ours."

Major Thomas handed Natalie another cup of coffee.

"I've switched to decaf," he said. "I hope you don't mind."

"Good choice."

They both focused on the radio. The repeating broadcast had changed. The call for soldiers to report to fire stations had been replaced by reports of fighting across America. The reports were of American military triumphs, but some places were never mentioned, and Natalie feared the worst: that some cities and states had fallen to the Immari militia.

Another report came: a caller claimed to have seen dark objects in the sky with his telescope.

The host laughed it off as a desperate attempt to distract the public from what was happening.

Kate was still pacing the corridor when Perseus peeked his head out. "We're ready for you."

She entered and stood at the head of the wooden conference table again.

"We've decided," Perseus said, "to administer your therapy to one group of our ships—a group fighting a lost battle. It's already underway."

"Thank you," Kate said. She wanted to hug him, but there was something she had to ask first. "I do have one request."

An awkward silence greeted her.

"That you save my world."

"We're already trying." The screen behind Perseus showed Earth. A hundred large Serpentine ships battled a fleet of many more triangular Exile ships. "We're losing though."

"I want to be there," Kate said. "I know we're losing but I have to be there in case there's anything I can do."

Perseus nodded. "A fleet of reinforcements is leaving in a few minutes. I'll join you. And I think the science team will want to as well—in case they have questions about the sentinel therapy."

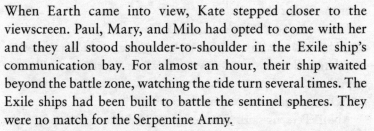

When Earth came into view, Kate stepped closer to the viewscreen. Paul, Mary, and Milo had opted to come with her and they all stood shoulder-to-shoulder in the Exile ship's communication bay. For almost an hour, their ship waited beyond the battle zone, watching the tide turn several times. The Exile ships had been built to battle the sentinel spheres. They were no match for the Serpentine Army.

Finally, Kate wandered back to the stateroom they had assigned her.

Even if the Exiles were able to turn the tide and save Earth from the Serpentine Army, her people would still be in trouble: the sentinel threat remained. Humanity would have to join the Exile fleet, living a nomadic life.

But if Earth fell and Kate's therapy were successful in neutralizing the sentinel threat, Kate, Milo, Mary and Paul would still be alone among the Exiles. She realized that no matter what, she would be alone again, without David. She wondered if it was all worth it, but sitting on the edge of the bed in the darkened stateroom, she knew that it had been. She had done all she could, what she thought was right. And she was proud of that.

# 55

Kate had almost worn a hole in the carpet of her stateroom when the doors opened.

"It worked," Perseus said. "The sentinel spheres have disengaged our ships."

Kate exhaled. "That's good news."

"The bad news is that we're losing out there. And another Serpentine fleet is on its way here. When it arrives, we'll have to pull out."

"Can you save anyone on the surface?"

"No," Perseus said. "I'm sorry. We're just not set up to fight the Serpentine ships or for planetary evacuations. Our ships were designed to defend against the sentinels." He waited in the sitting room for a moment, and Kate sensed he wanted to say more, but there was simply nothing to say and nothing he could do.

Finally, Kate took a seat in the club chair and said quietly, "Thank you. I know you tried."

Perseus paused at the doorway but left without a word. Kate sat for a while longer, unsure what to do, what she could do.

The double doors hissed open, and Paul, Mary, and Milo walked in. They had heard; Kate could tell from the expressions on their faces.

"What do you want to do?" Paul asked.

"I don't think there's much we can do," Kate said.

The door opened again, and Perseus strode through, excitement on his face. "You need to see this."

David had finally found what he thought was the command center of the Serpentine ship. It was a circular room with several hundred screens that showed Serpentine fleets hovering around hundreds of worlds. The Serpentine vessels drifted listlessly, and they were being obliterated by triangular ships.

Something had infected every link in the ring, severing it, as if the head of the snake had been cut off. That was the good news. The bad news was that he was trapped.

Kate stood on the Exile ship's bridge, staring at the Serpentine ships that drifted around Earth.

"Could this be connected to your therapy that removed the sentinel threat?" Perseus asked.

"No. I don't think so." In truth, Kate had no idea. "Well, maybe."

"Which is it?" Perseus asked.

"I don't know." Kate racked her brain. Something had killed the Serpentine Army from the inside out. Ares. His weapon. Isis' research. In a flash, it all came together for Kate. "It's us. Humanity. We're the ultimate anti-Serpentine weapon. Our DNA, the Atlantis Gene, the plague, it was all about this moment. When the Serpentine Army assimilated us, our DNA was an anti-virus. It killed them."

"That's impossible," Perseus said.

"Why?"

"They never made it to the surface of your planet to assimilate anyone."

It didn't make any sense. Kate was sure she was right.

"We're not taking any chances. The leadership has ordered us to destroy all the Serpentine ships."

"I think that's wise," Kate mumbled, still lost in thought.

She wondered how they could have assimilated…

David. When the military beacon had been destroyed at the Serpentine battlefield, they would have been able to see what was happening there. If they had recovered his body…

"I know what happened," Kate said. "They tried to assimilate someone from our team. His name is David Vale, and we need to find him."

"What are you proposing?"

"He's on one of the Serpentine ships. We need to begin searching—"

Perseus held up his hands. "Are you out of your mind? We don't even know how many ships there are. Millions, possibly billions. And this could be temporary or a trap. There's no way we're going to risk that for one life."

"You are. You're going to do it because I have something else you need."

Perseus eyed her skeptically.

"The location of the sentinel factory—their control center. And if I'm right, the resurrection ark that contains all the Atlantean survivors, as well as one of your own. Lykos."

Perseus stood there on the bridge, contemplating Kate's words. Finally, he said, "I'll take it to the high council. But even if they agree to search, they'll want that location first."

Kate nodded her agreement. At that moment, she realized the true genius of Janus' plan. He had spread the memories across the three locations that could reveal the full truth—the Serpentine battlefield, the sentinel factory, and the stranded lander on the ruined world. It had been his ultimate backup plan, his contingency against Ares. Kate hoped it would work this final time.

"They've agreed," Perseus said. "With conditions. They'll scan the Serpentine ships for human life signs before they destroy them. No life signs, they fire at will. If they detect human life signs, they'll send a robotic boarder to check it out. Anything fishy, they fire. If the robot finds your man, we bring him back under a heavy quarantine and do a thorough exam."

Kate ran to him and hugged him.

The hours that followed were the longest of Kate's life. She watched the triangular Exile ships maneuver the Serpentine vessels into a course for the sun. The black objects got smaller by the minute as they sailed into the burning star. She knew this was happening around hundreds, possibly thousands of worlds. She just hoped David wasn't on one of the ships.

Paul, Mary, and Milo had joined her in her stateroom, but no one said a word. The feeling was like a hospital waiting room. Everyone was there for Kate, but there was nothing to say.

In the Serpentine command center, David watched the triangular ships systematically destroy the Serpentine fleet. Of the hundred screens, only a handful still showed Serpentine ships. It was a massacre. On the central screen, which showed the rings of ships outside the one David occupied, a portal opened, and a fleet of triangular ships arrived.

They seemed to waste no time. Their shots immediately began tearing into the rings of Serpentine ships. The wave of destruction would reach David in seconds.

He watched the triangular fleet approach, bracing himself. At the back of his mind, he wondered if it was another illusion. A test. The lead triangular ship stopped, and David realized he was holding his breath.

Kate stood when Perseus entered.

"I think we've got something," he said. "One life sign, on the Serpentine central ring."

"Is he..."

"They're running him through a battery of tests now, but he looks healthy."

David sat in the decontamination chamber, waiting, debating what to do. If his rescue was another Serpentine illusion, what was the bait? How could he break it down the way he had the pit? He had to resist. He steeled himself. *It's all an illusion. No matter what they throw at me, I will resist.*

The doors opened, and Kate stood in the well-lit, white walled corridor. Her brunette hair hung down, spilling onto her shoulders, and her face was radiant, her eyes alive. She was healthy, vibrant, the same person he had met, fallen in love with. David stood still, unable to move.

She rushed in and hugged him. He felt Milo's arms around him too.

David decided that if it was a Serpentine illusion, they had won. It was too real to him. He couldn't resist her.

Kate pulled back and looked in his eyes. "Are you all right?"

"I am now."

At the sentinel factory, Kate and David paused at the wide window that looked out on the assembly line. The sentinel spheres were returning in droves. Kate wondered how many there were. Millions perhaps.

"What will you do with them?" she asked Perseus.

"We're still debating. We'd like to use some to destroy the remaining Serpentine ships. It could cut the process down by years. After that, we'll either scrap them or keep them in case another threat emerges."

Perseus led them through the factory's corridors. A trail of dried blood marked the path to the ark.

The outer doors opened, and Kate remembered the first time she had seen them, two miles under Antarctica.

In the decontamination chamber, she paused. She had torn her suit off here, placing it beside the two small suits Adi and Surya had worn.

Inside the ark, teams were combing every inch of the ancient vessel.

"Did they find Lykos?" Kate asked.

"Yes. They're still treating his wounds," Perseus said.

"Can I see him?"

Perseus agreed and led them down the dim, metallic corridors to a large room where medical technicians were setting up equipment.

"Lykos," Perseus said, "this is Dr. Kate Warner. She created the therapy that neutralized the sentinels, and she helped find you."

"We're in your debt, Dr. Warner."

"You're not. I want you to know that I was simply finishing the work Isis started. She was very, very sorry about what happened. Had she known the truth, she would have done things a lot differently."

Lykos nodded. "I think we all would. The past is the past."

"I agree." She eyed the equipment. "You're going to treat the Atlanteans?"

"Yes," Perseus said. "We think the treatment we used to cure your resurrection syndrome will work on them. We'll know soon."

"What then?"

"We were actually thinking that we would return to our homeworld. Everything on the surface of the Exile world was destroyed, and going back underground doesn't quite feel right. We're thinking we could all make a fresh start."

Kate smiled. She thought that a fresh start would have pleased Isis very much.

"There's one more thing we're hoping you can help us understand."

Perseus led Kate and David to the massive chamber that held the rows of tubes. Just beyond the double doors at the entrance, a pile of bodies lay. All Ares.

"We're still counting them. Cause of death was mostly blunt-force trauma, a few strangulations. Ship logs say he disabled his own resurrection."

"Did you find any more bodies?" David asked.

"One. Outside." Perseus held up a pad. Dorian Sloane's dead body floated through space, the sentinel assembly line in the background.

David glanced at Kate.

She thought about the hate Dorian and Ares had shared, the things they had done—on the Atlantean world and on her world. She thought about Earth making a fresh start and about the Atlanteans, reuniting and rebuilding their civilization together.

"What do you think?" Perseus asked.

"I think we reap what we sow."

# EPILOGUE

Atlanta, Georgia

Paul watched Mary walk through the home they had shared, a look somewhere between shock and amusement on her face. "You never took the pictures down?"

"I uh... no."

"I think we should."

"Of course, I could—"

"We'll put new pictures up."

"New pictures would be good," Paul said. It was the best idea he had heard in a very long time.

The front door opened, and his nephew Matthew bolted in, making a beeline for Paul. The boy hugged him, and Paul hugged him back with all his strength.

Natalie and Major Thomas followed. They looked tired except for the smiles on their faces.

Paul made the introductions.

"Mary and I were just discussing what we're going to do from here."

"Us too," Natalie said, glancing at Major Thomas. "We're going to report to the relief office downtown, see how we can help."

They said their goodbyes, and Mary and Paul began collecting the pictures. They carefully removed the old photos and placed them at the bottom of a dresser drawer. They kept the frames. They had been a wedding gift.

Kate didn't know if her hearing was going bad or if she had gotten used to the constant sound of hammering and power tools. And that commotion—from David's constant construction projects—was the only sound for miles around. There was no bustle of a city, no airplane noise, no stadium nearby. His parents' home was nestled on a large plot of land with a beautiful yard, surrounded by the greenest trees she'd ever seen.

She had wondered how she would like it. She'd never lived outside a city, but to her surprise, she found that country life suited her. Or maybe it was just the company. From the kitchen window, she could see Milo playing with Adi and Surya, being the big brother. He planned to move out in a few months, and David and Kate were dreading that day. But he had big plans.

David walked in. He was sweaty, white dust particles filled his hair, and a pencil rested behind his ear. Kate liked the look very much.

"Are we in destruction or construction mode today?"

David poured himself a glass of water and spoke between gulps. "It's demolition, not destruction but yes, major demo."

"Maybe that's what I'll start calling you: Major Demo. Or would you prefer Colonel Demo?"

He finished his glass and set it on the island, then grabbed her. "Oh, I think we both know I'm just a lowly private in this woman's army."

Kate tried to push away. "Hey, you're sweaty and dirty."

"Yes, I am."

The phone rang, and David released one hand just long enough to answer. Kate still struggled with the other hand's grip, but he released her several seconds into the call.

He spoke quickly, asking questions, listening, growing more serious by the second.

When he hung up, he looked at Kate. "They found it."

Kate had wondered if the call would ever come. When she had made David promise in Morocco, she had been dying then and had assumed she wouldn't live to see this day. Now she was filled with fear, and she knew why: she had hope.

---

The helicopter hovered just above the water. The pilot spoke to David through the ear piece. "We're here."

Kate glanced down at the water, then at David. He leaned across, kissed her, pulled his diving mask on, and jumped over the side.

For a moment, he floated just under the water, taking in the submerged city of San Francisco.

The readout on his arm marked the location, and he began pushing down through the water. When he reached the low-rise building, he swam through a broken glass window, careful not to cut himself. He snaked through the corridors, moving slowly, the light from his helmet illuminating his path. The doors were all open—this place had been evacuated quickly. The Immari labs were a collection of bizarre equipment and things David couldn't begin to understand. But he was quite familiar with what he was looking for. In one of the central labs, he came face to face with the four tubes Patrick Pierce had extracted from the *Alpha Lander* under the Bay of Gibraltar almost a hundred years ago. They were the same tubes that had held Kate, her father—Patrick Pierce, and the two men who would become their enemies: Dorian Sloane and Mallory Craig. The four of them had awoken in 1978, and the tubes had remained vacant since then, with one exception: Dorian had placed the infant he took from Kate in one of the tubes. Or so Dorian had told her in an interrogation room in Antarctica months ago. Kate and David still weren't sure if Dorian had been toying with Kate or if the infant really was in one of the tubes, but in Morocco, David had sworn he would find Kate's child—even if it killed him.

He swam closer and shined his light into the first tube, waiting, hoping. The beam went straight through. Empty. The second—empty. The third—empty. At the fourth, the beam of light met clouds of gray and white. David inhaled. The clouds parted, revealing an infant. The boy floated innocently, his eyes closed, his arms and legs straight out. David felt himself exhale.

Back at the U.S. Army base on the new coast of California, David could sense Kate's nervousness.

"They think they'll have the tubes extracted within a few weeks," he said. "They have an independent power source, but we have to be careful."

"I've been thinking… about what we should do."

"Me too. I think our son should have a brother or sister around his age." He raised his eyebrows. "I promise to finish the house before your second trimester."

"It's a deal."

# AUTHOR'S NOTE

You made it! To the end of the trilogy, that is. For a few months, I wasn't sure I would. I agonized at some length about where this book should go. I had planned the Atlantean backstory years ago, and my intention had always been to tell that story in the final book, but after the release of *The Atlantis Plague*, I was kind of nervous about it. *The Atlantis World* is different from the first two books in many ways (most of it doesn't take place on Earth and it's less about our science and history and more about our possible future and the myths that have driven us).

In the end, I decided to write the book I wanted to read, the book I hoped fans who loved the first two books would be delighted with. I hope you've enjoyed it, but I understand if it wasn't quite what you wanted or expected. I tend to swing for the fences. In this case, I wanted to write a book a small group of fans would absolutely *love* rather than a novel a large group of readers would just like. As a reader, that's what I prefer. I want the author to go for it: to take a little risk and either hit it out of the park or strike out at the plate. Life's too short for base hits.

I've learned a lot about writing and a lot about life in the last year. Being a writer hasn't been a cakewalk. But for now, I'm going to keep stepping up to the plate. I hope you'll stick around.

—Gerry

PS: If you'd like to know when I have a new book out, you can join my email list by visiting my web site: www.AGRiddle. com. I only send emails when a new book is released.

# ACKNOWLEDGMENTS

So many people contributed to this novel, and I owe them a huge thanks. They are:

Anna. Without you, I never would have been able to get this book into readers' hands so quickly and my life would be a lot less sane and enjoyable. I love you, and I appreciate you every day.

Carole Duebbert, Sylvie Delézay, and Lisa Weinberg, my alpha editors, for absolutely amazing proofreading, edits, and suggestions. Thank you again. You caught things I never would have and helped me see where I needed to keep working.

Juan Carlos Barquet for the stunning original artwork for the cover. You've been a pleasure to work with on this series, and I thank you for bringing my worlds to life and inviting people into my books.

To the best group of beta readers any author ever had. You all made this novel so much better than it was, and I will forever be grateful. You are: Fran Mason, Cindy Prendergast, Linda Winton, Leanne McGiveron, Emily Chin, Skip Folden, Dave Renison, Jane Marconi, NJ Fritz, Terry Daigle, Miora Hanson, Jeff Baker, Shawn Kerker, Michelle Duff, Kristen Miller, Duane Spellecacy, Virginia McClain, Vicky Gibbins, Brian Puzzo, Steven Nease, Jen Bengtson, Ron Watts, Kelly Mahoney, Lee Ames, Robin Collins, Sunday Moylan, Nikita Puhalsky, Paul Jamieson, Teodora Retegan, Karin Kostyzak, Rhonda Sloan, Christine Smith, Matt Fyfe, Scott Weiner, Christopher Kazu Williams, Paul Bowen, Peter Lynch, Dr. Akash Rajpal, and Katie Regan.

Mike Kohn, James Jenkins, Jared Wortham, Kathy Belford, Marco Villanueva, Michael Shekels, John Scanlon, and Donna Fitzgerald for your inquisitive minds.

Last but not least, to you, wherever you are, whatever time it is: I thank you for reading my first works of fiction. This trilogy has been equal parts hard work and fun for me, and I sincerely hope you've enjoyed it. Take care and safe travels.

### A letter from the publisher

We hope you enjoyed this book. We are an independent
publisher dedicated to discovering brilliant books,
new authors and great storytelling. Please join us at
www.headofzeus.com and become part of our
community of book-lovers.

We will keep you up to date with our latest books, author
blogs, special previews, tempting offers, chances to win
signed editions and much more.

If you have any questions, feedback or just want to say hi,
please drop us a line on hello@headofzeus.com

**@HoZ_Books**

**HeadofZeusBooks**

**www.headofzeus.com**

 HEAD *of* ZEUS

**The story starts here**